Blinding
the Ghost's Eye

Sara Maher

ISBN 978-0-6482591-4-5

Published by Africa World Books Pty. Ltd.
(www.africaworldbooks.com)

Design and typesetting: All In One Book Design
(www.allinonebookdesign.com.au)

For my families

Acknowledgments

There are many people who needed to be thanked for their support, feedback and encouragement. Special thanks to Victoria Adhar Arop – Adhar-dit, for the stories she told.

Also, and not in any particular order: David Nyuol Vincent, Akech Manyiel, Rita Awour Padang, Amon Dut Aluwal Back, Elizabeth Jang Biong Arob, Biong Deng Biong Akuol Noir, Alual Chol, Nyanbol Deng, Alice Abalo, Archangelo Nyuol Madut, Ayak Mawien, Lizzy O'Reilly, Susan Elgar, Ally Brown, Lee Spencer, Enya Gannon, Randall Watson, Emily Booth, Ann Bolch, Richard Holt, Malcom McKinnon, Edi Kurzer, Tony Tan, James Finnis, Peter Deng and Africa World Books.

Sara Maher is a writer and researcher
who lives in Melbourne, Australia.

'Assured writing, compelling reading; a window
to a community and story that needs to be known.'
Graeme Simsion, author of *The Rosie Project*.

Preface

Sudan suffered two civil wars. The first, from the end of colonialism in 1955 to 1972 and the second from 1983 to 2005. Sudan's southern population were predominantly African, Christians, the northern population predominantly Arab Muslims. In 2010, the southern population voted in a referendum for independence. In 2011 southern Sudan became the republic of South Sudan. As this story is set in 2005, the African characters are referred to as Sudanese, and their homeland as Sudan.

The characters in this book are entirely fictional.

1. Alaya

The murhaleen came on horses, machine guns screaming. We ran. My little brother in front. My mother behind. I prayed to God as the smoke burned my eyes. Let me become the kuei. I will carry us away.

Much later, when all was quiet, we returned. Our home was burned, smouldering. Dead bodies draped across the ground. I tripped over our neighbour. Part of his face was missing. The rest of it was dark with blood. His one eye gazed lovingly at the sky.

2. Ottavio

The meat works were okay for the short term. It had been easy to get work there while he was studying. In four years, the Sudanese had taken most of the positions. A few *kawaujas* remained. The tired, older men who'd worked there a long time were now in the packing department, boxing up the frozen meat. No effort, no blood.

As Ottavio left the building he fell into step with one of them. Fifties. Bald. A thin collar of greying hair around the base of his skull. He didn't quite reach Ottavio's shoulder. The man cast a friendly eye at him, 'Goin to the game on the weekend?'

'Na.'

'Who do ya barrack for?'

'Don't really. Prefer football … soccer.'

'Oh yeah. Most you fellas like soccer eh?'

'Yeah. And basketball.'

'Be bloody good at that. You're such tall bastards.'

Ottavio stiffened, but saw no menace in the man's soft, heavy body and nodded a farewell, but the man offered his hand. Cautiously he took it.

'Name's Brian.'

'Ottavio.'

'O…?'

'O t t a v i o.'

'Okay mate, see ya round.'

Mostly the *kawaujas* ignored the Sudanese. Why was one of them suddenly being friendly? Did Brian want something? Ottavio shrugged off the thought. Soon he'd get a real job. After years at uni he couldn't wait. He'd checked out a few suits, the kind a professional would wear, imagining he would be the one to break through, be employed as an engineer. Not working a shitty factory job. Or worse, being unemployed only because he was African.

His phone rang. The name of his oldest friend blinked on the screen. No doubt he was running late for his shift.

'Machar.' Malong's big deep voice boomed up at him.

Ottavio laughed silently, Malong always used his bull name, never his Christian name. He'd never heard him say Ottavio. Malong didn't have a Christian name. When a mass baptism had been organised in the camp, Malong had refused telling the minister, if God were real, they wouldn't be there. He maintained his rage as he grew. Later, claiming to anyone who would listen that religion was the cause for all the problems in Africa. Christian or Muslim, they were both colonisers. Things were fine until religion showed up. Ottavio didn't entirely agree, but for the sake of peace he didn't argue with him. Not anymore.

Ottavio scouted the car park, looking for his friend's car. The battered sedan was at the far end, near the gate, where the latecomers parked. Malong was getting out, flipping closed his phone. Ottavio gave him a playful salute.

'What did the *kawauja* want?' Malong growled.

'Just said hello.' Ottavio shrugged.

'Don't you be making friends with him. Only get you trouble.'

'Yeah, yeah,' Ottavio said softly. Malong was suspicious of anyone, *kawauja* or not.

'Come for a drink Friday night?'

'No way.'

'Don't be like that man, that wasn't my fault. You know that stuff happens when you're just walking down the street with your buddies.'

Ottavio shook his head. Malong's memory had always been selective. They hadn't been walking down the street, they'd been leaving a club and Malong couldn't keep his mouth shut when he was drunk. Loved a confrontation. Always had. Malong had stepped in front of a random guy and sneered; did he have a problem? The man's glare said he wasn't scared. He should have been. Ottavio got hold of Malong before he pushed the guy.

'You know I can't be getting caught up in that shit. I've got responsibilities.'

'You think you're setting an example for Alpha? He's not a little boy anymore. You let him go his own way. He's going to anyway.'

It wasn't just Alpha he was thinking about and Malong knew it. 'Whatever man, I'm still not drinking with you.'

Malong shrugged. 'You be at Zach's game tomorrow?'

'Why wouldn't I be?'

'Might want sit on the couch by yourself, thinking.'

'Meaning?'

'Machar, you gotta forget about Angelina. She's gone.'

The finality in Malong's voice stung.

'Dunno what you talking about.'

'You know. I know. See ya tomorrow.'

Ottavio took a breath in. He loved Malong, but man, he could be aggravating. Malong had a rule for women. Don't let them get close enough to hurt you. Any man dumb enough to let that happen deserved what he got.

Ottavio unlocked his car, careful with the key, not wanting even a faint scratch on the shiny, dark blue duco. Air hissed from the seat beneath him, the door closed with a comforting thud. Leaning back, he closed his eyes and breathed in the smell of the car, warm from sitting in the sun. There was a whiff of pine air freshener and something fainter, something female. He never wanted the car to lose that smell.

Ottavio was forever grateful to the guy who had bought the car new and a year later had to get rid of it quickly and cheaply, no questions asked.

He'd called himself Peter and they met in the car park when the shift ended. Peter talked quickly, pointing out all the features, keeping his eyes down as they walked around the car. Ottavio took in the fat tyres and gleaming alloy wheels, the back-sloping roof and flat, oval headlights. Peter started it up and tapped his foot against the accelerator for Ottavio to hear the surge of the engine. Ottavio got in and Peter gunned the car out of the gates, swerving onto the feeder road in a spray of gravel. They cruised to the intersection and when a gap opened up, he moved the car swiftly into the lane, overtook the truck in front of them and accelerated into top gear. Other than the whirring engine, the car was silent. Peter glanced at Ottavio, looking for his approval, but Ottavio didn't give it. He just stared straight ahead. Slowing down, Peter turned off the highway and pulled over. Ottavio got into the driver's seat and ran his hands along the smooth leather on the steering wheel. His long legs fitted, there was space between his head and the roof. Releasing the clutch, he eased the car back onto the tarmac and took it around the block twice before returning to the highway. Flooring the accelerator, the power of the engine pushing him back into his seat, Ottavio felt elated. Freedom wasn't a state of mind, he thought, it was being the one to decide when to move. How fast was entirely up to him.

Back at the factory, he had revved the engine half a dozen times before he parked. He had to own that deep rumbling sound.

Later that night Peter knocked at his door and Ottavio handed him an envelope of cash. Peter counted it, threw him the keys and walked off. Driving over to Malong's place, Ottavio could not stop smiling. He spent the evening showing off his prize, ignoring the buzzing sense of guilt. That much money could have made a lot of difference back home.

Ottavio checked his watch. On a good day it took forty-five minutes to get home. But the sky looked dark with rain and the traffic was already heavy. He turned the music up, letting the bass vibrate through his muscles. Being alone in the car was the best part of his day. It gave him time to zone out. After eight hours on the chain, his mind wandering anywhere it wanted to go, his hands moving through the routine, he wanted to claim them both back. Remind himself he was in control.

Turning the CD player off, he concentrated on the white line dividing the road. Coach Singh, his athletics coach, had trained him to follow the inside line on the running track. Try not to control your thoughts he had said. Just observe whatever appears: time, place or person. If something lingers, be patient and let it pass. Detach, Coach Singh would say, follow the line and detach.

In his mind Ottavio saw the girl he'd seen in the supermarket the night before. In front of him at the checkout, elegantly dressed, graceful hands, faint rose-scented perfume. The line of her neck made him want to move closer. Ottavio let the thought go and saw himself, sitting in a lecture at university, the only African student. Then he saw his sister, wearing a hijab, sweeping a floor. Malong appeared, ten years old, slapping him on the back, helpless with laughter. In camp he'd sneak up on Ottavio at night, hissing like a big cat. Scared the shit out of him every time and laughed his ass off at Ottavio's bug-eyed terror. Then he'd sing: 'You scared for no reason. Be strong like Malong. Be brave like Malong.'

That had always been Malong's plan—be scared of nothing. He didn't like to admit it, but he preferred working with Malong next to him. Usually they were side by side. It wasn't like Malong to work the second shift.

■

Making good time, Ottavio merged smoothly onto the highway and changed across three lanes in one fluid move holding the car at the speed limit. The world was a peripheral blur. Nothing could touch him.

Relaxing back into his seat, he let his mind settle back onto the white line. He found himself in Mayen Aben, his sister dragging him toward a pool in the swamp of bright green reeds. He hadn't wanted a bath. He'd wanted to keep playing with his age mates. The sun was going down. Burning dung was thick in the air, stopping the mosquitos from landing. Cows lowed nearby. Ignoring his protests, his sister dragged him behind her. She was in charge and she made sure he washed every day. Four years older and much taller, she could make him do whatever she wanted. Other kids splashed and laughed in the still water. He gave in, letting her yank off his favourite yellow singlet, and lather him with soap as he stood waist-deep in the warm, brown water.

Changing lanes, Ottavio indicated, took the off-ramp, left the highway and cruised into the back streets to the shabby suburb that was his home. Plain houses, their small patches of front lawn burnt by the sun. Low wire fences and scrubby bushes. Clapped-out cars in driveways. Tuesday was rubbish day and the trucks had been. Rows of green and yellow bins were strewn along the curb, waiting to be retrieved. On the corner of his street a lone gum towered into the sky. It seemed sad to him; a single majestic tree in a patch of dull, crowded suburbia. Pulling up outside his small cream house, Ottavio glanced at his watch. Fifty-two minutes. He rested in his seat, thinking of the day they arrived at his house, proud and pleased; a real house. Now it looked small and worn-out and the lawn was overgrown. He'd do something about it on the weekend after he polished the car.

As he got out of the car, Ottavio heard the music booming from the house. Anger flashed through him. He'd told Alphonso countless times to keep it down. The last thing he wanted was the neighbours complaining. But music was all his younger brother lived for. Called himself MC Alpha when he played an occasional Sudanese party. Wouldn't go back to school. Couldn't get a job, no matter how many times Ottavio told him to try. Alpha's reply never changed. The school didn't want him and there were no jobs for someone like him to get. Ottavio knew it was the truth. Alpha was as smart as anyone else but smart didn't matter - the school hadn't cared. Classes were based on age not level. The teachers expected him to be at the same level of the other kids in his class—they were the same age after all. But school in the refugee camp was nothing like school in Australia. He was years behind in the subjects he was familiar with, and there were subjects he had never heard of. He knew he was seen as a problem and the teachers didn't know how to help him or didn't want to. So he just stopped going. He would leave for school but not show up for class. The school didn't bother calling Ottavio until the end of the term. They told him Alpha had not achieved the marks required to move to the next year, and that he had been absent for over fifty percent of the term. Ottavio insisted on meeting with the principal. Mr Turner hurried him through the meeting and accepted no responsibility for the school's failure to keep Ottavio informed. Ottavio queried the school's role in supporting students like Alpha, and Turner had replied that 'you people might be better off in special needs schools'. Ottavio had swallowed his anger and insisted Turner give Alpha another chance. Alpha agreed, reluctantly. He tried, but didn't last long.

For the past two or so years Alpha had put his dole form in on time and hung out with his friends. Usually he'd go out on Friday night and show up again at home on a Monday or Tuesday. Ottavio would get calls; Alpha was drunk, he had to come and get him. But lately Ottavio had told Alpha's friends to stop calling. He hadn't really wanted to do that, but he hoped it might make Alpha become responsible. He wasn't a kid anymore. Ottavio didn't say it but he worried about Alpha, was scared that someday it would be the police calling. Alpha was the perfect target for them. Tall and broad, he looked like a tough guy. But Alpha had never shaped up to anyone. Loud noises and sudden movements made him flinch, and he was terrified of police. His breath became shallow at the sight of them. When their cars cruised by he watched carefully, his body tense – ready to fight or run.

Ottavio went straight to the bedroom, grabbed the mp3 player from the dock and threw it.

Alpha tried to catch it but missed and watched with glazed eyes as it spun across the floor.

'Oh man, what's ya problem?'

'When?' Ottavio yelled.

'When what?'

'When you gonna start behaving like a man?'

Grabbing the player off the floor Alpha did not look at his brother. He moved quickly out the front door, slamming it hard behind him.

In the kitchen there were dirty dishes on every surface. A cockroach skittered across the bench. Ottavio wrenched the fridge open. The juice and bread he had bought the day before were gone.

Ottavio filled the sink with soapy water and stacked the dishes to soak. Powering up his laptop, he went online and checked Facebook, skimming over posts, looking for Angelina. Nothing. She hadn't shown herself for weeks. He didn't care, didn't want to know her wedding plans.

The air was humid and sweat was trickling down his ribcage. A noisy flock of cockatoos landed on the lawn outside. Screeching, picking at the grass and striding about with half-lifted wings. Ottavio watched them suddenly fly off again and felt the quiet fill the house.

Lying down on his bed he picked up a battered copy of *A Catcher in the Rye* and flicked through the pages, looking for his favourite passages. But his eyes were heavy, and he felt himself falling into sleep, knowing the dream that came with it would be waiting for him.

Sitting on a bench in the rain he watched a slow spinning carousel, brightly coloured horses prancing lifelessly. With warm rain trickling down his face, he waited patiently for his sister to appear on one of the horses as they came around again. She would smile and wave for him to come join her.

The horses circled past, manes rigid, teeth bared. The carousel went around and around, but she did not appear.

3. Alice

There was a new face in the class. Alice went to him and shook his hand firmly, pronouncing her name slowly and clearly. He could only be from Sudan. Since volunteering to help in the English language class, she'd learned to recognise some features. The Asiatic eyes of the Hazara from Afghanistan. The black skin of the southern Sudanese. They were the tallest people she had ever met.

Not wanting to make him uncomfortable by asking questions, she took his elbow to guide him toward a chair at the long table the students shared, but he jerked his arm away and stepped back; eyes lidded, pride wounded.

Melissa entered the room and approached him with a wide smile, her hand out.

'Hello, you must be Ottavio? Melissa. I'm the teacher. Great to have you with us. You speak four languages? That's right isn't it?'

'Dinka, Swahili, English, Arabic.'

'Well, you're just what we need. Any more where you came from?'

'Ahhh, dunno, I just saw the call-out for volunteers.'

'Whereabouts?'

'Uni.'

'You're a student?'

'Graduated a few months ago.'

'In?'

'Engineering. Civil.'

'Congratulations. That's quite an achievement.'

'Thanks.'

'You've met Alice?'

Ottavio gave her a cursory smile.

'Good. Let's get started then. Just follow me. It's easy. You'll pick it up as we go along. If you have any questions, ask Alice. She's an old hand.'

Ignoring Alice's encouraging smile, he went for a seat at the far end of the table as the last of the students arrived. Alice sat next to her friend Batool, still mortified by her mistake. Ottavio introduced himself to the students as the class got underway and she snuck glances at him from the corner of her eye. As he ran the tip of his forefinger around the face of his watch, the pinched skin between his eyebrows relaxed. When he looked her way and caught her eye, he did not hold her gaze, and a hint of nausea hit her stomach. Alice didn't like upsetting people, she would have to make amends.

Slowly walking the length of the table, glancing over shoulders, encouraging the students with kind words, she made her way toward Ottavio. In her friendliest voice she asked him how he was going. He glanced at her, but didn't reply, turning instead to the student next to him.

Stung, Alice returned to her seat, anxiety blooming, mind racing. She really had offended him. Sipping from her water bottle she told herself to be calm, it wasn't her fault. Why wouldn't she think he was new in class? She had volunteered to help people like him, to be a supportive person who welcomed refugees, a good person who meant him no harm. How could he misunderstand her intentions?

At the break she thought to offer him a cup of tea, but his back was to her when she walked into the kitchen. He was listening to Achol, slender, pretty and Dinka. She was speaking in their language, even though the class rule was English only. Alice didn't interrupt. Making herself a strong coffee, she scooped up three shortbread biscuits. Standing by herself at the far window she ate them quickly, pretending to bask in the last of the afternoon sun.

4. Alaya

Nyath was my best friend and she had the sweetest voice. Just like a bird. Sometimes we played in the trees and pretended to be birds. I watched the kuei high above us. Such long wings, so graceful and proud, its lonely cry beautiful as its black and white feathers. It saw our suffering, yet it always came back. Slowly circling above us. Seeing everything. Nyath said if I moved like the kuei the boys would fight to be my husband.

5. Ottavio

Ottavio arrived just as the ref was about to start the game. Zach's team, the Reds, were playing the Titans, another local high school team. Adults and kids were scattered around the field. Groups of school kids in the stands, supporting their team, and teachers sitting together a short distance away. Malong had parked at the barrier and was leaning against the bonnet of his car, a cigarette in his hand. Ottavio pulled up next to him and stepped out, feeling his skin react to the sweaty, humid air after the coolness of the air conditioner. Malong nodded to him as he joined him on the bonnet.

Zach wasn't on the field. He was sitting with two other players on the lowest level of the stands, behind the coach, jiggling his legs, as the ref started the game with a harsh blast of the whistle.

'When they gonna give him a chance?' Malong asked Ottavio, blowing a stream of smoke high into the air.

'Maybe today?'

'Season will be over before he gets a start. That coach doesn't want him on the field. That's what it is.'

One of the Reds strikers dashed toward the goal. His long, black hair flicking out behind him, he weaved past two defenders and had only the goalie to beat. With a flick he put the ball neatly over the diving keeper into the top of the net. Cheering erupted from the stand. A group of girls squealed and clapped. The coach called out his approval. 'Good on ya Theo. Keep it up. That's what we want.' Theo smoothed down his hair, looking pleased.

Ottavio slapped Malong on the arm. 'Nice shot.'

'Zach would have dribbled around him. Wouldn't have needed to chip.'

Within minutes Theo found himself another space just outside the penalty box. On the end of a searching pass from the wing, he sidestepped a defender before neatly slotting another. The team was jubilant.

'I suppose that wasn't any good either?' Ottavio said.

'Plenty better than him.'

'You're so full of shit. It's not just African players that have talent.'

'You see any African players on the ground?' Malong glanced at Zach, sitting in the stands, looking bored.

'Maybe he should play basketball?'

'Why, when he plays this?' Malong was irritated. 'He could be a star if they gave him the chance. You know that.'

A car pulled up near to them and they both glanced over at the shiny black car with tinted windows. The driver killed the engine but kept the music thumping.

The teams were back in play and after the frenetic opening the teams settled for a period, swapping possession in the midfield. Ottavio let the debate with Malong drop and watched Zach on the sidelines, still jiggling his legs.

'You be there Saturday night?'

'What's on?'

'Keep telling you. Mawien's coming from the States.'

'Yeah. I'll be there,' Ottavio said.

'How many times you say you coming then don't?'

Ottavio didn't reply.

'I wouldn't care if a woman was stopping you, but I know it isn't.'

Malong was scheming. They hadn't spoken about Angelina but Malong knew. His networks were efficient.

They turned back to the game as the Titans moved the ball deep into their attacking zone. Theo yelled at his defenders, telling them to get in position. The coach did the same. A centered ball from the left corner evaded the Reds defence and the Titans striker headed the ball neatly past the goalie. The cheering subsided quickly when the Reds key defender was seen writhing in the penalty box, clutching his ankle. A lull fell across the ground as the ref stopped the game and the coach ran to the fallen player. After squeezing and prodding the player's leg, he helped him limp off the field, the crowd commiserating.

Two guys got out of the black car and stepped over the barriers, closer to the field. Malong watched from the corner of his eye. They were both about his and Ottavio's age. The driver wore thongs, a back-to-front cap over short hair, black Adidas pants, and a grimy muscle t-shirt that showed his heavily tattooed arms. He pulled hard on his cigarette. His mate's dark brown hair was short on the top and long at the back, he wore a faded red singlet and tied around his waist was a checked flannel shirt. Flannel shirt glanced at Malong. Malong got that feeling; the one that meant there might trouble and he tapped Ottavio's rib cage with his elbow in a way no one could notice. Without moving Ottavio flicked his eyes toward the two and nodded in the smallest way. He'd seen guys like them plenty of times. Seen how they'd kick something off in a moment, throwing their chests out, yelling, 'wanna go do ya mate?' If you backed down, you might get away with a lot of insults. If they'd had plenty of booze, there was no backing down.

Ottavio heard the coach calling out Zach's name and turned back to the game. Zach was bolting onto the field, the coach slapping him on his back as he passed, yelling, 'Get on and cover that kid with the long hair.'

'Now you're talking,' Malong said, grinning at Ottavio. 'We gonna see some action.'

The game re-started, and Zach moved down the field, tightly marked by his Titans opponent.

Intercepting a Reds through-ball, the Titans striker took off down the wing, heading for goal. Zach saw his chance to tackle. He left his man and was gaining fast, preparing to challenge for the ball when another Titans player grabbed the back of his shirt and pulled him down. Ottavio and Malong yelled in protest. The coach did the same but the ref hadn't seen the foul. Malong heard flannel shirt snickering loudly, 'nice play'. The game kept going and the Reds striker delivered a clever pass through the scrambling defence, allowing Theo to score again.

The crowd clapped the goal and the driver called out, 'yeah T, that's the way'. Ottavio wasn't sure if it was directed at Theo or someone else. The ref ignored the coach's sideline pleading and Malong kicked at the turf in disgust. 'What the hell? That man's blind. Can't be any other reason.' Zach's shoulders had drooped in disappointment, and Malong yelled out, 'bad call Zach.'

Zach got back in play, but the ref was losing control with both teams pushing and elbowing, parents crowding the sidelines, yelling directions. The ref plucked a soft foul against the Reds to howls of protest. Playing the ball quickly the Titans split the Reds defence again before finding the net. The crowd booed and cheered in equal measure.

At half time, with the score drawn, two goals each, Ottavio could hear the coach telling the team to cool down and concentrate. 'Work with each other. You can win this.'

Zach was a little outside the circle, behind the other players. Listening, his body hunched, he made no effort to stand with his team. It hurt Ottavio to see him not included. Zach was easily one of the best players, but he didn't assert himself. Not on the team, at school. Not with anything.

'Do you think he's forgotten?' Malong asked.

'Forgotten what?'

Malong sang his camp song. 'Play like a leopard. Attack like a leopard. So fast they don't see you coming.'

'You think Zach's still got some leopard in him?'

'Sure, he has, he's just on the wrong team. These guys don't know how to play. Dumb coach.'

The teams returned to the field, but play was scrappy, both sides unsettled by the first half. The coach paced the sidelines, shouting down the Titans coach. A series of late tackles left players from both teams sprawled on the turf. No fouls were called and neither team scored.

Ottavio started checking his phone, waiting for the final whistle. Malong lit another cigarette, checking the *kawaujas* on his periphery. Flannel shirt had got back into the car. There were shouts from the stands and the coaches yelled harder. Ottavio elbowed Malong to pay attention.

Eighty-five minutes in, a Reds striker got on the end of a through-ball and worked it into the penalty area, Zach close in behind. The striker took a shot. The coach leapt and the girls in the stand gasped, then squealed as the ball ricocheted off the crossbar. Zach pounced, trapping it. Stepping off, he sent the ball into the corner of the net. The coach threw his arms into the air and bellowed. The girls screamed, calling out Zach's name. Disbelieving, Theo stared at Zach as the rest of the team rushed to slap him on the back. Malong punched the air and grabbed Ottavio by the shoulders.

'Yeah leopard. Yeah!'

With time running out the Titans took the ball forward.

Zach confidently streamed into defence. He dispossessed the Titan's centre forward and cleared the ball long, but the Titans took the ball back off the Reds. The ball moved swiftly down the field, and Zach moved to intercept again. The crowd stirred with anticipation, the Titan's forward ducked around

Zach, but before an attempt at goal was made, the ref blew the final whistle.

With pride Ottavio watched Zach jog from the field, the coach clipping his shoulder approvingly, supporters clapping and chanting their team's name. A red-haired girl beamed at Zach as he jogged into the change rooms, but he kept his eyes to the ground as Theo walked over to the girl, his hands on his hips.

The two guys got back into their car, firing the engine, music thumping. They rolled slowly backwards out of their park, stopping just behind Malong's car. Ottavio and Malong turned together, watching the passenger window slowly slide down to halfway. His eyes glowering, Flannel shirt puckered a kiss towards them as the driver jammed the accelerator, peeling out of the carpark. Ottavio didn't need to look at Malong, he could feel the anger radiating from him, matching his own. Malong spat hard on the ground and leaned back on the bonnet, lighting another cigarette. Ottavio swallowed his anger as he always did. His mind racing in the silence, finding the right words to cool Malong down. 'Don't even bother with those two …'

'Shut up Machar. Don't give me one of your speeches.'

6. Alice

Late, Alice weaved through the white-clothed tables of the hushed restaurant. Elspeth was alone at her table. A waiter delivered her mother's coffee just as she arrived. Turning to Alice, he pulled out her chair.

'Good afternoon madam.'

Alice sat down, bristling at the formality. The waiter took a step back, hovering, awaiting instruction. Impatiently, Elspeth unfolded her napkin, 'Get her a latte, thank-you, we don't have much time.'

Alice felt the criticism, she always did. Elspeth did not like tardiness, there was never an excuse for it.

'I can't stay long. Your father and I are having dinner with the partners.'

'Hello Elspeth.'

When Alice turned sixteen, Elspeth had insisted that she stop calling her Mum and use her first name instead. It felt awkward and formal and Alice didn't like it, but complied without question. Questions were not allowed.

'It's at our place and I have to get back.'

Alice smiled tightly at the thought of her Dad and his two ex-partners from the days of McKenzie Crocker. She didn't like thinking of him at the boozy, monthly get-togethers. Wives were supposed to quietly excuse themselves after dinner when the heavy drinking began. Karl would be there of course.

Karl was a new partner in the firm, when she started as a file clerk in her first year at university. Six to eight pm, three nights a week. Karl was rather handsome, with large dark eyes and a cheeky grin. She was usually alone after six-thirty or seven; until Karl started working late. He was going through a nasty separation from his wife at the time. As she organised documents for filing, Karl told her stories about the 'bitch' and the disintegration of their marriage. Sitting on the edge of his desk, flicking a pencil against the palm of his hand, he didn't hold back. Alice felt uncomfortable with the fine detail; the screaming and throwing things, how he would try to calm her down. But she was flattered too, that he chose to share his heartache with her. Not for a moment had she thought he might be manipulating her. She was nineteen, and here was this handsome older man confiding in her. One night he told her his wife had demanded a divorce, and he'd seemed distraught. She had not hesitated when he asked her to join him for dinner. It was an expensive French bistro. Over the trout with flaked almonds in a butter sauce entrée, she found herself confiding in him. She'd never really wanted to go to university. It was only to keep her parents happy. She'd rather be in Africa, teaching people to read, she had always wanted to help people. She also wanted to tame wild animals, but she didn't mention that.

'Lucky Africa,' he'd said with a smirk, pressing his napkin against his buttery lips and pouring generous glasses of wine. They had more wine with their steak and oyster main. By the time they'd finished their dessert, crème brulee, Karl's eyes were gleaming. He grasped her hand and drunkenly kissed the tips of her fingers. His desire made her tingle.

In bed Karl had said she tasted like champagne, her wet softness like a ripe, raw fig. She felt floaty, like a balloon tied to a string Karl held, bouncing about any way he yanked her. They met as often as he could manage, the sex would happen anywhere in his barely furnished flat, and Karl liked to involve food. Sensual, delicious food. Licking honey off her stomach was a favourite. He fed her a chocolate croissant during slow sex on his sofa; pressing into her each time she took a bite. Being wanted gave her a buzzing energy. She paid more attention to how she looked, dressing to please Karl. He liked to see her naked in very high heels and bought her a pair; hot pink and so high she could barely walk in them. When not in use, they were hidden in the back of her wardrobe – best that Elspeth did not see them. The shoes were in her bag when she had arrived for work, exactly three months and two days after their affair had begun. She was planning to wear them while doing the filing, anticipating Karl's eyes on her as she moved about the office. However, Karl had met her at the door, with his briefcase in one hand and his overcoat in the other. He bluntly told her he'd reconciled with his wife. They were going to try again, then kissed her on the cheek and left her to the filing. He never made eye contact with her again.

The numbness that had enveloped Alice at that moment, had never really left. She continued on at McKenzie Crocker, but the more Karl ignored her, the more diminished she felt. After a month, she told her father, she wanted to concentrate on her studies. She tried to counter the numbness by indulging in the food he had loved, but the only thing she gained was fat. Fat she couldn't lose.

'Well, how are you?' Elspeth asked.

'Quite good.'

'You look tired. Are you working too hard? You shouldn't have taken up that volunteering thing. You've already got enough on your plate.'

'I enjoy it.'

'What is it you do there?'

'I help people learn English. You know … new arrivals.'

'New arrivals? You mean immigrants?'

'Refugees actually.'

'You didn't tell me they were refugees!'

'Well they are.'

'Why do you do this sort of thing? Going all that way on the train.'

'I don't know what you mean.'

'You shouldn't get involved with other people's problems. It's not your business. You don't know what those people have been involved in.'

'They are perfectly ordinary people, Elspeth. It's not their fault they became refugees.'

'No, I'm sure it isn't, but what's it got to do with you?'

Alice remembered she'd told Karl how she wanted to help people, but she had never shared that with Elspeth. Now, here they were staring at each other like they were strangers. Elspeth had that look, the one she bullied her with. But it had taken Alice years to work up the courage and actually do something she wanted to do. She had only just begun, and she was not going to give it up because he mother didn't approve. If Elspeth paid any attention at all, the "volunteering thing" should be of no surprise. Nor the complete lack of interest Alice showed in working her way up a corporate ladder. Alice wasn't interested in which ladders her old school mates or their husbands were climbing either. But Elspeth was. She still attended the bi-monthly mothers' lunch and reported back to Alice the details of her former classmates' lives. Alice couldn't imagine how Elspeth answered the concerned inquiries about her daughter's varied interests, lack of a proper career, and complete lack of marriage or motherhood prospects. There was no disguising the sly and nasty competition that lay behind it all. Alice had no idea why she kept going.

Elspeth knew nothing of her daydreams, let alone her ordinary life. Her weekly reports had all the pointy bits trimmed off. Alice entirely omitted the petty rebellions.

When the mood arose Alice threw some mild risk-taking into her day. The risk of being caught doing the wrong thing gave her a rush of energy. It lifted her spirits in a way she did not understand. A few days before she'd caught the train without buying a ticket. She remembered every moment of the trip. Feeling light-headed, she'd squeezed between two workmen on a three-seat bench. The carriage rocked slightly as the city and the possibility of getting caught got closer. Two stops before Central Station a group of surly inspectors got on. The type who loved wielding their thuggish authority over passengers. The tallest of them blocked the exits as others worked their way through the carriage, asking to see tickets. When they reached her, she feigned innocence. With the packed carriage listening, she worked up a few tears and told a wide-eyed story. At the station, she'd realised her wallet wasn't in her bag. Somebody must have taken it when she was on the bus. But she had to get on the train. If she were late, she'd lose her job.

It was thrilling, lying to the man's face, gaining the sympathy of the other passengers. After taking her details, the inspector issued a verbal warning and lumbered off. One of the workmen gave her a friendly nudge. 'Bloody goons', he'd said with a wink.

She didn't do it often. Better to spend her money on a good red than a fine, or getting arrested for shoplifting a beautiful silk scarf from a posh boutique. Cornered, she'd convinced the manager she wasn't stealing, she'd simply forgotten it was still in her hand. She'd thought it was the perfect gift for her only sister who was dying of cancer. The woman looked at her with such pity, that Alice nearly gave herself up, but managed to maintain a look of bewilderment and despair.

Elated, she left the shop with a little rope-handled monogrammed bag, the scarf neatly wrapped in tissue inside; a gift from the manager. When the guilt settled in a few hours later, she decided she couldn't keep it and gifted it to her mother for her birthday.

The scarf was draped around Elspeth's neck, complementing her elegant wool suit and expensive, Italian-made court shoes. Elspeth's world was neat and close fitting. Would she unravel if she knew how her daughter had acquired the scarf? What about the outrageous lies she occasionally told? Would that bring her undone? Alice didn't think it would. Elspeth wouldn't imagine such aberrant behavior had anything to do with herself. It could be Alice's fault and no one else. Alice imagined Elspeth would cut her off without much difficulty.

Alice wished she'd ordered some cake with the coffee, normally it would be a large slice of something gooey and rich, but she did not dare in front of Elspeth. She held back a sigh. For a wistful moment, she imagined Elspeth was a mother who noticed when her daughter needed comforting.

Elspeth folded her napkin and pressed the edges together, placing it carefully to one side Alice recognised the careful arranging of her thoughts.

'You shouldn't be involved with these people.'

'Helping them learn English doesn't mean I'm involved.'

'I just want you to ...'

'... to what?'

Elspeth spoke carefully. 'To do something with your life.'

'Elspeth, I am doing something.' Alice readied herself for the argument, but instead of the usual tension, she saw something that looked like concern in her mother's face and it made her uncomfortable. She backed down.

'Look, it's been two months and so far, so good. Besides, you're not allowed to get involved. The rules are strict. I'm just there to help them learn the language.'

Reaching for her handbag was Elspeth's signal that their meeting was over. And the subject was closed—until next time.

Outside, Alice caught a whiff of her mother's French perfume, the one with the three-tiered name she could never pronounce. Elspeth had worn it for as long as Alice could remember. Couldn't leave the house without a dab on her neck and wrist. Said it was her signature. All women should have one.

Every birthday, perfume was Elspeth's gift to her. That she never smelt it on her daughter did not deter her. This year, Alice thought, I'll ask her to give it to someone who likes perfume.

'Bye darling. Are you off home now?'

'Actually, I'm going to the centre. A meeting for volunteers.'

'Really? Don't let them keep you too long then. See you next week. You are coming for your father's birthday, aren't you?'

'Of course, I am.'

'Well don't be late.'

7. Ottavio

Zach arrived home from school, dropped his skateboard and backpack at the door and slid onto a chair at the kitchen table.

'You help me with my homework?'

'What you got?' Ottavio asked playfully.

'Maths.'

'Want the genius to take a look huh?'

Giggling, Zach hunched his skinny shoulders up and twisted away from Ottavio.

'Ok my man, let's do it,' he said as Zach pulled his books from his backpack and stacked them on the table.

'But you got to make me some tea first.'

Zach jumped up and put the kettle on and rattled some cups from the cupboard. He seemed to be getting taller by the week, but there were no signs of him filling out. At fourteen he was already at Ottavio's shoulder. His legs were reed thin, his chest and hips the same narrow width. Zach filled the cups, left the teabags in, heaped sugar into them and passed a cup to Ottavio who took a small sip. The sweet, hot rush of the tea scoured around the emptiness that had been in him all day. The familiar feeling of circling, of going around and around and around. He tried to focus on Zach who was leaning his chin on his hand, smiling his doubtful smile. Even when he was little, he smiled like that. As though he never quite believed people meant what they said. Zach spread his books out across the table and as he looked intensely at the page patted the table, feeling for his pencil, Ottavio smiled to himself. He had been the same age as Zach when he had moved to the boarding school. He couldn't believe what he had found. Actual textbooks and trained teachers. Brand new notebooks. Pens and pencils. He had wanted, more than anything, to learn. Books and pens meant more to him than anything else.

'How did you get to be a genius?' Zach asked smiling.

'I worked hard.'

Zach waited for Ottavio to continue.

'I didn't understand Maths at first. Or Physics. I'd just stare at the board, feeling like the dumbest kid in the class. But Mr Kalasi said he wouldn't let any student fail. He made me work hard. Gave me homework every day and one day I realised how numbers work and how they could be used to build things.'

'What things.'

'Bridges, roads, all kinds of things. In the van when the athletics team went to a meet at another school, it would take hours. I know it's hard to believe but Nai's traffic was worse than here. I'd try and figure how we could get there quicker. Make the roads wider and smoother. Build tunnels, bridges. Mr Kalasi showed me how to make a model of what I wanted to build. To calculate the dimensions. He was a cool guy.'

'Rosa still wants me to be a doctor.' Zach said with the same doubtful smile.

'I know, I know. But you don't have to decide now.'

Ottavio didn't want him to feel the same pressure he had; to make sure what he did would provide for everyone.

Only three years had passed since Zach and his sister Rosa arrived in Australia. Rosa smiled more easily now, but Zach had not lost his restive caution or the sheen of sadness in his almond-shaped eyes. He worked hard and caught up on all the schoolwork he'd missed living in the camp, but he'd made no real friends. He hadn't learned to relax.

'Leave this till later. Let's go get some burgers.'

Confusion played out across Zach's face.

'You heard me.'

'But I got to hand it in tomorrow.'

'Don't worry, we'll get it done.'

Zach looked at the books, worried.

'Come on now. We got to celebrate a winning goal. It's the Australian way.'

But Zach was not swayed. Shaking his head Ottavio gave in, 'Bring it with you. We can do it there.'

Loading the books into his bag, Zach slung it on his shoulder, ready to go.

'Hold on, hold on. You think I'm going out with you in your school uniform? Go get changed.'

Zach dropped the bag and ran to his room.

Ottavio's phone rang. It was Paulino, an elder of the Twic community.

'*Cheebuk* Uncle. *Cheebuk.*'

'*Cheebuk* Ottavio. *Ekadee?*'

'I am very well Uncle Paulino.'

'Thank-you for sending this money to the camp. They know they can rely on you.'

Ottavio had constant requests from relatives. Everyone did. He sent what he could, always feeling bad that it was not more. But he knew – that was not why Paulino had called.

'My boy I've heard you are volunteering.' It wasn't a question and he didn't wait for a reply. 'This is good. All the young people should contribute; give Australia the best possible impression of us. They will see what good people we are.'

Ottavio squashed his irritation, wishing Paulino would get to the point. He wasn't calling about the respect of *kawaujas*. The community were gossiping about him.

'When will you start working as an engineer?'

Paulino knew black men couldn't get real jobs in this country, Ottavio thought bitterly, but the old man's pride would not let him admit that. Ottavio told him a half-truth. 'I've applied Uncle, am just waiting for an interview.' Ottavio had put in thirteen applications in the past few months and not had a single response.

'Son, now is the time to buy cows.'

Ottavio smiled. The clever old man wanted to arrange a marriage, a counter move against Angelina's family.

'Don't worry about the dowry. It is not your burden alone.'

Paulino took Ottavio's silence as encouragement. 'There is a girl. I know her family. She still lives in the village and she's not like the girls here who have forgotten where they come from.' Ottavio shook his head. Elders like Paulino complained that the traditional ways were being lost. Families breaking up because women could do whatever they liked in Australia. They could get their own income. Have babies without getting married. Young men did not offer cows.

It seemed to Ottavio that maintaining tradition in this country might not be possible. The best the elders could hope for was the young to respect what they no longer related to.

'An engineer deserves a good wife. One who will be admired.'

Paulino's slight towards Angelina and her family bit deep. It wasn't her fault their engagement had ended but he was letting Paulino blame her.

Angelina had asked Ottavio again and again. When would they marry? What day? Her family was waiting for their announcement. Her sister Adut had asked the same questions when Angelina had given up.

It was only six weeks since Angelina had called. Her voice was sad and quiet when she told him. She could not wait any longer. Ottavio had not protested and she got angry with him. He'd heard her voice break and her tears come before she abruptly ended the call.

Ottavio and Angelina had chosen each other. Luck had brought them both visas to Australia, but two years apart. Angelina was studying when he arrived. She could have been any man's wife but she wanted to do a degree and had rejected two marriage offers before she and Ottavio started seeing each other. She was his first real girlfriend. Paulino had protested their relationship – the elders should decide who would make a good wife for a man like Ottavio. But others pressured Paulino to accept their decision. Let the young people choose. Their lives had been such a struggle. Let them be happy.

Well, now Paulino would decide. He would make sure things were done in the traditional way. As the oldest clan member in Australia, he would make the right match for Ottavio. Angelina's rejection had marred the clan's reputation. Ottavio needed to marry a bigger prize, worth more cows than Angelina's family had asked for her.

Ottavio did not ask about the girl in the village. Paulino would bring her up again, now he was just planting the seed.

'I'm making good money at the meat works Uncle.' Ottavio told him, 'Every week I put some aside.' Ottavio let him think he was referring to the dowry.

Paulino was pleased, 'Machar, we know you are more responsible than most your age.'

'Thank you, Uncle.'

'How are Rosa and Zachariah?'

'Fine, Uncle, fine. Rosa is doing well in her studies. Zach scored the winning goal for his team this week.'

'Good news, good news. That young man will make us all proud. His parents will be watching. They will know it was you who bought him and Rosa here. A man looks after his family first. You have not forgotten this.'

It was not possible to forget. His cousins were the only members of his family he'd been able to help. The letter from immigration saying the visa application had been successful had been a proud moment. He'd waited for over two years for that letter. Without hesitating he went straight to the bank for a loan to buy their plane tickets.

At the airport, with one small bag between them, Rosa and Zach walked into the glaring lights of the arrival hall, terrified. They had taken the same journey as he had with Alpha and Malong eight years before. From a hut in the desert camp they'd taken a two-day bus ride to Nairobi, then a twenty-two-hour plane trip to the other side of the world. They were groggy with exhaustion, too overwhelmed to speak. Zach clung so hard to Malong, Ottavio had to drive.

'Everyone who can, will contribute.' Paulino said, returning to the dowry. 'Even those still in the camp will.'

'No Uncle, they are too poor.'

This did not deter Paulino. 'They may not have the resources now, but they will make a pledge and pay it later. It is a matter of honour. Everyone will gain from your marriage.'

Ottavio tried not to seem rude but cut him off before he could go any further.

'Thank you, Uncle, but I have to go now. I have someone waiting for me.'

'Don't worry my boy. Off you go. I will call again soon.'

Zach was waiting at the door in black jeans and his number nine Chicago Bulls shirt. Ottavio knew he'd been listening but said nothing to him, he wasn't going to draw Zach into the politics of marriage.

Driving to the shopping centre, Ottavio couldn't stop thinking that Paulino was wrong. Angelina would've made a very good wife. He wanted to defend her. Tell Paulino it wasn't her fault. She broke their engagement because of him.

As Zach chewed his way through a cheeseburger and a pile of too-salty chips, Ottavio sat next to him sipping a coffee from a paper cup. There wasn't much he could tell his cousin about Maths, watching Zach deftly use his calculator. Ottavio made him repeat a few equations. Just to be sure. He waited for him to finish then went and got him a chocolate sundae. Zach's eyes glazed over as he spooned the creamy goo into his mouth. He didn't even notice his pencil roll off the table. Ottavio scooped it off the floor. Next time he took Zach out they would leave the books behind.

As he finished his coffee, his thoughts returned to Paulino. His Uncle's praise had left a leaden weight in his chest. He was not the man his Uncle thought him to be. Here he was sipping coffee, money in his wallet and an expensive car parked outside. A highly-educated, free man. Rosa and Zach were doing okay, Alpha wasn't. Ottavio would always have his back, but he didn't see what more he could do for his younger brother at the moment. Things looked good from the outside, but inside was the same indescribable feeling. The feeling you get when you do not keep your word.

Ottavio dropped Zach home and headed for the community centre, pleased to have something to concentrate on. Being a volunteer was easy. He'd been surprised how much he'd enjoyed the first class. It was a simple way to help someone and he liked simple. The life of his community was not. He'd stopped going to the some of the meetings because they made him feel like he was sinking. So much was wrong. A new life in another country was hard, for everyone. But sometimes he wished young people would just get on with it. There was no way around the difficulties. They just had to go through it. Like crossing the Nile at its widest point. You couldn't see the other side and had no idea if you could make it, so you just had to keep paddling. He wondered if people were forgetting how it used to be. Nothing could be worse than what they had lived through.

Nothing.

As he walked into the classroom the plump, blue-eyed woman who had mistaken him for a student the week before came straight up to him. He did not like her fake warmth and patronising manner. Her low self-esteem and her flat, ugly shoes.

'How are you enjoying the class?' she asked nervously.

'It's fine.'

'You speak very good English.'

He nodded but said nothing. She looked uncomfortable, which is how he wanted it.

'Did you learn here?' she mumbled.

'No.'

He went to turn away, but something in him softened. 'I learned English in Kenya.'

'Oh, I thought you were Sudanese.'

'I am, but I went to high school in Kenya. A boarding school. On a scholarship.'

'Right.' There was a note of surprise in her voice.

He knew that she was defining those words in the way she understood them; rich kid, privilege. He wasn't going to explain, how a few lucky kids got out of the camp and into Nairobi schools on scholarships from churches or sport coaches, searching for talent in the Sudanese gene pool which had formed in the northern Kenyan desert. They regularly visited Kakuma: the massive, sprawling camp of hungry, desperate refugees. Over a hundred-thousand, choking on the dusty wind under the scorching sun waiting for something to happen. Anything. Even death. There were plenty of days when that seemed like the better option. He wasn't going to explain anything to her. There was nothing she had that he wanted, certainly not her kindness and sympathy. She should offer it to someone who did.

At the table he took a seat next to Mohammed. Mohammed smiled, pleased to have another man in the room, for once he wouldn't have to accept a woman's help. Achol arrived just as the class was starting and had no choice but to take the only remaining seat—at the other end of the table. Ottavio was relieved, he wanted to keep his distance from her in case she got the wrong idea. She had arrived only a few months ago and still had the look of a startled kitten wanting to be picked up and petted.

About twenty minutes later Ottavio glanced over at Achol, saw her staring at Mary and recognised the look in her eye. It was a hard fuck-you glint. Mary caught Achol's stare and held it for a moment too long. Achol clenched her hands and jumped out of her seat, lunging toward Mary, the room exploding with her furious energy. A chorus of voices gasped, and a woman screamed as Achol landed against Mary, knocking her flat, then straddling her chest. Ottavio could hear Melissa shouting at Achol to get off, as she ran toward the women. Mary's long legs splayed beneath her, the bright fabric of her long dress pushed up around her knees as she tried to twist her body away, grunting each time Achol's fist thudded against her head.

Ottavio forced some air into his lungs and pushed himself out of his chair, yanking Achol off Mary, tossing her to one side. But Achol turned and went for Mary again. Ottavio wanted to smack her down. Make her stop. But he couldn't, not in front of these people. Grabbing her again, he hauled her up and pushed her back against the wall, scattering the students bunched there like frightened cattle.

Mohammed and Melissa pulled Mary to her feet. She staggered as they led her away. Hair braids were scattered amongst the pencils and notebooks on the floor.

Achol's eyes shifted like a bird looking for a hole in the cage. She was barely breathing. He wanted to yell at her. 'Look what you've done. You stupid bitch. Now everyone will be scared of you. Of us.'

'No more. You hear me?' Ottavio spoke in Dinka, his voice low and harsh. The other students watched, dazed and anxious. Houda and Batool sniffed and wiped their eyes with handkerchiefs, correcting their headscarves, consoling each other. As Ottavio pulled Achol out of the room, he heard someone say, 'She have knife, she kill her.'

Waiting for the lift, Achol turned away from their shimmery reflection in the silver doors and stared at the ground. Her body sagged, hands hanging loosely at her sides, anger gone. Ottavio's hadn't. He knew it would be a petty grievance of some kind, maybe a feud between their families, or a story from the camp. He knew she didn't fully understand the implications of what she had just done.

'Ottavio! Please, please wait.'

Alice was rushing toward them. The lift arrived and Ottavio pushed Achol ahead of him. The doors were closing as Alice appeared, her eyes wide and frightened. He let the lift doors close between them. Watching the red numbers change as they dropped to the ground floor, he realised he was shaking.

8. Alaya

I think of other girls in other places. What are their lives like? Maybe they go to school? Once I held a pencil in my hand. A boy had dropped it and I picked it up. I want to know how to use it, to write with it. I want to know how to read. One day, when God returns, I will go to school.

9. Ottavio

Melissa's call had caught him by surprise, asking him to a meeting about the fight. He wanted to say no, this stuff happens, you don't need to pay it any more attention, but he felt obliged and reluctantly agreed. Obligation was the problem with volunteering Ottavio thought, as he pulled up outside the centre. Surely if you do something for nothing, you shouldn't be asked for more? That's what Malong would say, in fact, he would refuse to do it in the first place. Work for no money? No way. Ottavio had not mentioned the weekly class. But no doubt Malong would hear about it from someone.

Melissa and Alice were waiting for him in the empty classroom. Mugs clasped in hands, they were talking quietly but turned to him as he walked in, looking serious and concerned.

'Can I get you something. A cup of tea?' Melissa asked with a careful smile.

Ottavio shook his head politely.

'Thanks to both of you for coming in.' Melissa said, 'I wanted to make sure you were okay about what happened the other day. Give you a chance to debrief.'

Ottavio could feel Alice's eyes on him but he did not look at her. Melissa continued.

'Well, I've talked to the director and we have agreed to ban Achol. We can't have violence in the classroom. If she can't control herself, she can't be here. Ottavio, you know her. Any ideas about why she did that?'

Sitting back in his seat Ottavio folded his arms over his chest. 'I don't know her. I met her here. Three weeks ago.'

'Yes, but she's … isn't she the same tribe as you?'

'Yes, she's Dinka, but I don't know her.'

'We were hoping you might be able to give us some insight into the violence,' Melissa said. Ottavio looked to the ground. The blue carpet was faded and tired and there was a faint red fleck in it that he hadn't noticed before. He would keep it brief and get out of there as soon as he could.

'Have you asked her?' Ottavio spoke to Melissa.

'I plan to. I called and she agreed to come and see me, but she didn't show up. I think I'll visit her at home. How do you think she'll react to being banned?'

'I don't know,' Ottavio replied, trying to sound neutral.

'Do you know any of her family?'

'It's better if you speak to her.'

'Okay. Well, like I said, this is more of a debriefing for you and Alice. I wanted to make sure you were both okay. It's never happened in my class before. I hope you both keep coming.'

Ottavio was counting red flecks.

'What about you Alice? How have you been?' Melissa asked.

'Fine, I'm fine, but I was a bit shocked. I've never seen anything like that before. But I'm okay. I'm worried about Achol though. If she can't come here, where can she go?'

'I can find another place for her, but I'll have to tell them she's been banned from here. They'll have no obligation to take her and I'll explain that to her but if she can't guarantee there will be no more violence, I'm afraid there's nothing I can do.'

The room fell silent again. He knew they wanted him to speak but under his breath he kept counting.

'Would she go to counselling?' Alice asked him directly. 'Do Dinka people know what a counsellor is?'

Sliding the tip of his finger around the cool glass on his watch, Ottavio did not look up. 'I'm sure she knows what a counsellor is.'

'Do you think something has happened to her?' Alice asked, her voice thick with concern.

Loosening his jaw Ottavio stopped counting. 'Yes, "something" has happened to her. "Something" has happened to all of them. That's how they got to be refugees.' Immediately, he regretted his sarcasm. There was no need to be rude. And excluding himself? He could pretend he wasn't a refugee, but the thing about this country; you're never allowed to stop being one.

Alice looked like she wanted to cry and Melissa was watching him with quizzical eyes.

'Look, I'm sorry, but I can't help you understand Achol,' Ottavio said carefully. He wanted to ask them about the women they knew. What did they fight about? Wasn't it always about the same shit? Men? Jealousy? Dumb, petty stuff? Why did they think it was different because Achol and Mary were refugees? Maybe Achol was a bit crazy? He didn't know and didn't care. 'You need to ask her, and I need to go.'

'Stay a bit longer thanks Ottavio,' Melissa said. 'Alice can you give us a moment.'

Grabbing her bag and coat off the back of the chair, Alice rushed from the room.

Resentment flooded through Ottavio. If Melissa chastised him, he would not be coming back.

Taking a drink Melissa cleared her throat. 'Alice might not have said it well, but she was asking a reasonable question. We aren't blaming you, we're asking for your help.'

Ottavio replied carefully. 'I'm sorry, but I don't know why she attacked Mary. It might be personal, maybe a family thing. A feud? I don't know, but I don't want to get involved.'

'I wasn't asking you to. I'll deal with it. But I do want you to keep coming. You're a great help in class.'

'Thanks.' Ottavio got up to leave. As he put his bag across his shoulder, he paused for a moment, then glanced at Melissa. 'See you next week then.'

'Great, thanks Ottavio, see you Thursday,' Melissa smiled gently, and he nodded farewell.

As he came out of the room, he saw Alice move as if to block his way.

'Can we get a coffee? I mean do you want to… Do you have time? We seem to have gotten off on the wrong foot and I would like to make it up to you. Or just buy you a coffee.'

'Thanks, but I can't right now. I have to go.' Ottavio waited for her to move.

'Please.'

She was motionless, her face tight and pale. What could she want? Ottavio took a breath in. 'Ahhh.... well next week?'

'Before class?'

'Okay.'

'Thank-you. I can meet you in that place across the road if you like. Say an hour before class. Is that okay?'

'That's fine. See you then.'

In his car, Ottavio rested against the seat. Eyes aching, mind cluttered; he needed music. Flicking through the few CDs he kept in the glove box, he chose a favourite; Run DMC. Sixteen years old, using Vaclav's Walkman, he'd lie on his bunk and listen to the same track again and again, chanting the chorus, loud and out of tune. *It's like that. It's just the way it is.* The other kids in the dorm would throw their pillows and yell at him to shut up. But he ignored them. It was the song he always chose to cool down when his head ached with anger.

He let his eyelids droop, felt his scalp tightening against the coming headache. *It's just the way it is. It's just the way it is.*

Tapping replay, Ottavio started the engine and glanced in his side mirror. Angelina was standing at the bus stop, her long legs in tight jeans and high-heeled boots, a handbag on her shoulder, arms casually folded across her chest. If she had seen him she was pretending otherwise. With his heart beating wildly he pulled the car into a U-turn, stopped beside her, turned off the engine and got out. Ottavio tried to appear calm.

Angelina took a step back. Her black eyes gleaming as she searched his face, trying to gauge his mood.

'How are you Ottavio?'

'I'm fine. How about you?'

'I'm good Ottavio.'

'What have you been doing with yourself?'

Angelina gave him a wry smile and dropped her eyes.

'Can I give you a lift home?'

'That's okay. The bus will be here soon.'

Why am I even asking? Ottavio thought. Because she'd chosen Dut so quickly?

'You sure?'

'I'm sure Ottavio.'

'You look good Angel.'

Her gaze stayed cautious. 'You have something you want to say to me?' she asked.

'Yeah, I do. There's something I want you to know.'

'And what's that?' Angelina said, raising her chin. Her smell reached his nose. Breathing in lightly, he cleared his throat. 'I'm going home. To Sudan.'

Her eyes shifted off him and back again. She waited for more and so did he, but it didn't come. His throat was dry and the words he wanted her to hear were so far away he couldn't form them, couldn't ask her to leave Dut and wait for him to find his way there and back. She had already waited too long.

Angelina did not move. Ottavio wanted to pull her close to him and press her softness against him. But he cleared his throat and got back into his car.

'Look after yourself then.'

'You too Ottavio.'

He watched her in the mirror as he drove off. Turning her head, she wiped her cheek brushing something away.

He slammed his foot down on the accelerator, wanting to get the hell out of there.

The speedo was climbing and he kept nudging it until he saw a police car turn into the street. Lifting his foot, he turned the music down to a whisper. He would not tempt them. He would not think of Angelina.

It's just the way it is. It's just the way it is.

At home he showered and collapsed on the couch, a headache gripping his scalp. Would it have made any difference to Angelina if he'd told her the whole story? If anyone would understand wouldn't it be her? But how could he tell her, when he barely understood himself. He had to go back, to find out. There was nothing to stop him going. Other than being scared.

His phone blinked up Malong's name.

'Machar.'

'Hey Malong, what's up?'

'Nothing man. What you doing?'

'I'm at home.'

'The guys are coming over. Mawien's here.'

'Okay, I'll come by.'

Malong paused. 'What's wrong?'

'Nothing. I said I'd come.'

'You come it'll be first time in months.'

'So?'

'Something's happened. I know. You won't tell me but I know.'

'Whatever man. Give me an hour.'

'You still not drinking?'

'I'm bringing some Hennessy.'

'Oh man. You saw Angelina. That's it. I know it is. She made you small, didn't she? Man, you can't let a woman do that to you.'

'Shut-up Malong. You want me to come over or not?'

'Yeah man, get over here.'

10. Alice

As she blow-dried her hair Alice reminded herself it wasn't a date. He was a good-looking guy, broad across the shoulders and long limbed. Confident. Okay, so she was attracted to him and was curious about what he would look like without any clothes on, but it wasn't just his body. There was something in his eyes, like he was here and in another more distant place at the same time. Alice wondered about the other place.

Flicking the mascara brush through her lashes, she sighed. It had been a long time since she had seen anyone naked. Last year or the year before that? Applying a ruby-coloured lipstick, she imagined Ottavio in the prelude to naked—slowly unbuttoning his shirt, his long slender fingers moving down the zip of his jeans. Closing her eyes, Alice rested her forehead on the cold, smooth glass of the mirror.

The train was packed and Alice had not been able to get a seat. Standing in the aisle, swaying in motion, she tried to seal her mind off from the chatter of the school kids near her. Further down the carriage two junkies were loudly whining about someone who'd ripped them off. A man in a suit yelled into his phone as he undid his top button and loosened his tie. By the time the train pulled into her station, she was desperate to get out. The muggy air of the western suburbs came as a relief. She was fifteen minutes early, so she went to the café anyway and took a seat at the window, watching people pass by, trying not to check her watch. Then she saw a clock in a shop opposite. Ottavio was ten minutes late. Trying to not feel sad, Alice decided to wait two more minutes, then go back to the train station. Just as she was about to leave, she saw him pull up in a shiny blue car and reverse park in one precise move. Lithely stepping out, he slipped his bag across his shoulder and checked his watch.

Annoyed, Alice concentrated on her phone, pretending not to notice when he walked in. He waited for her to raise her head, then cleared his throat when she didn't. Casually looking up, Alice feigned surprise.

'Oh, hello.'

'Sorry, I'm late.'

'Are you late? I hadn't realised.'

The chair he pulled out from the table scraped loudly on the wooden floor. 'Well, at least you didn't make a joke about African time.'

Alice wasn't sure if he was being serious or not. A waiter appeared and took their orders. The silence was awkward and the room stuffy. Alice could feel her face getting warm.

'So, you wanted to talk about something?' Ottavio said.

'No, I mean I thought we could just get to know each other a bit better.'

Ottavio shifted in his seat.

'Maybe you could tell me something about Dinka culture? I don't know much, and lots of the students are Dinka.'

'Sure. What do you want to know?'

Alice had no idea. 'What brought you here? There was a war?'

'Yeah. Two actually. But there were a few years in between.'

'A civil war?'

'That's right.'

Alice was relieved to not sound completely ignorant.

'It's a long story but basically southerners rebelled against the North. Arab rule. There's a lot of tribes in the south. Dinka are the largest.'

'How long did the war go on for?'

'Together? Almost fifty years.'

'Who won?'

'No one really. Officially it ended this year. There's supposed to be a referendum in 2010.'

'About?'

'Independence. If the vote goes that way, the southern region will become a republic.'

'If the war's over don't you want to go back?'

'There's not much to go back to.'

His answer was so resolute she changed the subject. 'You look like you enjoy helping in the class.' Alice asked, still feeling self-conscious.

Shifting in his seat again, Ottavio cleared his throat, 'It's easy. Anyone could do it.'

'Not anyone. It takes a lot of patience, don't you think?'

'I guess.'

Their drinks arrived and Alice watched him spoon three heaped teaspoons of sugar into his black tea. She only allowed herself one. 'Gee, thought I was a sweet tooth.'

He shrugged, 'It's the Sudanese way. All sugar, no milk.'

Alice smiled, stirring her coffee, wondering what to say next.

'So, you just finished uni?'

'That's right.'

'Engineering?' Alice already knew the answer, yet she couldn't stop her nervous questions.

'Yep.'

'First degree?'

'Lots of Sudanese start their education late.' He sounded defensive.

'I just thought it might be a Masters.'

'I'd like to do one sometime. But first I want to get some experience. I'm a bit sick of study.'

'Yeah. I couldn't wait to finish. Desperate to get out of there and into the world.'

'What did you do?'

'English. Literature.'

'Novels?'

Alice heard a note of interest in his voice.

'That's right.'

'You like books.'

'I love books. Well, reading them. I mean reading fiction. Always have. I chose Lit so I could keep reading. Loved the idea I could go to uni and study stories.'

He was listening, his prickliness retreating.

'You must have read a lot?' Ottavio said.

'Yeah, you have to. But you get to compare all kinds of different styles and authors. I did a course on post-colonial writers,' Alice paused for his response.

'What was that like?'

'Great. I didn't even know what colonialism was, let alone what happened after it.' Embarrassed by her own naiveté, it was Alice's turn to shift in her seat, noticing the glimmer of the overhead lighting on his smooth scalp.

Ottavio made a comment that Alice didn't catch. 'Pardon?'

Fingering the face of his watch, he softly repeated himself, 'I like books too.'

'Oh, so you read?' Alice groaned inside. 'God, I'm sorry, that sounded terrible. Of course, you read. I meant do you read novels? Fiction?'

'Yeah. I read novels.'

'What's your favourite book?'

'That's hard. There's a few.'

'There always are. Top three?'

'*Catcher in the Rye.*'

'Really? I love that book. I still have the copy I stole from my high school library.'

Ottavio smiled a little.

'What else?'

'*Things Fall Apart.* You know that? Chinua Achebe.'

'No.'

'Every African who can read has read that novel. Achebe's the godfather of African literature.'

'I'd like to read it.'

'Yeah, you should.'

'Was there a third?'

'Ahhh … Chimamanda Ngozi Adichie, *Half a Yellow Sun.*'

'Don't know him either.'

'Her.'

'Oh sorry. Should I read her too?'

'You should if you're interested in post-colonial writing. Achebe was the first African novelist to be published in the nineteen-fifties. His books were about the effects of colonialism, but Adichie's the next generation. What happened after the colonialists left. She writes about the civil war in Nigeria. She's good.'

Alice sipped her coffee and looked at him again. All of what she had assumed about him was wrong. He was not a vulnerable person that she needed to guide.

'So what are your three?'

'Oh, umm, well, it is hard isn't it?' Alice paused, 'Umm, *Love in the Time of Cholera.*'

'*Love in the Time of Cholera?*' Ottavio looked perplexed.

'It's a love story.'

'Really?'

'Yeah. Sorry. I guess that's obvious.'

'What else?'

'Um, well, *Babette's Feast* by Karen Blixen.'

'Karen Blixen?'

'She's most famous for *Out of Africa*.'

'The film?'

'The film was based on her book. But she wrote a lot of books. Actually, she was a colonialist herself. Had a farm in Kenya in the 1920s, but she went broke and had to go back to Denmark. She wrote beautifully.'

'The third?'

'As clichéd as it sounds, I have to say *Pride and Prejudice*.'

Ottavio broke into a wide smile.

'You've read it?' Alice said.

'Of course, I have. Funny book. The best marriage for a daughter. Dinka mothers are just the same. It could have been set in Sudan.'

'Really?'

'Different era, different culture, same story.' Ottavio drained his cup, set it back on the saucer and asked the waiter for the bill. Alice noticed his hands and the elegance of his long fingers.

They walked to class together, saying little. She hoped he might sit near to her, but he took a seat at the other end of the table.

11. Alaya

The sun was bright in the sky and we were walking, my little brother and I, to the river. We should not have been at the river at that time of day. Water should be collected at dawn and in the evening before the sun goes down. But everything had become confused. The way we did things was getting lost.

We filled the water bottles. Then I told him to undress. But little brother was scared. He did not want his bath. I said the hippos would not bother us; they are lazy from the sun. And he must not think about those men on horses. If we hear them coming, we will run. They will never catch us.

We removed our clothes and walked into the dark water. I rinsed the red dust out of his hair and scrubbed him with my hands. He was whispering a song under his breath, one his Auntie taught him. Then he froze, staring across the river. I looked too and they were a long way away, but we could see them clearly on the opposite bank; three horses making their way down to the water to drink. The riders had cloth wrapped around their heads and machine-guns slung across their backs. They had not seen us.

12. Ottavio

Crows burst up from a tree as Ottavio left the house. Their strange, slow cry always sent a shiver through him. He didn't like those birds, their shiny little eyes and glossy black feathers.

As he drove to work, he thought about how he came to have a copy of *A Catcher in the Rye*. When he first arrived in Nairobi, he couldn't believe the size of the buildings or the number of cars on the road. His brain felt numbed by the sounds of the city. He'd only known his village, which he could barely remember, and Kakuma. Nairobi was the biggest place he had ever seen. In his first week at boarding school he spent a lot of time in the library, flicking through books, taking in the smell of the paper and ink. He chose the book because he liked the green cover. There was a drawing of a boy in a red hat watching a young girl running toward a carousel. The girl was looking back at him. There were tall buildings in the background. He started reading it in the library then asked if he could take it to the dormitory. At night, using a torch, he read the book again and again, lingering on Holden Caufield's adventures in New York. Unlike Nairobi, New York seemed like a place of magic. On every street, there were magical things. Holden was free to do anything he wanted. He made choices; he drank, danced, and could have had sex with a girl. His teachers wanted to know his opinion. Even though he had a family, he didn't really seem part of it. His father was a distant concern who did not frighten him. His mother worried like any mother. Holden didn't have a clan bearing down on him, watching and judging his behaviour, always checking to see he was becoming a responsible man. When his teacher had tried to apply pressure, Holden just left. The only person he listened to was his little sister Sophie – she was the girl on the cover. Holden was actually interested in what a little girl had to say.

And then there were the ducks. Holden wanted to know where they went when the pond froze. The people he asked didn't know, but he kept asking. Ottavio did the same, asking his teacher if a lake could freeze like an ice cube. Mr Kalasi gave him a picture of people skating on a frozen lake. Ice so deep and strong, nothing could break it. Ottavio stuck the picture on the wall next to his bunk. The very thought of skating on ice made him laugh so hard he had to bury his face in his pillow, so he didn't wake any of the other kids. He kept the book under his mattress and read it again and again, a little bit every night. When he heard that he was going to Australia, he did not return the book, even though he knew it was wrong. He felt guilty, but he'd wanted it with him. Years later, a friend who'd helped out in the library told Ottavio, the librarian referred to the kids with overdue books as the Book Keepers. When she knew a kid was leaving school, she usually made a point of collecting their books, but for some reason she did not pursue him. It was a gift of sorts. Ottavio wondered if Alice felt guilty for not returning her copy. Maybe she was a bit like him.

Ottavio turned into the car park and pulled up beside Malong. He checked his watch. Malong tapped on his window, imitating to him, pointing to his own bare wrist with a quizzical face. Ottavio got out and locked the car.

'You late Machar,' Malong said with a sly smile.

'No, I'm not late, you early. Boss give you another warning?

'No one warning me. I don't give a shit about time.' Malong said defensively.

'Money is the only thing you do give a shit about.'

'Man, that's harsh.'

'It's the truth.'

'Maybe, but you be nothing without money.'

'Yeah, yeah. At least you back on day shift. Drank all the extra money you made on evenings?'

Malong feigned shock, like he had no idea why Ottavio would say such a thing.

They wove their way through the car park to the main entrance and Malong changed tack.

'Saturday night was awesome man. Why you miss it? You crawl back into your hole? One night on Hennessy and we don't see you again for months?'

'I had stuff to do.'

'Staying at home by yourself, reading those shiny magazines about how to build bridges? That stuff? Volunteering is not going to get you what you need. You gotta come out. There someone you gotta meet.'

'Who?'

'Remember Rachel? In Adelaide?'

'With the skinny legs?'

Malong snorted, laughing at the memory. 'She all grown up now… and moved to Sydney.'

'You be pleased then. You always had your eye on her.'

'C'mon man. Just meet her.'

'Malong, how many times I gotta say this. Leave me out of your dating services. Please.'

'You think I'm gonna let you sit at home and think about things?'

Ottavio didn't reply.

'You gotta get back out there man. There're plenty of ladies for you. They be hanging off you if you let them.'

'Malong, let me do things my way. Okay?'

'If I let you do things your way, you be at university your whole life learning how to be a *kawauja*.'

Ottavio threw a fake punch to Malong's ribs. Malong swerved and playfully looped his arm around his friend's neck pulling him into a headlock.

'No way I'm gonna let that happen, Machar. No way,' Malong said, letting him go.

'You're so full of shit man,' Ottavio laughed, pulling open the factory door and pushing Malong through it.

Changing into overalls, they pulled on boots and gloves, slid papery caps onto their heads, checked their knives and took their place on the line for the first carcass to slide their way, swinging from the ceiling hook. Ottavio skinned the animal, peeling off the pelt, pushed it on to Malong. He slit open its belly, scooped out the internal organs and spilt the rest into the disposal chute. Next to them, their buddy Achek buzz-sawed the head off, cut the carcass in half from top to bottom and pushed the pieces along. From worker to worker, each man did his part, until the animal was reduced to small pieces for human consumption. The skin, blood and bones ready for sale elsewhere.

Ottavio let the work numb him. The hissing of hydraulics, bone-cutting machines, high-pitched saws, and the stench of warm blood dulled his mind and kept the constant murmur of guilt and memory at bay, until the buzzer for lunch break sounded. When they returned, the men settled in quickly, concentrating through the afternoon hours, the hum and clang of machinery setting the rhythm of their routine. If they all maintained the same pace, they'd get through the quota and finish on time.

The last hour the energy picked up. Men started calling out. What you doing tonight? A drink after work? No, I gotta get to soccer training. How's that team doing? Yeah, alright, alright. They pushed on until the buzzer sounded again. The line stopped and they were out of there fast. The next shift was ready. Another thousand animals waiting to be slaughtered.

In the car park Malong told Ottavio goodbye, punching his shoulder.

Ottavio checked his watch. At this time of the day he had only one goal. Without cheating or speeding, no short cuts, purely on his own skill, Ottavio had forty-five minutes to get home.

13. Alice

'Happy birthday Dad.'

'Thank you darling.' Thomas winked. 'I hope you didn't get me anything. No point wasting your money on an old man.'

Alice gave her dad a quick hug. 'There's no one I'd rather waste my money on.'

'I was hoping there might be.'

Her father's tone was playful, but Alice still winced. 'Dad please. I'm not the only close-to-thirty that's still single.'

'I know love, I know. But you can't blame me for hoping can you?'

Alice took his arm and he led her to the dining room.

'Got a wee surprise for you,' Thomas said ruefully.

Aunty Bronwyn and Uncle Jack were seated at the formal table and with them was their son Stefan.

Alice could not hide her surprise. Why hadn't Elspeth told me he'd been released? She always called as soon as there was any news, enjoyed conveying additional details of her nephew's spectacular failure, even though she'd always end her calls the same way, 'Poor Bronwyn. I don't know how she copes.'

Alice exchanged kisses with her Aunt and Uncle. Stefan stood up and pulled out the chair next to him, 'Hey cousin, long time,' he said, pecking her cheek. His expensive aftershave making her nose twitch. A sneeze threatened.

'You look well Stefan.'

'Don't lie. You've always been too polite. But you look great. Life treating you well?'

'Oh, you know, nothing to complain about.'

Carrying a large platter of antipasto, Elspeth bustled into the room.

'Isn't it lovely to have Stefan with us Alice?' Elspeth said, not expecting an answer. Fussing over the platter, she herded the green olives back into a pile away from the buffalo mozzarella, before marching back to the kitchen. Alice saw the tension her mother's stride and guessed that Bronwyn hadn't warned her she was bringing Stefan. This was going to be more of a strain than usual.

Alice took an even breath and caught Stefan's eye, and he gave her an exaggerated wink. Alice had never visited him in jail. Even though she had not planned to, she was relieved when he had written asking her not to come. They'd been best friends growing up. He'd been a sweet and mischievous kid, just a few months older than her.

Elspeth was back at the table passing the platter around. Her lipstick was fresh and she'd had her nails done. Alice wondered if Stefan had noticed. As a teenager, he'd made a habit of complimenting his aunty on her appearance and Elspeth often said how lovely it was of him. In her first year of high school she'd overheard Elspeth on the phone, telling a friend that she thought Stefan was gay. Alice was shocked. How could Elspeth say that? Not because of Stefan's compliments? Besides, he couldn't be gay. He'd never have kept something like that from her.

'Some wine love?' Uncle Jack didn't wait for an answer. He filled her glass with wine, one of the prized reds he kept for birthdays. Jack's face was flushed, and she could smell the wine on his breath. He's well on his way, Alice thought. Stefan was holding a tumbler of sparkling water that rippled from the slight tremor in his hand. He didn't look nervous and certainly not like someone who had just come out of prison. Clean-shaven, the crisp blue shirt matched his eyes. He could have just come from working in a company office. Two years can't have passed, he must have been released early.

'So Stefan,' Alice began, but Bronwyn looked at her with pleading eyes and she stopped. Stefan gave her a small smile and Alice took a sip of wine. 'So, what are your plans Stefan?' she asked, keeping her tone bland, avoiding Bronwyn's gaze.

'Let's not talk about it now Alice, it's your father's birthday,' Bronwyn said brightly. Elspeth passed the platter again and the tension eased a little amongst the clatter of serving spoons, plates, and throats clearing. Stefan took several long gulps from his glass.

Alice remembered being in court. His lawyer described Stefan as so drunk he couldn't remember breaking his wife's arm and three of her ribs during an earlier assault. Hearing there had been previous charges, which Carmel had dropped, made Alice feel sick. Carmel had made eye contact with her once during the whole time they'd been in court and had quickly looked away. She hadn't been heard of since the day Stefan was sentenced.

'How's work Alice?' Uncle Jack asked. 'Keeping you busy?'

Alice blinked away tears and smiled at her Uncle Jack; always the peacemaker.

'It's fine,' she said.

Alice gazed at her wine, trying to take in an easy breath. She looked around the room, at her family pretending everything was normal. Why couldn't they talk about what happened? Right now? Here at the table? Alice put her glass down, a mixture of the shame and bafflement that she had felt in court, rising up in her again.

'What about your flat love? Ever think about selling? Moving back this way?' Alice shrugged weakly and kept her eyes down. Growing up, they'd been best friends, had started university together. Stefan dropped out in first year after discovering all night dance parties and the drugs that fuelled them. At some point he'd met Carmel. A whiney voice, but pretty with dyed red hair and a big smile. Alice had no idea what her cousin saw in her, other than maybe being his drug supplier. Dealing would have been a perfect sideline to her job promoting clubs.

Elspeth cleared the platter, then served small bowls of crab bisque with garlic croutons. They seemed to have barely finished when she was up again, stacking the bowls, tacking them back to the kitchen. Lobster tails with a blue cheese sauce followed. Uncle Jack's compliment to Elspeth was slurred, and Alice glimpsed Bronwyn's annoyance.

Her father hummed his appreciation of each course, but Alice knew he didn't care much for fine food. A dish of Kung

Pao chicken at the local Chinese would have made him happy. Alice grinned at her Dad and sipped some wine as she thought more about Carmel.

When his lawyer had listed the incidents of Stefan's violence towards her, Alice refused to believe it. It had just not seemed possible that Stefan could be like that. But as the evidence was presented, the truth lapped at her like a cold wave. She tried to back away from it, but there were photos of Carmel's bruised face, records of complaints to police, a restraining order he had ignored. Stefan pleaded not guilty, but the judge said the evidence was undeniable. As the judge sentenced him to jail, the wave surged up and swamped her. Watching him being led away, a man who had brutally beaten his wife, she saw them both in a totally new light. Stefan was a bully and Carmel had had the strength to stand up to him.

Jack was topping up the glasses again and Alice placed her hand over her own when he unsteadily offered the bottle. Stefan refilled his glass as Elspeth delivered the tarte tartin, with a candle carefully placed in the centre. Thomas blew it out to a small round of applause.

Alice offered her father a carefully wrapped gift.

'Oh love, you really shouldn't bother. I'm too old for gifts.'

Alice ignored him. He would have been hurt if she hadn't bothered. And since it was her father who had encouraged her love of books, every year her gift was the same.

'Ah, a book. What a lovely surprise.' Thomas gave her a cheeky smile.

'Che … chin-a-wah, A…che…be. *Things Fall Apart*. What have you got us there, then?'

'Nigerian writer Dad. The first one actually. I mean the first African novelist ever published. Back in the fifties. I thought you might be interested. It's very good.'

'Well I can't say I've heard of it. But I'll give it a go.'

'Your mother said you are doing some volunteer work? With Africans?' Uncle Jack said.

'Refugees.' Aunty Bronwyn added, her voice flat with disapproval. She would never admit how much she and Elspeth were alike.

'Yes, they are. Or were. Strictly speaking they aren't now. They are migrants.'

'Why on earth would you do that?'

'I wanted to do something… useful. It's a lot more interesting than my work.'

'You always were a sucker for a sad story,' Stefan said. It was the first thing he had said all night.

'It's a long trip, the train to Parramatta. Is it safe?' Bronwyn asked.

Thomas intervened, 'It must be interesting meeting people from all those different places.'

'It is. I enjoy it. They are really nice people who've been through an awful time.'

Bronwyn glanced at Elspeth. She would be on the phone to Elspeth in the morning.

'Had a chance back in the seventies to go. Got offered a job in South Africa. New mine. Would like to have gone,' Uncle Jack slurred.

'Oh, for goodness sake Jack,' Bronwyn said. 'You didn't want to go any more than I did. Terrible place. Always running around killing each other. Dreadful diseases. Starving children. You wouldn't have lasted five minutes.'

Alice wondered for a moment if her childhood dreams of going to Africa had come from Jack.

'No sense of adventure in our house,' Stefan said mildly.

'It has nothing to do with adventure Stefan,' Elspeth said, in a rare show of support for her sister. 'Those places aren't for white people. The climate is just too hot.'

'Well the colonialists didn't mind the heat,' Alice said, bolstered by the wine. 'Plenty of white people went there. Plenty benefited. Whole countries got rich from Africa.'

Lips pursed and tense, Elspeth sliced the tarte tartin into narrow triangles, placing each piece onto her most delicate china plates; small, pale-yellow ovals with hand-painted violets. She passed each plate with a small silver cake fork on each one.

'Well, I for one, will look forward to reading it. Thank you darling,' Thomas said turning the hard-covered book over in his hands.

Elspeth passed the double cream.

14. Ottavio

Zach was standing back from the crowd of kids at the school gates when Ottavio saw him glancing at a group of girls walking by. One of them was the redhead from the soccer game. She gave Zach a shy smile as she passed and Zach dropped his eyes.

Ottavio sounded his horn so Zach's classmates would notice the car. Zach loped over and jumped in and Ottavio released Zach's window, so he could casually lean on his arm as they drove away.

'Man, you gotta work on your form.' Ottavio said.

Zach looked at him confused.

'When a pretty girl is smiling at you, you gotta smile back.'

Embarrassed, he flicked his eyes away and peered out the window.

'Come on now. Don't be like that. Nothing gonna happen if she thinks you don't like her.'

'I don't like her.'

'Well, you looking at her.'

'No. I wasn't.'

'Nothing to be ashamed of my man.'

'I wasn't looking at her.'

'What's wrong with her?'

'Nothing's wrong with her. But I wasn't looking at her.'

'Doesn't matter if she's *kawauja.*'

Zach didn't reply.

'I saw the way she smiled at you. She likes you.'

Zach folded his arms over his chest and twisted in his seat. Ottavio could see there was more to this than a shy teenager not knowing how to handle the situation.

'There a problem here Zach?'

'No.'

'Come on.'

'Everybody knows you get trouble.'

'Listen to you sounding all worldly. You got to have a girl before she can give you trouble.'

'I don't mean her.'

'Who do you mean?'

'Nothing.'

Ottavio ignored Zach's hedge and went back to the tease. Put Zach under pressure and he'd stop speaking altogether.

'If you like her just smile at her.'

Zach slowly shook his head no.

Ottavio wanted the problem to be a fourteen-year-old's shyness, not a white girl being off limits. Or some idiot white kid telling Zach to stay away.

'You do know how to smile don't you?'

Zach glanced at him.

'Put your lips together and then pull them tight at the corners until your teeth show. Like this.' Ottavio made a grotesque face. Zach tried to hold back a laugh.

'And then after you smile you say hello. You know that

word, right? You say, hello my name's Zachariah. I know your name. All the boys know it cause they all talk about you.'

Zach shook his head again. 'I ain't saying that.'

'They talk about you all the time. You're so pretty. It's that beautiful red hair.'

'I'm definitely not saying that.'

'You want to spend some time together. We could go to McDonalds. You know, hang out. Maybe catch a movie. You busy this weekend? We could catch the train, go to Bondi beach.'

Zach giggled.

'That's what Malong would say. Sometimes it even works. You just have to be confident. Be your leopard self. Don't matter if she's a white girl. No different to any other girl. They're the same all over.'

Laughter subsiding, Zach looked at Ottavio again.

'So you gonna ask her?'

'No.'

'Come on Zach. You can do it.'

'She's someone else's girl.'

'You sure about that? Why she smiling at you if she got someone?'

'No one messes with him.' Zach said, wary again.

'What's his problem?'

'Theo hasn't got any. He rules. Everyone is scared of him. They do what he says.'

'That kid from the game? I wouldn't worry about him.'

'You don't know him.'

'I don't need to. I know his kind. He thinks he's a big bad dude who owns the world but really, he's all scared inside. I've met plenty of Theos in my time. I'll have a word with him.'

Zach's head jerked back, 'No!' he said, voice tight and loud.

Ottavio looked at him hard. Zach never raises his voice.

'You do that you get me killed.'

'Oh, come on now.'

'You don't know him. Everyone stays away from him.'

'You got trouble with him?'

'No. And I don't want any. I don't want trouble with him.'

'Okay. Calm down my man. There's no problem here.'

Zach sat back in his seat and leaned his head back against the headrest. Ottavio watched him from the corner of his eye. His thin body still and tense.

Pulling the car into the driveway, Ottavio killed the engine and put his hand on his shoulder.

'Zach.'

'Yeah.'

'You'd tell me if there was?'

Zach didn't reply.

'If there's a problem. You tell me. Right?'

'You think you can fix things, but you can't.' Zach said in a small voice.

Ottavio didn't know what to say. Zach sounded so weary.

'You tell me what's happening, and we talk about it. Okay?'

'Okay.' Zach got out of the car and let himself into the

house. Ottavio waited, listening to the engine tick as it cooled down, telling himself there wasn't anything to worry about. Zach had always been nervous. This was nothing new.

Then Ottavio thought of the two *kawaujas* at the game. Was the guy with the tattoos Theo's brother? Is that why Zach's so worried? Theo got some muscle behind him? Shy kids get picked on for sure, but shy and black? Zach was a target for anyone looking for one. Especially someone who hated blacks. He wondered if anything had happened that Zach hadn't told him about. He thought of calling Rosa but decided to wait until they were both home. He had to choose the right time with Rosa, she could easily spin off into her rituals of prayer and worry.

Given the chance Zach could do anything he chose, there was nothing to stop him. But he wasn't a fighter. He couldn't stand up for himself. His spirit was too thin. It wouldn't take much to break it.

15. Alaya

*The horses snuffled and snorted their noses in the water. I wanted
the day to turn black, so we could disappear into it. My little
brother stared at me, his eyes huge. I put my hand across his mouth,
sucked air into my nose and pulled him under the water with
me. He was clever my little brother, he picked up his feet. I held
onto him and let the river carry us away. Little brother began to
struggle but I held him down. I did not want the men to see us.*

*We could have stayed under the water. Lived forever with the
fishes and the crocodiles. But my chest hurt like it would break
apart. It wanted the sky. We burst above the water and I tried
to stand, but my feet could not find the bottom of the river. The
water carried us on. Little brother's eyes were closed. His head was
floppy.*

*We swerved into a bend and the water pushed us to the side,
leaving us behind as it rushed on. We collided with a tree. I
reached for it and it rolled. I reached again and held on, telling my*

little brother to wake up. I needed him to wake up. There was land under my feet. I stood up, little brother under my arm like a sack of dura.

The branch rolled again, and I saw that it was a man with a hole through his chest. Next to him there was another man, and another and another. Among them was an old woman. Her face was burned.

The river had pulled them all into this quiet bend.

I shook so much I could hardly drag little brother from the water. I wanted to take him into the bush, so he did not see the floating people when he woke up. But he would not open his eyes and I got angry. I slapped him and pushed him. Water came out of his nose and mouth. He rolled over and coughed and spat out more. His eyes were confused.

I slapped him again. Told him he was a stupid, lazy boy.

16. Alice

Alice had butterflies in her stomach as she waited at the lift for Ottavio. He came down the corridor and acknowledged her with a curt nod. Pushing the lift button repeatedly he asked coolly, 'How you going?'

'I'm good.' Alice pulled the novel from her bag. 'Thought you might like to read this.'

Taking the book, he flicked open the pages.

'In my top three. Gabriel Garcia Marquez.'

Ottavio turned it over with his long, slender fingers and cast his eyes across the back cover.

'One of the characters is a doctor trying to find a cure for cholera.'

'I've had cholera.' Ottavio said with a smirk, 'Didn't make me think of love.'

Alice did not give into her nervousness. 'I think you'll like it.'

'What makes you think that?'

She hesitated, unnerved, he was hard to read.

'I'm genuinely curious.'

'Umm, well. It's about tradition. And um love, well… spiritual love.'

Ottavio face changed. As though a veil had dropped away, his limpid eyes brightened. It felt like he was looking at her, for the first time and shyness overcame her. 'Anyway, I'll leave it with you.'

'Thanks. You on your way home?'

'Yeah. To the station. I get the train to Central.'

'West for me,' Ottavio said dryly. Alice swallowed. 'Ok then, see you next week.'

'I can drop you at the station if you like. It's on my way.'

'Umm…no, that's okay. You don't have to.'

'I know.'

Alice swallowed again.

His sleek blue car was parked nearby. It was nothing like hers. There were no drink bottles on the floor or junk on the backseat. The interior was spotless and smelt of air freshener. The engine rumbled quietly.

The seats were low and slung back. Conscious of his sudden closeness, Alice tried to inch her skirt down over her knees. She put her handbag on her lap. 'So, how long have you been here? In Australia.'

'Eight years now.'

'You must miss home.'

'Not exactly sure where home is. Was about five when I left Sudan. Lived in camps in Ethiopia and Kenya for nearly fifteen years.'

Alice tried to make sense of what he was saying.

'Have you been back to Sudan?'

'No, but I'm planning to now that I've finished uni.'

'Do you remember it?'

'Some. I grew up near a big swamp. Lots of water and bright green reeds. Used to play 'pretend battle' there with my age mates. I remember that well.'

'When will you go?'

'I'm not sure. When I get organised.'

Alice waited for him to continue, but they drove on in silence. Ottavio cleared his throat, 'So you're an Aussie?'

'I guess so, though both my parents came from England.'

'They were immigrants?'

'Yeah. They were ten-pound Poms. That's how much they were charged for a ticket on the boat out here.'

'Ten pounds?'

'That's about thirty Australian dollars in today's money.'

'From England to Australia? Thirty dollars?'

'This was in the early seventies.'

'Sounds okay to me. When I bought my cousins out from Kenya the plane tickets cost over three thousand.'

'Really? You had to pay that? I thought the government did?'

'You wanna bring your family here, you pay.'

'Can people afford that?'

'They take out huge loans.'

'That's what you did?'

'Yep.'

'And now you have a uni debt?'

'That's right. That's how it is for lots of people. Big, big debts.'

'I didn't realise.'

'Why would you?'

Alice didn't answer. Her parents paid her fees when she was at university, gave her an allowance and bought her a car as a graduation present. They bought her another for her twenty-fifth birthday. It was parked in the garage of her flat, which they had paid the deposit on.

Ottavio pulled over near the station. Behind, a driver leaned on his car horn, protesting loudly. Alice got out quickly and before she had a chance to thank him properly, Ottavio drove off with a wave goodbye.

She watched his car speed through an orange light and turn the corner.

17. Ottavio

Ottavio stirred a third teaspoon of sugar into the strong black tea, wondering where Alphonso was. Last night he'd been home but they hadn't spoken, he'd been listening to music in his room with his headphones on. Alpha had a tight bunch of friends and they looked out for each other, Ottavio told himself. If there were any trouble, he'd know about it quickly.

Pouring a tea for Rosa, he knocked on her door then pushed it open with his foot. Rosa was at her desk; a lamp threw a bright circle of light on it and the papers she was working on.

'You want this?'

'That's sweet Ottavio, thank you. I didn't hear you.'

'And you never will, cause that car's a gazelle.'

He snickered and handed Rosa the tea. 'You been at work this morning?'

'Yeah. They said there's some more hours.'

'More cleaning hours?' Ottavio said in disbelief. 'I thought they were always cutting your hours?'

'Don't be like that Ottavio, I am grateful for it.'

Rosa's passivity, her compliance made him uncomfortable. He changed the subject. 'How's the study?'

'Fine. Can be hard, but I like it.'

'Back in camp you couldn't even count.'

Rosa smiled at him. She didn't mind the ribbing. 'How's work?'

'Work is work. Lots of dead animals and blood.'

'You haven't heard about the jobs?'

'Nup.'

'God willing. I'll pray for you.'

'Thanks Rosa, but share your prayers around.'

'Like who? Alpha?'

'And Zach.'

'Something's wrong?' Rosa's voice hushed with concern.

'No Rosa, I just want him to do well.'

'What is it?'

'No, he's just fine.' Ottavio did not want to mention the red-haired girl. Rosa would not approve.

'Ottavio?'

'You know what kids are like. He doesn't seem to have many friends.'

'He wouldn't say anything to me. He keeps everything close.'

Ottavio wished he hadn't mentioned it. Rosa would worry now. She worried about everything.

'Don't worry Rosa.'

'Something wrong for Zach, you tell me.' Rosa fiddled with her pen.

'There are other Sudanese kids at that school. He's friends with them.' Ottavio tried to sound light. 'You speak to Samuel this morning?' Rosa smiled. A one hour call was their weekly ritual.

'Fine. Working hard.'

Samuel was studying theology in Nairobi. They were planning to marry when they had both finished school the following year.

She would return to Kenya for the ceremony, then they would apply for a visa for him to come to Australia as her spouse. She would come back, and he would wait for the approval, and when he arrived they would have another ceremony. The families were negotiating the dowry, the final number of cows had not been settled, but it would be high. Rosa was pious, quiet and had a good heart. Both families were highly regarded and before the war, their fathers had many cattle. They had been prosperous men. At home, the family's resources were being slowly restored and Rosa's dowry would be keenly anticipated.

Rosa cleared her throat. 'Saw Adut yesterday.'

'Angelina's sister?'

'Yes.'

'How was she?'

'Fine. She asked about you.'

Ottavio had avoided this moment. Rosa knew the reason Angelina's family had broken the engagement was because he delayed the wedding again and again. Adut would have been polite to her, it was beneficial to both families for things to remain calm. But Rosa would not let Angelina's family make hers look bad. She didn't understand why he'd delayed, nobody did. It looked like he'd had doubts about Angelina, but the doubt was about himself, about being the man Angelina deserved. He'd wanted her family to lose patience, then she could call it off. Dut had been in the background, hoping for a chance. Dut would be a better man for her.

Rosa waited for him to speak, but when he stayed quiet,

she said, 'Uncle has been speaking to a family. Next time I see Adut I will tell her your marriage is being organised.'

Ottavio shook his head. It was no surprise that Paulino and Rosa had been plotting.

'Good night Rosa.'

'I'll pray for you Ottavio. Pray to God to marry soon.'

Ottavio closed the door quietly behind him. There was a light on under Zach's door. He took a slow breath and knocked gently on the door.

'Is the leopard in there?'

'Yeah.' Zach sounded sleepy. Ottavio stuck his head around the door. Zach was in bed, looking like he was about to fall asleep.

'How's things?'

'Good.'

'What's happening at school?'

'Nothing'

'Everything fine?'

'Yep. Fine.'

'Your coach going put you on again?'

'He said so.'

'That's good news. So you going on a date this weekend?'

Zach played along. 'I'm too busy. Got an English assignment. Have to write a genius essay.'

'Is that all?'

'Have to score for the Reds too. And find a cure for malaria.'

'Now you're talking. You have that done by Sunday night?'

Zach sniggered.

'Then you can ask that girl out. Tell her how you cured malaria. She already knows you smart and she's seen you score.'

Zach's smile was shy and lopsided. 'Ain't gonna happen.'

'Come on now. What's her name?'

'Kelly.'

'And what you know about Kelly's family?'

'Not much. She works at her aunt's bakery after school. The one at the shopping centre. They make chocolate cake there.'

'She bring you cakes? Is that it?'

Zach didn't reply so Ottavio eased up.

'Well, Kelly don't know what she's missing. Goodnight, leopard.'

Pulling the sheet up, Zach rolled over and Ottavio turned out the light.

In his own bed Ottavio yawned and closed his eyes, wanting sleep to come quickly, but the ache opened up in his chest as it did nearly every night. He felt it most at night, in the dark, when he was alone. He rolled onto his side, then his back, then his other side, trying to keep his breathing slow and deep, but the restlessness would not leave. Ottavio yawned and blinked in the darkness. Why was he delaying? Sudan was just a plane ticket away. Mentally he packed his bag.

18. Alice

Alice hurried down the fire stairs to the foyer. Gail was waiting. Once a week, in their lunch break, they spent half an hour power walking around the city. Gail was the only friend from university Alice had stayed in touch with. In fact, she was the only true friend she had. It was Gail she rang in a panic, three years before, when she'd resigned from her previous job on a whim and booked a round-the-world ticket. The moment she had, her daydream of solo travel to far off places dissolved. She didn't admit to Gail the possibility of freedom had terrified her, she didn't need to. Gail got her the job in the insurance office.

'Come on, I've been down here five minutes,' Gail yelled as Alice reached the foyer.

'Sorry, couldn't get off the phone.'

Gail charged out of the double glass doors; fists aloft, elbows pumping, hips rocking side-to-side, Alice trailing behind her. Stopping for a red light, Gail turned toward her friend, walking on the spot, breathing deeply through her nose waiting for her to catch up, so she could start on her favourite subject.

'Come on, keep up. You're supposed to be leading the way, keeping me motivated. If I don't drop a few kilos I won't fit into the dress I got for Charmaine's birthday party.'

Gail's daughter was turning twelve. Alice had held Charmaine just after she was born. She was such a tiny red-faced thing. Her cry was so loud she seemed to be protesting her arrival. Gail and her husband Tony were hugging each other, weeping. Alice also cried as she handed her back to Gail. Charmaine was born in their last year at uni, so Gail never finished her degree. Tony got a construction job and now ran the entire company. Gail's life seemed so full and busy even though she complained constantly about how bored she was. She was comfortable and loved in a way Alice could not comprehend. Other than slimming down a size or two, she didn't know what else Gail could want, although she didn't mind all of the clothes Gail passed on to her because they were just a little bit too tight.

'Maybe one day you'll buy a dress that fits?' Alice asked dryly.

'You know I need the motivation. Otherwise I'll be a sixteen all my life. Size fourteen will do. If you manage it, so can I.'

Alice didn't reply, mentally ticking that subject off in her head. Gail's mild envy of her friend's lesser weight had stopped being complimentary years before. Alice waited for Gail to move onto the other items on her treasured list of complaints. There was an order to it, her body, and her inability to control it or her children, followed by Tony's problems at work, and her clearly unbelievable claim to not minding that he was never at home.

The lights changed and Gail raced off again, turning the corner into a cool breeze, her glossy hair flicking over her shoulders. She spent a fortune on the dark, honey-coloured highlights and her French-polished nails. Her personal grooming was relentless. Alice couldn't be bothered with any of that anymore. Streaking her hair had become the sole remaining ritual of its kind and she was relieved to have finally given it up a few months ago. Gail had noticed the mousey brown growing through, but said nothing, probably out of pity.

They crossed the street into the park and Gail dropped the pace.

'So, how's it going at the centre?'

'It's good. Interesting.'

'So, what are they like?'

'The students?'

'No, the cleaners.' Gail's voice dripped with sarcasm. 'Of course, the students, who else would I be talking about?'

Alice ignored her, 'They're mostly from Africa, some from Iraq and Afghanistan.'

'Really? Any nice-looking fellas?' Gail raised her eyes suggestively.

Alice took a breath in, hoping this was not going to lead to anymore revelations of her frustrated sexual fantasies. She hadn't forgotten the last confession. Gail handcuffed to a four-poster bed, ready to be serviced by three policemen in riot gear.

'What about the Africans? Always fancied a black man myself. Big buggers, are they?'

'Gail, please. I think it's a bit inappropriate to be talking about people I'm working with.'

'Oh, lighten up. You're such a prude. Always have been. I can't believe you're still single and not shagging yourself silly.

If I had my chance over, I wouldn't get married.' Gail paused thoughtfully, 'Well maybe I would. But there'd be a legal contract stating after the seventh year, hubby wouldn't mind if I went out in search of a good root every couple of months.' Gail burst into giggles. Alice couldn't help but smile, hating to admit an admiration for her friend's crass honesty. Alice would never confess to her own sexual fantasies. They seemed so pedestrian in comparison.

'So, are there?' Gail asked, puffed.

'Are there what?'

'Any lookers?'

'Well…'

'I knew it! Go on, tell us.'

Alice gulped. 'There's one guy. He isn't a student, he's a volunteer. African.'

Raising her eyebrows Gail egged her on.

'He's really tall.'

Gail squinted at her. 'What? He's really tall? That's it?' Exasperated and breathless Gail went on. 'Tony's "really tall",' Gail said, striking her fingers in the air, quoting Alice. 'Lots of blokes are "really tall". I don't care how tall he is, I want to know if he's hung like a donkey.'

Alice rolled her eyes. 'I've only just met him,' she gasped exasperated. 'He seems like a nice guy.'

'Oh my god.' Gail's sarcasm returned. 'Seems like a nice guy? You're such a bloody romantic. Too many books that's your problem. You should never have done Lit at uni. Waste of time.'

'Not following you Gail? What should I have done? Sexy science?'

'What you should have done was slept around a bit, instead of all those private tutorials with that sleazy lawyer.'

'He was a barrister,' Alice winced at herself. She sounded pathetic.

'He was a bloody sleaze bag and he ruined you for anyone else. Filled your head with romance and fairy floss.'

'Karl wasn't sleazy.'

'Oh, I don't believe you. Karl even tried it on with me.'

Alice winced. 'Karl came onto you?'

'Karl came onto everyone Alice. Every teenage girl who ever walked through the door of McKenzie Crocker got the eye from Karl. Elizabeth Munro got pregnant to him.'

Alice froze.

Gail paused, gazing at her friend.

'She had a termination,' Gail said bluntly. 'Blurted it out one day when I found her crying in the bathroom.'

A chill rolled down Alice's spine. 'Why didn't you tell me?'

'What you don't know can't hurt you.'

'What?'

'I didn't think you would handle it. It was all so bloody long ago, what does it matter?'

Gail increased her speed. Alice felt woozy. Breathless, she had to push herself to catch up. Gail slowed and waited for her, looking perplexed, 'Don't tell me you still carry a torch for him?'

'Of course not,' Alice said weakly.

'You do! Oh Alice, I'd understand if he was a great guy.'

Alice felt like a net had been dropped over her. How could she not know?

'Elizabeth Munroe?'

'Yep.'

'Elizabeth Munroe?' Alice repeated. 'The skinny brunette with her big eyes and long lashes?'

'Yes. Elizabeth bloody Munroe.' Gail sped off again.

Alice blinked away tears. Of course, Karl had others. All those work experience girls hoping his dark eyes might linger a moment longer than necessary. The tears came back. Gail did a U-turn and put her arm around Alice's shoulders.

'I can't believe you didn't tell me?' Alice sniffed. 'Did you really think I wouldn't cope?'

'Alice look…'

'Do you think I'm weak? Do you? I want to know.'

'No. But back then…. You were just a kid and you thought he was God. I didn't want to be the one to break it to you.'

Alice looked at her friend, searching her face, unsure if she should accept what she was saying. 'What happened to Elizabeth Munroe?' Alice asked, wiping her eyes.

'Lives in the States. Two kids. Divorced.'

Gail took her by the hand and pulled her along. 'Doll don't let it upset you. It was a long time ago. I think you should just ask Mr Really Tall out on a date with the express purpose of getting laid.'

'I've had a coffee with him,' Alice said meekly.

'You sly dog. Why didn't you tell me?'

'It was just a coffee.'

'You asked him?'

'Yeah. We needed to talk about something that happened in class.'

'Well, go you! So, what did you talk about?'

'Ahhh… books mainly.'

'Oh God! Alice, please! You must be the only person I know who gets turned on by books.'

'What were we supposed to do, shag each other in the cafe?'

'You're supposed to flirt with him. Get him interested in your body. Smile and show off your boobs.'

They stopped at lights again, Gail's elbows still pumping. 'It's Karl isn't it? You still think he was the best root you've ever had.'

'I've had other men,' Alice said, squirming.

'Oh please, not that drip from the bookshop? That accountant? I mean a real man. Someone who knows what he's doing in the sack.'

'God Gail, you think because he's African he's good in bed?'

'Yes, I bloody do. But who gets the chance to really find out? Do it, the girls will be green with envy.'

'Gail, it's not all about sex.'

'Yes, it is Alice. You've just had your head in the clouds for too long. Ask him out, get drunk and get naked with him. Okay? And then ring me immediately with all the details.'

Delighted at the thought Gail giggled, lost her balance and slipped off the curb.

19. Ottavio

Ottavio saw Alpha coming out of the mall and pulled over. For a moment it looked like he might not stop. Ottavio sounded the horn and waved. Alpha paused, stuck his hands in his pockets and strolled over to the open window on the passenger side.

'Haven't seen you for a week. Where you been?'

'Nowhere.'

'You must be somewhere cause you not at home.'

'Bin staying with friends.'

'Who?'

'You don't know them.'

'They're not friends then.'

Alpha's lip curled and he took a step back. Ottavio got out of the car and rested his elbows on the roof.

'You smoking weed?'

'Not your business what I do.'

'Your business is mine brother. If we were at home, you wouldn't behave like this.'

'We not at home.'

'I didn't drag you all the way here for nothing. Our parents would be ashamed.' Shame was the only way to get to Alpha.

Alpha dropped his eyes and stared at the ground.

'I can get you a job at the works.'

'I tried already. They didn't want me.'

'I'll vouch for you. Malong will too. Just put your name down.'

'I did that.'

'Try again.'

Alpha folded his arms across his chest and jutted his chin. Ottavio could see there was no point going on. He'd said his piece. 'Get in. I'll give you a lift.' Alpha took his time.

'Wanna drive?' Ottavio revved the engine, almost laughing at the pleasure sweeping Alpha's face.

'Me drive your beloved?' Alpha said, unbelieving.

'You know I will kill you if you harm it in any way?'

'Oh, I know that more than anything.'

Ottavio pulled on the handbrake. They ran around the car and took each other's seats.

'Seatbelt,' Ottavio said as Alpha let off the handbrake. Alpha did as he was told. The CD came on playing Run DMC. Alpha laughed in scorn.

'What is this shit? Man, you can't listen to this.'

Ottavio took the bait. 'These guys are legends. It all started with them.'

'Whatever, it's old. You should listen to new stuff. That's where it's happening.'

Ottavio turned the music up louder. Alpha laughed and accelerated through an orange light.

'You got no respect for the past. That's your problem,' Ottavio said, pleased to have Alpha next to him. Couldn't think of the last time he had been.

'You obsessed with the past. That's your problem,' Alpha scoffed. Reaching out, Ottavio playfully clipped the back of Alpha's head.

'Don't be treating me like I'm a little kid,' Alpha laughed.

'You'll always be little brother,' Ottavio scoffed. 'Even if you're taller than me.'

At home, they found Rosa and Zach sitting at the kitchen table. Rosa's hands folded in prayer. Zach looked like a small animal startled by headlights in the dark.

Alpha stood behind Zach's chair and put his hands on his shoulders.

'How you doing little man?' Alpha said gently. Zach did not reply. Alpha folded his arms and leaned back against the bench waiting for someone to speak. Ottavio pulled out the chair opposite Zach and sat down.

'What's up?' Ottavio made sure he sounded calm. Zach said nothing. Rosa looked at Zach. 'You can tell him, or I can.'

Zach's eyes flitted away from Ottavio's eyes, paying respect to his older cousin. Zach would never disrespect an adult by looking them in the eye.

Acid churned through Ottavio's stomach. It was something bad. Something had started. 'What is it Zach?'

Zach would not look up. Rosa let the silence build before she spoke. 'The school called. A phone was found in his bag.

He wanted to come home, so I went and got him.'

Ottavio almost laughed, what she'd just said was ridiculous. Didn't she hear how wrong it sounded? Of all people, she knew Zach would never steal.

Alpha moved his head from side to side in disbelief.

Ottavio saw fear ripple through Zach. It was not the low buzz of anxiety that usually hovered around him, or the fear of displeasing his family. This was something new, something sharper.

'Come on Zach.' Ottavio waited for him to reply but Zach didn't say a word. Alpha put his hands on Zach's head, tilting his face toward him. He spoke playfully, 'Might as well tell us now, save me having to beat it out of you.'

Dropping his head into his hands Zach remained silent. Rosa intervened, 'School said a girl's phone was missing and they searched all the bags. It was in Zach's backpack.'

'Well someone else put it there,' Ottavio said, his voice tight. The red-haired girl, Ottavio thought. It was Kelly's phone, he knew it, he just knew it. Ottavio turned to Zach, 'You know whose phone it was?'

Zach shrugged, misery was all over his face.

'Let's go down there now and tell that dumb fuck principal,' Alpha said.

Rosa's head jerked up. She spoke harshly, 'Alphonso, that language.'

Shrugging his shoulders in a sort-of apology, Alpha loosely massaged Zach's shoulders.

'Zach, you listen to me carefully now. There's no way I'm gonna let anyone say our family are thieves. They say you are – they're saying it about Alpha, about Rosa and me. I'm gonna see that principal whether you want me to or not, so you might as well tell us what's going on.'

'I don't want any trouble,' Zach said, his voice high with panic.

'You already got it,' Ottavio said. 'You gonna get more if you don't tell us.'

'I don't know who put it my bag.'

'Did you tell your teacher that?'

Zach nodded that he had.

'What did he say?' Alpha said.

'He said I had to see the principal.'

Ottavio had not forgotten Turner and how easily he had written off Alpha. It wouldn't have mattered to him that the phone was in the bag of the quietest, best-behaved boy in the class.

'What did Turner say?' Ottavio asked.

'I didn't see him. I got sick and Rosa came.'

Ottavio knew why Zach felt sick. It would be hard enough for him to speak to someone in authority, let alone the terror he had for getting into any kind of trouble. And Turner wouldn't have cared to look into it. In his mind the problem would have been sorted. Phone gets found, end of story. He wouldn't look into it more than that. It wouldn't occur to him that Zach's name had just been smeared. Or that there might be someone else involved.

Ottavio stood up and reached for his keys. 'Rosa come with me. Alpha, you stay here with Zach.'

Zach sat up, open-mouthed with fear, but Ottavio did not look at him.

Sitting with Rosa outside the principal's room, Ottavio could feel anger jangling through him. The woman in the office said Turner wasn't available, but Ottavio quietly told her that the principal needed to talk to him first if he was going to accuse his little cousin of theft. She asked them to take a seat, 'he might be a while; end of a busy day.'

Clasping her hands tightly, head bent, Rosa silently moved her lips in prayer. Ottavio concentrated on a spot on the opposite wall, making his mind go blank so something else could leap into the space. It was a game he had played with himself when he was little. What would appear? Of course, it was Zach; in camp, about five years old, skin blotchy with ringworm, pot-bellied and dragging a stick through the dust smiling as though they weren't living in the worst place in the world. Ottavio would take Alpha and Malong to visit Rosa and Zach, in a section of the camp only for women and children. The blue plastic walls of their hut flapped in the hot wind and the dust swirled across the ground. Zach was always pleased to see his cousins but he truly loved Malong. He would ignore the dust, grabbing at Malong's T-shirt, wanting his friend, famous for beating up older and bigger kids, to play chase. Adults in the camp said Malong was crazy, told Ottavio he had to control his brother. Ottavio lost count of how many times he had dragged Malong off someone. But Malong wasn't crazy, he just couldn't hold the anger in. It was bigger and stronger than him. But he was kind to little Zach. Told him if he had any trouble he would come and sort it out. Zach would giggle. Proud to be the only kid not scared of him. Malong would take him down to the dried-out riverbed to play on the lifeless tree trunks that lay there. If any of the kids had a ball, Malong would take it off them and kick it to Zach, showing him how to tap it off the side of his foot or dribble it across the hard ground. And he would get him to shoot for goal, then nudge it along when the ball stopped. When Malong was about fifteen he was moved to the army training camp. No one objected and Malong couldn't wait to go, but Zach was broken-hearted. The next time Zach saw Malong was at the airport on the day he and Rosa arrived in Australia, more than ten years later. Malong had thrown him over his shoulder like a sack of maize and carried him out to the carpark. A few nights later Zach sat with Ottavio in the backyard and shyly told him of the day they left the camp; a man had told him that Malong was not Ottavio's brother. Ottavio told him how they came to be at the camp.

After the attack on their village, the wandering, the horses, after all that, Ottavio was exhausted, alone and terrified. He had run for hours through the dawn, into the early light of day. When he could run no more, he climbed a tree and slept in the canopy for most of the day. He woke to gunfire and screaming, and the sweat of horses, then realised it was in his head. The day was fading and silent. He tried not to think of anyone in his family, of where they were and what happened to them. He got down from the tree and moved carefully through the bush, ready to run again. When he heard a sound that might have been horses, he panicked. Shaking with fear, he climbed into a tall tree and waited, but the sound faded away. When the sun had dropped fully and the last shadows of light were leaving, he climbed down to drink the swamp water. It tasted muddy, but it was cool, and it made him realise how hungry he was. Then he heard another sound. Was it singing? Ducking into the tall reeds and staying very still, from his hiding place he saw a kid wandering past and in the fading light he thought it looked like Malong, his friend who lived near him in their village. He saw the boy stopping to smash a stick against a rock. His song was weary and sad; 'Be brave like Malong. Be strong like Malong.' Ottavio couldn't believe it was his age mate. 'Malong', he whispered, 'Malong, is it you?' Malong's eyes bulged with fear as Ottavio stepped out of the reeds in front of him. Neither were sure the other was real. Ottavio edged closer and Malong swung his stick, hitting Ottavio across his chest, knocking him to the ground. He went to strike again but Ottavio caught the stick and pulled him down on top of him. Both lay there panting. Neither had the strength to fight. They could barely speak. 'It is you Machar?' Malong said quietly. 'It is me,' Ottavio whispered back. They lay beside each other, listening to the sound of each other's breath, until they fell asleep where they lay. Ottavio woke in the night to hear Malong muttering his song in his sleep.

The principal swung his office door open and buttoned his suit jacket as he offered Ottavio his hand.

'Mr Bol, good to meet you.'

'We've met before Mr Turner, Alphonso Bol is my little brother.'

Turner paused and Ottavio saw him trying to place the name.

'He left school about two years ago.'

'Ah, yes,' Turner replied.

Ottavio could see he didn't remember Alpha.

'Please come in.'

Ottavio and Rosa sat in front of his large desk as he made himself comfortable in his high-backed leather chair.

'How can I help you?'

'We'd like to know what happened with Zachariah today.'

'Well, as the office would have told Rosa when she picked him up, there was a complaint of theft from a student – an expensive phone. We are obliged to search if something goes missing in the classroom. Zach became very upset when the phone was found in his bag. Said he didn't take it. Complained of a sore stomach. Said he wanted to go home. We thought it best until it got sorted out. So, the office called Rosa.'

'And how long will that take to sort out, Mr Turner?' Ottavio asked.

'Well, it's hard to say. But these things are best resolved in the school.'

'There's another way?' Rosa asked.

'Well, police can be called for theft and they have been in the past. But I don't think we need to involve them; the item has been found.'

'So, you'll be looking for the person who took it?' Ottavio asked, pushing him, he wanted a guarantee.

In her softest voice, Rosa interjected, 'Mr Turner, Zachariah is a good boy. He would never steal from anybody.'

'However, the phone was in his bag ...'

'Zach didn't take it. Someone else did. They want to make Zach look bad.'

'Mr Bol, we will look into it.'

'Zach's probably your best-behaved student. He didn't take it.'

'Yes, he's known as a....'

'He knows who did, but he's too scared to say.'

'Mr Bol ...'

'We want Zach back here, but he's not coming back with people thinking he's a thief. The school needs to find the kid who took the phone.'

'I will speak to the social worker tomorrow and ask her to get involved,' Turner said. 'I'm sure we can sort this out. His teacher does think highly of him.'

'Who does his teacher not think highly of?' Ottavio said, unable to hide his resentment.

Turner ignored the implication; his voice became warmer and smoother. 'Leave it with us, Mr Bol. I'll get the office to write a referral to the social worker, Julie Miller. She's in tomorrow so she can follow up then and call you as soon as she has some news.'

Rosa stood and dipped her head, 'Thank you, sir. Thank you for your help.'

Ottavio recoiled as he watched Rosa demean herself. Turner smiled and offered his hand. He did the same to Ottavio, who did not want to take it, but Rosa looked at him with hard eyes and he took Turner's hand.

'Thank you for taking the time to come in,' Turner said, squeezing his hand firmly.

The corridors were eerie in the absence of any students. Agitated, Ottavio went outside to wait, while Rosa spoke to the secretary, giving Ottavio's number as the contact. Rosa watched anxiously as the secretary wrote it on the referral for the social worker. The secretary gave one of the forms to Rosa and told her Ms Miller would receive the other.

Outside Ottavio saw a few students lingering at the front gate. Kelly and Theo were amongst them. Theo's arm was looped around Kelly's neck. A sleek black car pulled up on the other side of the street. Ottavio recognised it immediately, it was the car from the football game. The guy with the tattoos got out and let the seat fall forward. As Theo, Kelly and a third kid piled in the back, he saw Ottavio. Staring hard at Ottavio, he got in and as the car pulled out, he leaned out the window and yelled, 'Ya black cunt. Go back to where you came from ya fuckin' monkey.'

Ottavio heard laughter from inside the car and watched the car speed off down the street. He stayed still. It wasn't the first time and it probably wouldn't be the last. At least now he was sure. He let it wash over him. Let it all fall into place.

20. Alice

Alice had parked a few blocks away from the café. As she made her way, she caught the scent of creamy vanilla and stopped at an enormous purple wisteria overhanging a high fence. Leaning in she took a deep slow breath. The fragrance was delicious. It lifted her spirit, helped her prepare for their meeting.

'Kill two birds with one stone,' Stefan said, explaining why they were meeting in Taylor Square. 'Check out the old stomping ground and see my favourite cousin at the same time.'

'Your only cousin,' Alice said, sounding colder than she had intended. They were sitting outside so Stefan could smoke. The air was thick with heat and car fumes. People streamed past their table. The tremor in Stefan's hands was more obvious than it had been at dinner.

'So, what does a claims officer do? Sounds important.'

Alice shrugged. 'Elspeth's been filling you in then?'

'I asked. She told me. We weren't gossiping, I know how you hate all that.'

'I handle insurance claims, that's all. Someone who pays their premiums for years, finally makes a claim, and I try every trick in the book not to give it to them. No doubt Elspeth gave you a much grander version. Probably didn't mention I'd quit my lowly public service job for the big overseas adventure, only to chicken out and end up number crunching in an insurance office.'

'She didn't mention that.'

'No, she wouldn't, because I didn't tell her at the time. She's probably still mortified that I quit without any plans except a trip overseas. She would have talked me out of packing my bags if she had known. The mortgage, superannuation, career continuity, the ticking clock, marriage and only having myself to rely on when her and Dad passed on. As it was, she didn't need to. I did that myself. Turns out big adventure terrifies me as much as it does her.'

'You could do anything you wanted.'

'Oh please.'

'You were always the smart one.'

'No smarter than you and look where you ended up?'

Stefan winced.

Stirring more sugar into her coffee, Alice waited.

'I'd spend the whole weekend around here. Handful of E's, dance all night, chill all day, then off I'd go again. Shame you missed it. I think you'd have had fun. Spent too much time studying.'

'Taking handfuls of drugs to stay awake for days doesn't sound like fun to me,' Alice said sourly. Truth was, the whole scene had scared her. There had been one time she had agreed to meet him and his friends in a nearby bar. They were glamorous and full of confidence; flamboyant, loud and unrestrained. It was a Friday and they started the weekend with cocktails at the same bar each week. They offered to share their party pills with her. Telling her 'not to be so boring, come out, have some fun.'

She'd felt a little envious of Stefan back then, he'd seemed so fearless and so… bright. Immaculately groomed, with bleached hair and a number one blade crew cut; the future didn't concern him.

'They were the best times of my life,' he said sadly.

The waiter passed by and Stefan ordered another coffee. Alice declined a second, annoyed by his maudlin reminiscing.

Alice smoothed out the fabric of her skirt. She'd agreed to meet him for only one reason. The queasy sense of shame that took control of her when she thought of Carmel. When they were young, she had adored Stefan for not caring what others thought. Had the adoration stopped her noticing who he really was? How had she not seen the violence in him?

Her stomach fluttered with nerves, but she was not going to let that stop her. She would insist if necessary—as hard as that might be. All her life she had choked on restraint. Elspeth had taught her well.

Unshaven, his face flaccid, fingers stained from nicotine, Stefan stared blank-eyed at the passing traffic. Leaning across the table, Alice took a breath.

'Carmel.'

Her name hung there like a hovering bee deciding to land or fly off. Unfazed Stefan took his cup in his hand. Alice gathered herself, ready to try again, but Stefan spoke first.

'Have you heard from her?'

'Nobody's heard from Carmel.'

Stefan nodded a little, looking down at the table.

The butterflies in her stomach disappeared, 'She must hate our whole family.'

'What do you mean?' Stefan sounded genuinely confused.

'Not one of us believed her.'

Stefan held Alice's gaze for a few moments. She saw nothing in his eyes she understood.

'I'm sorry cous, I didn't mean it.'

'Is that it? You didn't mean it?' Alice replied.

'I don't know why I married her.'

'Jesus.' Alice shook her head in disgust. 'Are you gay?'

Stefan glanced up. 'Not really.'

'Not really?'

'I've had a few men…' Stefan shrugged.

'Do you hate women?'

'No.' Stefan answered flatly.

'So, what then?' Frustration surged through her. Smiling carefully, Stefan shrugged again.

'I can't figure it out. Good family, great education, lots of friends. No obvious reason to become a violent, sadistic bastard and all you can say is "I didn't mean it."'

'Thought you might have stuck by me,' Stefan said, stubbing out his cigarette.

Alice bristled at the whine in his voice. She'd felt cowed by it when they were younger. 'You completely destroyed everything you had. You did it. No one else.'

'I've thought about it every day.'

'Really? And what did you come up with?'

'I thought I was in love with her, but I wasn't. She was besotted with me and I liked that. I liked being adored. She said she loved me and no one had ever said that to me.'

Alice couldn't believe what she was hearing. 'You'd never felt loved so you beat up the woman who loved you?'

Stefan rubbed a spot on the table with his thumb.

'Plenty of people don't feel loved but they don't lash out. You broke her arm and cracked three of her ribs. God knows what else you did before she finally called the cops on you.' The queasiness surged through her again. Just for a moment she thought she should stop, but the momentum carried her on. 'But I didn't believe it. I couldn't imagine that you, of all people, could do something like that. I thought she was a lying sicko. But it turned out to be true.'

Stefan kept rubbing the spot.

'You behaved like an animal. Worse than an animal.' Alice gasped, pressing the tips of her fingers against her temples.

'Men are animals. Some just know how to control themselves,' Stefan sounded hollow.

'That's what they say in prison is it?'

Stefan didn't reply.

Picking up her bag, Alice called for the bill, and for a brief moment she saw Achol smashing her hand against Mary's face. She flicked the image out of her mind and sat back in her chair. 'How could you do it?'

Stefan would not look at her.

'You have to give me some kind of answer. One that makes sense.'

Clearing his throat, Stefan spoke quietly. 'I had to go to a program in jail. We'd all sit in a circle. The guy who led it was tough, wouldn't let you talk shit. Didn't let you blame drugs or alcohol. You had to accept responsibility for what you did. And I did. What I did was wrong.'

Stefan stubbed out his cigarette. 'I was angry all the time. I took it all out on Carmel because I could. I wanted it to be her fault.'

'Wanted what to be her fault?'

'Everything.'

Alice felt the enormity of that single word.

Stefan tried lighting another cigarette, flicking the plastic lighter again and again without it sparking. He shook it until a tiny flame appeared and puffed his cigarette into life before the flame died altogether.

Crossing her legs then uncrossing them, Alice fiddled with the ring on her finger. Blame. It was such an easy out. How often had she blamed someone when something was not right with her? Usually Elspeth was her target.

Alice pressed her spine against the hardness of the chair, wanting the discomfort to go away.

Stefan sniffed. 'I wished I hadn't. I wished I could take it all back.'

Alice didn't have anything more to say. Standing to leave, Stefan glanced at her with a spark of curiosity in his dull eyes.

'Why did you think I was gay?'

'I never did. It was Elspeth's theory.'

'Elspeth never liked me.'

'I'm not sure Elspeth likes anyone. Her life is dedicated to a battle of one-upmanship with your mother. The possibility of you being gay just gave her ammunition for the next round.'

'You think?'

'I know.'

'Who's gonna win?'

'It's to the death.'

21. Alaya

It has been said that we have always been taken north, to the land of the Arabs. Arabs think all black people are alouny. They like to take children and sometimes their mothers too. Their families never see them again. Everyone knows a child who was never seen again.

The children must work for nothing. They are given Arab names, must speak that language and must pray to the Arab god.

But once some children did come back. It was such a long time ago that our grandfather said his grandfather was a little baby.

A chief went to the north and found the children behind the wall. He brought them back. Everyone in Dinkaland knows the story of the children behind the wall.

22. Ottavio

Every call to Julie Miller went to message bank. Each time, he left his name and number and told her when he was available to call. After work was best, or before if she could ring before 8 am. It had been two days since they met Turner, and Zach had barely left his room. Ottavio had not stopped thinking about the car, he had no doubt the driver was Theo's brother and he was somehow involved. Ottavio had also been thinking about Kelly, toying with the idea of going straight to her and making her tell the truth. He knew the bakery Zach said she worked at. But the thought of Theo's brother stopped him. He wasn't scared of guys like him, but he didn't yet know how far he was prepared to go.

Ottavio decided to wait for the social worker to call. He got ready to go to the ESL class, making one more call to Julie Miller as he left. No answer.

Sitting next to Mohammed, he tried to pay attention to the lesson, his phone was in his pocket on silent and he waited to feel the buzz of a silent call. At the tea break he stayed at the table chatting with Mohammed, until Alice approached and Mohammed politely moved away.

'Strong, black and three sugars?' she said, handing him a mug. 'How are you?'

'Fine, fine,' he replied blandly annoyed at her attention. 'You?'

'I'm good. How's that novel?'

'Novel?'

'*Love in the Time of Cholera.*'

'Oh, the book you leant me. Sorry I haven't even started it. Haven't had time.' Ottavio realised the book was still in his bag. Hadn't thought about it for a moment.

'That's okay. I don't need it back in a hurry. There's no rush.'

She was speaking quickly and seemed nervous. Stepping closer, in a quiet voice she said, 'I was wondering if you'd—.'

Ottavio felt the buzz of his phone and sprang from his seat. Yanking it from his pocket, the screen said Social Worker. He moved away from Alice to a space by himself and took the call. Julie Miller introduced herself. She sounded rushed. Ottavio asked to meet with her the next day.

'I'm sorry, Mr Bol but tomorrow's not possible. Could you tell me what it's about?'

'You don't know? The school didn't tell you?'

'Well, I do have a referral. A phone was found in your brother's bag and he is now on probation?'

Dismay dropped through him. 'Zachariah's my cousin. He lives with me. He took nothing so he cannot be put on probation. He is not a thief. He came home on the day it happened and he hasn't been back - he's not going back until it's sorted out.'

'I'll have to look into it.'

'Miss Miller what is it exactly that you do?' Ottavio asked, not hiding his frustration.

'Ms Miller.'

'Sorry?'

'Ms not Miss. Kids get referred to me who are having problems in their family, that sort of thing.'

Ottavio took a breath. 'Our problem is with the school. Saying Zach's a thief is saying his whole family are too.'

'I don't think anyone is saying that.'

'Being put on probation is saying just that!'

'Mr Bol, please stay calm.'

Ottavio ignored her, 'Someone put the phone in Zach's bag. Zach did not steal the phone.'

'If there is another student involved, I'll have to talk to Zach, but I do need to speak to his teacher first. I can do that tomorrow.'

'I'm pretty sure he knows who put it there.'

'Okay. Well, I'll talk to his class teacher tomorrow. I could make a time to see you and Zach in the afternoon after school has closed. Okay?

'He is not coming to the school until this is sorted out.'

'Mr Bol, I'm here to help. How is four-thirty?'

Ottavio paused, trying to hold in his frustration. He was not going to take Zach to that meeting. Agreeing to the time, he hung up and called Rosa immediately, telling her she would go to the meeting with him, not mentioning that the social worker was expecting Zach to be there as well. Rosa sounded relieved, and they agreed she would tell Zach about the call. Knowing something was finally happening might help him feel better. Ottavio took a deep breath and went to retrieve his tea. Alice was waiting.

'Sorry about that.'

'Everything okay?'

'Yep. Fine. You were saying something?'

'Could we get a bite after class?'

'A bite?'

'Dinner.'

'Dinner?'

He hesitated. 'Sorry, ahhh…I can't tonight. I have to get home. But thank you.'

Embarrassment flushed across her cheeks. Ottavio realised two things at the same time. She liked him and he had just hurt her. Ottavio let the first realisation click over in his mind. He'd had no idea. There was nothing in the way she moved when she was near him and he hadn't noticed her watching. He looked at Alice closely and saw shyness in her. It had taken courage for her to ask and he had turned her down flat. But the invitation opened up his curiosity. He hadn't liked her at first, her good intentions and sloppy clothes, but he had no real reason to be unkind. And she loved *A Catcher in the Rye*. Ottavio took a mouthful of lukewarm tea, 'Next week instead?'

Her eyes brightened. 'Great. Okay, next week then.'

In the car, Ottavio's thoughts jumped from Alice to Malong – he had to tell him about Zach. If he heard it from someone else, he'd go straight for Theo. And that would be one mess Ottavio couldn't clean up. Everything depended on the meeting the next day. If Zach wouldn't tell them who put the phone in his bag, he would need to do something before Malong did.

When he got home Ottavio saw no light under Rosa's door. She had been going to sleep early. That's what she did when things got too much for her.

Alpha was listening to music in the bedroom he shared with Zach. He could hear the bass thudding softly from his headphones. Alpha had been home each night since this thing had started. Three nights in a row. Since he had left school, that might have been a record.

Zach was lying on the sofa, reading a comic he'd read a dozen times before. Propping himself up on his elbow, he looked at Ottavio, worry all over his face.

'How's things little man?'

Zach didn't reply.

'Rosa told you about the social worker? That she wants to speak to you?'

Zach's eyes darted around the room.

'Come on now. Everything's going be alright.' Ottavio tried to sound reassuring. 'You just need to tell her who put that phone in your bag and it will all be sorted. You go back to school then.'

'I don't know who put it there.'

'Theo put it there.' Ottavio said, following his hunch. 'I know it and so do you. He wants to set you up? Why? Jealous? Or is there something else?'

There was no sound in the room. Ottavio wanted it to be jealousy and nothing else.

'That's it isn't it? He wants to scare you off. He's not going to make you carry this Zach. Rosa and I are gonna see the social worker tomorrow. She wants you to be there but you are not going back to that school until your name is cleared. If she can't sort it out. I will.'

Zach was looking at the ground, his shoulders hunched. Ottavio didn't want to pressure him, but he had to say it. 'If we were at home now, you'd be getting marked soon. The war stopped me getting any, but I still had to behave like a man when I was your age, and now it's time for you to. You got to toughen up Zach. In the village, you wouldn't bring trouble home. It's your job to protect your home. It's no different here. Not really.' Ottavio had more to say but stopped there. Zach did need to be stronger. For his own sake. He was a stranger in a strange land. Ottavio didn't want to make him feel guilty. He would deal with the school, with Theo or whatever problem came their way. It was his job to protect the family's reputation, not Zach's, but Zach had to understand what was at stake here.

Zach got up and went to his room and Ottavio dropped down onto the sofa.

Looking around the room he saw the framed photograph

of Zach on his first day of high school on the wall opposite. Smiling in his gleaming white shirt and grey shorts, Rosa next to him beaming with pride, the first in their family to get a proper high school education. There was nothing to stop him. He was smart and clever and hungry to learn. The school had good teachers and all the resources it needed. There would be no interruptions or worries, Zach would finish in the top class, get into university and become the doctor they wanted him to be. They all knew it was possible. He was going to make sure of it.

Ottavio's thoughts flicked to Alice and her awkward invitation. Why had he gone soft on her? Was it pity or genuine interest? He should be wary of her. Zach was the only person he should be thinking about. Dinner with the white woman was a dumb idea. A really dumb idea. But he couldn't stop himself wondering what she meant by dinner. Surely it was more? It was no different here than any other country. Some of his friends might be envious of a date with a *kawauja*. He'd heard of a few guys with *kawauja* girlfriends but didn't like the way they were described as lucky, like somehow a white woman was a prize they had won. He hated that shit.

Malong would be delighted if he knew. White women were fair game. If anyone got the chance, they should take it. Malong would play it that way. He would go out, eat a lot, let her pay, then go back to her place and do the deed. Wouldn't stay the night. 'Just giving her what she wants,' he'd say innocently, laughing and high-fiving his friends.

If that was the offer, maybe he should try it? He had to

admit he was curious. Did creamy white skin feel the same?

Ottavio fell asleep on the sofa and woke in the night, startled and disorientated. Riderless horses had been pounding toward him through flames and smoke. Their chests heaving and slick with sweat. A girl screamed his name.

23. Alice

No unnerving quiet, not tonight. As Alice let herself in she heard the sound of Thomas at work with his hammer. She slammed the door to let him know she was home. Her father stepped out into the lounge wearing pristine blue overalls.

'Hi Dad.'

'Hello love.' Thomas gave her a peck on the cheek as Alice hugged him, smelling wood dust and hair oil. It was good to see her father in his overalls. The only part of retirement he enjoyed was pottering about, fixing things. Being a carpenter suited him far better than practising law. He was much more relaxed when he worked with his hands.

'How's it all going?' Alice asked, dropping her handbag and coat on the lounge and following him back into the bedroom, relieved she'd shoved all her dirty clothes under the bed before leaving that morning. Thomas had covered the carpet with a dustsheet and on top was a towel with his tools neatly laid out. Bookshelves now covered the narrow wall next to the windows.

'Dad, that looks great. Thank you so much.'

'My pleasure love, quite an easy job really, five more minutes and I'll be done.'

'Can I get you a cup of tea?'

'That would be lovely.'

Alice went to the kitchen, put the jug on and emptied the vase of wilting yellow flowers. Millie was hiding under the table, unnerved by the building noise. Alice gave her a reassuring scratch behind her ear. Opening the window, Alice waved her hand through the jasmine vine creeping along the sill, breathing in the sweetness. Glimpsing one of her neighbours arriving home, she ducked out of view before he saw her. Alice preferred to keep her distance. Even when she felt horribly lonely, her flat was her sanctuary and she wanted to keep it that way.

Thomas tightened the last screws as she took him his tea. He leaned against the bedroom windowsill, sipping carefully, clearing his throat a few times. Alice sat on her bed and pressed her back against the headboard. She could see there was something on his mind.

'Your mother and I were thinking you might like a bigger place love. Maybe get a house over our way. We could help you out with the cost, there'd be no problem there.' Her father paused and Alice pondered how much of this was her mother's idea.

'Surry Hills is very nice these days and it's convenient I know but, well, we were just thinking… the inner city isn't very safe is it?'

So it was Elspeth's idea. She'd worked on him, made him anxious. There must have been a story in the news she'd used to pressure him. Alice hated Elspeth using him like that, she knew just how to get to him. He was such a gentle man, it was easy to do. He seemed unable to protect himself from Elspeth's manipulations but always tried to protect her. When she was a girl, after one of Elspeth's tirades about … anything, Thomas would give her a reassuring wink. He made sure Elspeth never saw these small signs of support. The fondest memory of her childhood was when he had time to take her to the park. They would sit on the bench chatting, Thomas telling her stories from his work, making it sound silly, sometimes even fun. They would feed the ducks and walk home with an ice-cream they would finish a block before their house. Thomas would take his handkerchief and wipe any evidence of it off her face.

'Oh come on Dad. I've been here six years. Nothing bad has ever happened. Nothing that couldn't also happen in Bellevue Hill.'

'Well, I take your point, but at least think about it. This is nice but it's a bit small isn't it?

'Have you started reading your birthday present?' Alice said, changing the subject.

Thomas looked relieved, 'Actually I just started it last night. The names are a bit hard, but it's about wrestling so I'm happy.'

Looking at her father, Alice wondered if he had ever been happy. He rarely seemed it. She was sure that Elspeth had never made him happy. She had never seen them hold hands or even kiss each other on the lips.

'Just think about it Alice. You won't need bookshelves in your bedroom if you have a bigger place.'

'I like books in my bedroom,' Alice replied.

Alice couldn't tell her father how often she thought about moving. Her daydreams of other places had continued, despite being unable to actually do anything about them. She thought of her grandmother who had lived her entire life in a small terrace near the East End, had raised Thomas there. Stayed in the same job until she retired. Died in the house. Alice envied her lack of restlessness.

Meowing for food, Millie leapt onto the bed. Alice scooped her up and carried her back to the kitchen as Thomas finished packing his tools. She opened a foil-sealed tab of salmon and spooned it into Millie's china dish. Why couldn't she just be happy with what she had? There was nothing wrong, not really. She'd never struggled or lived through tough times, but she felt stuck. She wanted for nothing, but she didn't feel like she was really in control of her life. There'd always been choices and options, but they had not inspired her. How many times had Ottavio been without options? She could only imagine what life had put in front of him, and he had migrated to another country, finished a degree. He had motivation and determination. Was volunteering going to give her some of that? She hoped so. She didn't know how much longer she could stand the sense that she was drifting without any purpose. Alice sighed and yanked open the fridge looking for the half bottle of white wine left over from the night before. She emptied it into her largest glass and decided to make her favourite pasta with a cream and bacon sauce.

'You gonna stay for dinner Dad?' Alice yelled, knowing he would say no.

'Sorry love but I have to get back,' he yelled back.

Alice toasted herself a small congratulations for asking Ottavio out and took a gulp of wine. She wondered if she should suggest a home cooked meal. If she stuck to Gail's idea, dinner at her flat would make the getting laid part easy. Getting laid. She hated that expression. It sounded so crass. But maybe Gail was right, she just needed to lighten up, get naked and relax. Enjoy it for what it is and not what she imagined it could or should be.

Alice had been passively compliant with the men who had wanted her but Ottavio was a different matter; she had no idea if he was interested. But all men took the option of sex if it was offered didn't they? He had looked quite surprised when she'd asked him to dinner. Alice hoped she'd sounded casual; a simple invitation from a new friend.

'Okay, love. It's all done. Want to have a look at the finished product?' Thomas stood in the doorway holding his toolbox.

'You bet.'

The shelves looked strong and even. Thomas had wiped them clean of dust. Alice ran her hand along the smooth wood, then turned and kissed her father's cheek.

'They look great Dad. Thank you. I'll haul all the boxes out of the closet and those shelves will be full by the time you get home.'

'Alright love. I should be going. Beat the traffic.'

At the door Thomas took off his work boots, placed them in a blue plastic bag, slipped on his loafers and kissed his daughter farewell.

Alice returned to the kitchen and her thoughts of Ottavio, shelves forgotten. His frame was slender, shoulders only a little wider than his hips, forearms smooth and hairless. Was the rest of his body the same?

Catching her reflection in the window, she stopped, not liking what she saw. She couldn't describe herself as anything other than frumpy. Another word she hated, but it was accurate. There was no definition in her face. It was simply round with fat hiding her cheekbones and pointed chin. Her pale blue eyes were perhaps slightly larger than average. Her hair was a mess, slowly returning to its original mousy state since she decided to never face another preening hairdresser again. It just wasn't worth it. The bleach stank and having her hair dragged through the little holes in the rubber cap with that nasty hook just plain hurt. She would tie it up and keep it out of the way. Alice lifted the long, loose black top, purchased solely for the purpose of hiding her wobbly thighs. Underneath, the footless black tights aided in the camouflage. She stripped off the top, then the tights, and considered herself in her underwear.

The knickers had been expensive, but they were faded and tight, the elastic gone on one leg. She preferred sets, but the knickers were black, and the sports bra beige, the one she resorted to when extra kilos caused the others to pinch and press red marks into her back. She couldn't deny it, she had 'let herself go,' that horrible expression women of her mother's generation used. Nearly thirty, with no children or husband, and a flabby, dimpled body. She couldn't see a single redeeming feature. She took another gulp of wine and faced her wardrobe, trying to rally herself. Her sexiest dress hadn't been worn since dinner with Craig, the manager of the bookstore she used to frequent.

The pale blue, gauzy material matched her eyes. Alice slipped it over her head and worked it down around her hips. Smoothing the fabric across her thighs, she checked a long mirror, twisting around to get a better view of her bulging backside. It was discouraging. Still, the fat could be moulded into curves by some shape wear. Weren't African men supposed to like big women?

Alice lay down on her bed. Men liked women who were confident and full of fun, risk takers who did adventurous things. That's what she'd read on the internet. But not all men could have the same taste in women. Some liked bland, overweight women who bought their clothes from Target where there were plenty of cheap choices for the larger sizes. She'd seen plenty of women like that, walking hand in hand with men at the supermarket, on the train. Trouble was, the men were usually a mirror image, pudgy and unremarkable. All their disappointments and frustrations piled onto their bodies, creased into their faces.

Pulling the dress off, she threw it into the back of the wardrobe and changed into her pyjamas and ugg boots. In the kitchen she fried bacon and onions for the cream sauce and finished the white wine. Any excitement at the prospect of dinner with Ottavio was gone. She would stop thinking about him. It wouldn't work anyway.

With a large bowl of steaming pasta, a fresh glass of red, and a small plate of soft cheeses for after, Alice lay back on the lounge to watch the news. As she wolfed down the pasta, Millie made herself comfortable on her lap. Putting the bowl aside, she picked up her glass and sniffed the wine. The dark rich aroma did not soothe her. Instead, it opened up an ache in her, a scouring bitterness that led her to Karl.

For almost ten years she'd daydreamed of the sweet, poetic way he'd compared her body to sumptuous, delectable foods. The scent of freshly shaved truffle, the melting softness of a room temperature Brie. The memory of her very first orgasm tingled deep inside her for a few seconds. Maybe Elizabeth Monroe has a similar memory? Had she received the same sugary attention, heard the same breathy descriptions? Did she have the texture of fine yellow pear or a succulent black cherry, the spicy snap of a freshly picked chilli? Gail was right. She had never let the idea of him go. Whenever she had been with a man since, she'd thought of the worldly, clever Karl stroking her unworldly innocent self into an elated stupor. Not the Karl she had seen through a café window just before she quit her job, balding with a paunch, sharing a chocolate torte with an elegant woman who may or may not have been his wife.

Alice sipped some more wine, and picked at the cheese, trying to concentrate on the news instead. It didn't work. Blurry from the alcohol, Alice decided she could not go through with the date. It was a stupid idea; she would tell Ottavio something had come up and she had to cancel. Why would Ottavio want to get naked with her? A gorgeous man like that would have his pick of women. Probably had dozens of girlfriends. Her mind wandered back to his forearm. Alice sighed. Since dinner wasn't going to happen, there was no harm in dwelling on that arm. No risk of disappointment since she wasn't going to actually see his body.

She'd never thought of a forearm as sexy before. The skin was taut and smooth, the muscle corded. The rest of his body must be the same. Alice let her mind wander a little more.

She pushed Millie off her lap and lay out on the lounge. Closing her eyes, she conjured Ottavio in front of her. He stripped off his shirt, dropping it to the floor, loosening his belt, unzipping, letting his pants slide down his long legs.

Then it was her turn. Flicking her long hair off her shoulders, staring straight into his dark eyes, thrilled at the desire she saw in them. Slipping her dress off over her head in one easy move, she held it aloft between her finger and thumb, then let it flutter to the ground. Moving her hands over her lacy, black underwear, she tipped the bra strap off her shoulder.

Alice was concentrating so hard it took a few moments to recognise the sound of her phone. She sat up, dismayed to see her mother's name flashing. Maybe she could ignore it. But it was late. Elspeth never called late. Alice picked it up.

'Alice?'

Elspeth voice was strained, trying to sound calm.

'What's wrong?'

'It's Stefan.'

'What?'

'Meet us at the hospital.'

▨

The doctor was explaining that Stefan had overdosed on heroin. By chance, a passer-by had seen him slumped over the steering wheel. Ambulance officers had revived him. He was now resting; any potential side-effects would be known in the morning.

'Stefan will be discharged in the morning if all is well and it would be better for him if he was to stay with a supportive person, family, if that is appropriate.' The doctor continued in his business-like manner. 'You might want to look at some of the available services.' Handing them a pamphlet with the heading: 'Drug Overdose.' Giving them a kind smile, he moved off to the next clump of worried people.

Looking at the bewildered faces of her family, Alice ached. Uncle Jack had his arm around Bronwyn, who was wiping her eyes with a tissue. Elspeth looked blank and Thomas continually shook his head, gazing at his shoes with his hands thrust deep into his trouser pockets. They'd all be thinking the same thing. Had he taken too much deliberately or was it a mistake?

'Let's just leave him to sleep.' Alice said as she corralled her family off the ward. No one protested.

At the ground floor café, Alice sat them in a quiet corner and ordered at the counter. It was a creepy feeling, but she was sure it was no accident. Stefan had tried to kill himself with heroin. As far as she knew he hadn't had a heroin habit before jail. He could have developed one while he was in there, but maybe it was the first time he used it? Maybe that's why he chose it, because he knew it would kill him? Alice tried to slow down her thinking. How he had done it didn't matter. Spurred on by the bloom of guilt she'd felt the moment she heard her mother say hospital, Alice had decided on a plan by the time the waitress handed her the change.

Elspeth shuffled along the bench seat to make room, squeezing Thomas up against the wall. They all looked exhausted in the bright glare of the overhead lights. Their son had led them back into a sea of bewilderment and they, once again, were out of their depth.

Jail was one thing. As grim and ugly as it was, Bronwyn and Jack had been able to pretend it wasn't real. Their son may have been hidden behind high walls and locked doors, but he could just as well have been overseas, due back at some vague date in the future. They had remained stubbornly befuddled, refusing to believe they had any part in the long, slow drama of their son's disintegration, despite their ringside seats.

Alice looked carefully at her aunt's face trying to assess what position she was going to take. Was she going to stand by her son or turn away? She didn't wait to find out.

'Stefan can come and stay with me. I'll pick him up when he's ready and keep my eye on him. I can take the week off work.'

Bronwyn's eyes flushed with fresh tears. She dabbed at them with a sodden tissue.

'Alice, do you really think that's the right thing to do?

'You haven't got much room, love.' Thomas said.

'It doesn't matter. He can have my room. I'll take the couch.'

Reaching across the table, Bronwyn took her hand and squeezed it hard, still unable to speak.

'Do you think he meant to?' Uncle Jack asked, his voice wavering.

'Yes,' Alice said, feeling her mother squirm beside her. Her father cleared his throat and they all waited. 'Yes, I do. I think it's all catching up with him.' Alice felt the fine grain of her own guilt wash through her again. She had been so cold toward him. How much had she contributed to the Stefan who was asleep in that bed, upper body slightly raised, drip taped to the back of his hand?

24. Ottavio

Rosa and Ottavio were leaving to meet Ms Miller at the school when Zach came out of his room in his uniform, Alpha close behind him.

'I'm coming.'

Moving over to Zach, Rosa put out her arms to pull him close, but he shrugged her away.

Ottavio nodded, taking in both Alpha and Zach, proud that they'd worked out a plan together, but his mind was made up. 'You go back to school after the school apologises. If you want to tell the social worker who put the phone in your bag, she can come here and hear it from you. You choose.' Ottavio slipped his bag over his shoulder and picked up his car keys. Zach and Alpha looked at each other.

'Let's go Rosa.'

'Ottavio.' Rosa pleaded.

'You all heard what I said?' Ottavio's voice was hard.

Alpha crossed his arms. 'You said you wanted him back in class. Why you making more of this than it is?'

'That Theo kid's just waiting for another chance.'

'Zach's not scared of him.' Alpha said, nudging Zach. 'Are you?'

Zach said nothing and Rosa went to his side. 'Ottavio please. He wants to come.'

Ottavio opened the front door and waited for Rosa to go ahead of him.

Ms Miller leaned over her desk, notepad and pen ready. The top button of her crisp cotton shirt was undone; a small gold cross rested at the base of her throat.

'I'm sorry Zach didn't come with you today.'

'Ottavio didn't think he should.' Rosa said quietly, glancing at her cousin. 'But Zach wants to speak to you.'

'Well, I'm pleased to hear that. I can come and see him tomorrow, if that suits. I have spoken to the class teacher. He said he was surprised Zach was involved in anything like this and doubted very much if Zach took it. Thought it would have been another student.'

Relief dropped through Ottavio. He held back a smile and waited for the apology. It didn't come.

'However, the owner of the phone said they had seen Zach take it.'

Ottavio saw Rosa's mouth go slack. 'I don't understand?'

'It's their word against Zach's I'm afraid.'

Furious, Ottavio stared at Ms Miller in a way that made her look to her notepad.

'Look, I'm not saying Zach took it, but the owner of the phone maintains it was him. I'm afraid we don't have much choice. Zach can only come back on probation.'

Ottavio couldn't believe what he was hearing.

'Zach can't come back to school until everyone knows it wasn't him who took the phone.'

'Zach is not a thief.' Rosa said quietly and firmly. Clasping her hands, she turned to Ottavio and waited for him to find a solution. Ottavio was taking in what the social worker had just said. Kelly had betrayed Zach. Either she was in on it, or Theo made her say it and she was too scared to refuse. He cleared his throat and spoke as calmly as he could. 'Someone did this to Zach to make him look bad and Zach's scared of that someone. He was going to tell you who that kid is. But he won't now. Now that we know two people are in on this.'

Kelly and Theo together. Why hadn't he seen that?

'Zach doesn't deserve this.' Ottavio said, anger twitching behind his eyes. 'None of this is his business.' Rosa reached out and placed her hand on Ottavio's urging him to be calm.

'I know you are trying to help, and I thank you for it,' Rosa said. 'We worried about Zach. He's a good boy and very quiet. He's barely said a word since this all started. He just stays in his room.'

'I know he's a good student Rosa. I want to see him back in school. We all do.'

'Zach's not coming back here on probation.' Ottavio said resolutely. 'We both know Theo is involved in this. Are you going to talk to him, or you just gonna accept Kelly's word? You gotta know she's lying to cover up for her boyfriend?' Ottavio knew he was on difficult ground. Accusing two students. He wasn't going to mention the guys in the black car.

'Mr Bol, can you explain to me why you would think that?'

Ottavio wasn't sure how well Miller knew who was who in the zoo. But how could she not? Everyone knows who the school bully is. And the girls they hang out with.

'Kelly's sweet on Zach and Theo is jealous.'

Rosa looked at him with such shock, Ottavio was instantly sorry to have said that in front of her. But to him it seemed obvious and simple. It couldn't just be that Zach was an easy target for a bully.

Ms Miller was considering what he had just said. She clearly had not thought of it as a possibility.

'Well, Mr Bol, if you are sure, then I'm going to have to speak with both parties and we might have to involve their parents.'

'I'm sure.'

What Ottavio wasn't sure of, was if Kelly was scared of Theo and just did what she was told. Or, if she was in on it with him and enjoyed humiliating Zach. For Zach's sake, Ottavio wanted Kelly to be scared.

'I will be in touch.' Ms Miller stood and shook both their hands, then walked them to the front door.

They drove in silence until they were almost home.

'I'm sorry Rosa. I should have told you.'

Rosa was as anxious as he'd ever seen her. 'I've only just worked it out, okay? Maybe I'm wrong, but from what I see, Theo is the school bully and Zach is scared of him—apparently everyone is. But Theo's got him in his sights, because he knows his girl Kelly is sweet on Zach.' Ottavio hesitated, wondering if he should tell Rosa the full story then decided to say it, so everything was out in the open.

'Zach likes her too.'

'Why didn't you say?'

'It's just a teenage crush Rosa. It's not like they want to get married.'

Rosa folded her arms. 'So, what will happen now?'

'I don't know Rosa. If Kelly admits she lied and Theo had made her, then Zach's name is cleared, and he can go back to school.'

Ottavio knew how unlikely that sounded. If Kelly did that, Theo would want revenge against her and Zach, but he kept those thoughts to himself.

Rosa sounded meek and a little scared. 'Maybe Zach could go to another school?'

'Rosa, Zach has done nothing wrong. If the school won't do anything, I will.'

'Please Ottavio, we have to wait. That's all we can do. And pray.'

'Sure Rosa, sure.'

'Being angry is not going to change it, Ottavio. Promise me you're not going to do anything.'

Ottavio said nothing.

When they pulled up outside their house both Zach and Alpha were sitting on the front step.

'Well?' Alpha said as they got out of the car. Zach was hollow-eyed and silent.

'We spoke to her,' Ottavio said, 'She said the owner of the phone saw Zach take it.'

Alpha's face crumpled. Zach looked like he was about to cry.

'It's okay my man. It's gonna come good. Nothing to worry about.' Ottavio knew he did not sound convincing

Zach got up and went inside. Rosa followed.

Alpha stood up. 'What the fuck?'

'Be cool Alpha, I'm working on it.'

25. Alaya

At the end of the day, as the sky turned black, our Grandfather told us stories. But my little brother and I only wanted to hear about the chief who brought the children home. That chief had tried to live with the Arabs without fighting. He made friends with them because friends do not fight each other. Arabs brought their cattle and goats to water and to eat our grass when their grass was gone, but even this did not stop raids.

Then the Mahdi came. He took charge. Said the raids would stop. The Arabs would no longer think of black people as alouny. The Mahdi said if the chief would follow him and tell all his people to do the same, the raids would stop. He would set the alouny free.

So, the chief walked all the way to the house of the Mahdi. It was large and hidden behind a high wall. The children were there. The slave master had scarred their face, so everyone knew they were alouny. They slept under the trees. They were hungry and had not been loved.

The chief took the children back to his home and they stayed with him until their families came. Then he gathered his wives, and his children, and the whole village, and told his oldest son to catch two big white bulls. They were sacrificed to thank the spirits for the children's return, for the end of the alouny. It was a great day and they were all happy.

But the raiders came back. They came when our grandfather was a child and later when he was a man. Now they come all the time. They burn our tukuls and crops and take the cattle. The people they don't want, they kill.

26. Alice

In the morning she woke to the sound of Stefan crying. The sound paralysed her. Alice wished she'd thought her plan through. She did not know how to comfort him. She'd only imagined that her company might somehow return him to a better frame of mind. Getting up, she made sure Stefan could hear her moving about, turning the radio on, opening the wardrobe doors. Stefan had insisted he take the couch and she'd heard it squeaking as he'd tried to get comfortable. She'd woken again in the early hours and he was smoking on the balcony. Alice lay in the darkness, not able to go back to sleep. She couldn't stop thinking of how much he had changed. Memories bounced toward her like a child's rubber ball. Her hesitation at primary school. Not knowing how to make friends. Stefan always there to drag her into games, his playful confidence running roughshod over her constant, niggling doubt. Alongside his confidence Stefan also had courage. Standing up for her – to her parents and his, and the kids who'd turned on her. Scrawny, with dirty blonde hair and defiant blue eyes, he'd planted fists on hips and yelled at Krystal Williams, Carla Bowmont and Lucy Nutall to leave her alone or he'd bash them all.

In the lounge, Stefan was lying on the couch, eyes closed, face waxy and drawn. Doubtful that he was actually sleeping, Alice waited for him to open his eyes and acknowledge her presence, but he did not move. Alice let him be, went to the kitchen and cooked a large breakfast. As she added toast to the plates of scrambled eggs and sausage, she heard him stirring, his cough building to a gasping hack then calming down again. Then he appeared in the doorway, blanket about his shoulders, crumbled with fatigue.

'Morning cous.'

'Morning, Stefan. Did you sleep well?' Alice asked cheerfully.

'Not bad,' Stefan lied.

Alice swallowed. So, they were both going to pretend.

Clearing the overflowing ashtray from the balcony table, Alice served breakfast in the still-soft morning sunlight. She maintained a steady stream of banalities: Gails daughter's birthday party, the devious clients at work. But Stefan seemed far away. Picking at his food, he said little.

Washing and drying the dishes, Alice put everything away then tidied the flat while Stefan remained on the balcony, drinking his second and third cup of coffee. She didn't know what to say to him. How do you begin a conversation about wanting to die?

In the shower Alice thought a sumptuous meal might be a good distraction for both of them, after having barely any breakfast, he should be ravenous for dinner. And as there wasn't much in the pantry it was a good reason to leave the flat. Singing cheerfully as she blow-dried her hair, Alice mentally planned a menu. Dressing in track pants and t-shirt she went out to the balcony. 'Feel like anything special for dinner?'

'Na mate. Not much appetite.'

'Well, I have to go get some things. I won't be long.'

Stefan gave her a small smile.

'You'll be okay?' Alice asked and he waved her away.

Outside in the jasmine-scented air Alice took a deep breath and exhaled loudly. It was difficult to admit, but her flat, her little haven, felt claustrophobic.

At the market, despite Stefan not sounding interested in dinner, she filled her environmentally friendly shopping bags with a free-range chicken and organic vegetables. The past twenty-four hours had felt like she was on a ship suddenly hit by rough weather. Tilting one way and then the other, trying to keep her balance. She didn't like to admit it but she was scared. How could she be strong for Stefan, when she spent so much time feeling weak? She thought about going overseas. How many times had she thought of doing that? Going somewhere else. Seeing how other people lived. Cutting her ties to Sydney, to her family. Alice stopped outside the open doors of the flower shop, taking in the scented air. Did she only think about going somewhere else when she was desperate? When she was overwhelmed and wanted to escape? When she was a girl and fantasised about being somewhere in Africa, is that what she was doing? Imagining Africa to be somewhere where she could be a completely different person. She went inside the shop and took a large bunch of yellow roses from a bucket. The dark-haired woman behind the counter wrapped them for her, chatting away, but Alice barely heard her. With the roses tucked under her arm she crossed the road to the lingerie shop. Plastic torsos were adorned with elaborate silk and lace contraptions. Women who wore silk underwear were sure of their erotic selves weren't they? Perhaps, she had time to try something on?

The blue silk negligee dropped to mid-thigh, its slinky fabric so deliciously cold, a rash of goose bumps appeared. Alice swayed and watched the silk gently shift in the mirror. It was beautiful. She tried to see her reflection as beguiling, but after a few moments, she carefully took the negligee off and left it in the dressing room.

Stopping next at the bottle shop, she did not hesitate over her favourite bottle of red. Alice did not want to ply her fragile cousin with alcohol, but she badly wanted it herself, so bought just the one bottle and at the check-out added a giant bag of hand-cut potato chips. As she was paying, Alice saw the clock on the cash register and a thin line of panic shot through her. She'd been away far longer than she'd thought. Rushing back with the loaded bags bouncing off her shins, her anxiety was peaking as she put her key in the lock.

Stefan was back on the couch with the TV on. Alice tried not to look relieved as the pulse of her concern slowed. Stefan looked at her sheepishly. 'It's okay cous, I'm still here.'

Alice put her shopping bags down, dropped her head to one side and considered her cousin with his three-day growth and crumpled sweatshirt. She sat down next to him. 'Well, I for one, am pleased you are.' She squeezed his hand and looked him directly in the eye. 'Please tell me you're not going to do it again, Stef. Promise me.' Tears built, but she blinked them away.

'It wouldn't matter would it?' Stefan said, part question, part statement.

Alice felt queasy.

'If I wasn't here it wouldn't really matter.'

There it was. Selfish pity. Diamond clear. Alice looked at him, but he was not able to hold her gaze. Taking the cigarette from behind his ear, he went to the balcony. Alice stayed on the couch, the queasiness coiling into a burning anger. Trying to remember the person who had been her best mate. Not this pitying, awful, poor-me. She took the shopping into the kitchen and let some of her rage loose as she unpacked. Slamming the cupboard door, shoving the chicken and vegetables into the fridge. She opened the wine to let it breathe. Then reached for a glass in the cupboard, paused, and put it back. Ripping open the bag of chips instead, she crunched through a handful trying to contain herself. He's vulnerable and needs my support, she told herself, taking more chips from the bag. When she saw her reflection in the kitchen window, she stopped eating and dropped the bag on the bench. Yes, he needed her support, but that didn't mean not saying what she thought, did it? Could she do that? Just once, could she say what she really thought?

Alice put the roses in a vase, arranging the stems. She held her nose amongst them, breathing in the heavenly scent, letting it calm her down.

She made tea, taking her time, practicing in her head. Breathing evenly, she took the mugs to the balcony and handed him a cup, taking the chair next to him, looking out over the red tiled and rusted tin rooves of Surry Hills. She took a sip of her tea. 'Do you remember those holidays at Jervis Bay?'

'Yeah, course I do.'

'You remember how we would just take off for a day at the beach. You'd tell our parents that we'd be okay, you'd look after me?'

'I don't remember saying that, but yeah, I remember mucking round all day at the beach, ice-cream, sunburn. They were good days.'

'Well, now I'm trying to look after you, but honestly Stef, I don't know how to. I keep thinking, what happened to that person? Where did he go? Because now, all I see is someone who is selfish. Selfish and self-absorbed.'

Stefan's face was blank.

'I trusted you completely then. Could tell you anything and you didn't flinch. You made me feel good about myself. I was so proud to hang out with you. But now… now I'm ashamed of you.' Stefan crumpled but Alice didn't stop. 'What you did … you deserved to go to jail. To be punished. And I can see why you might feel depressed since you got out, or even in despair. But why pity?'

He stubbed out his cigarette.

'It breaks my heart seeing you like this. I can't imagine what your Mum and Dad think. Or what you think about them. Is it their fault? Is that it?'

'I'll go stay somewhere else.'

'No Stef, I want you to stay. What I don't want is for you to feel sorry for yourself. All of this is self-inflicted.'

Stefan lit another cigarette with shaking hands.

She picked up her cup and held it firmly in her hands, letting the warmth seep through her. She'd said exactly what she had wanted to say, yet she felt calm and steady.

Stefan wiped away tears with the back of his hand. His voice was barely above a whisper. 'It just seemed easier to finish it. I've fucked up my life and I don't know how to put anything straight.'

Alice felt a rush of concern. She got up and looped her arms around him, giving him a quick squeeze. This was the moment she was supposed to tell him everything would be okay, but she couldn't bring herself to say that word. Everything. A lot had changed in a week, but not the enormity of that word.

27. Ottavio

Ottavio sensed the tension in Malong the moment he stepped out of his car. Monday mornings he was usually brimming with energy and stories from his weekend, but he was sullen and did not wait for Ottavio to fall into step. He charged through the door and into the change rooms. Ottavio knew what was coming.

Side-by-side they put on their work clothes. Malong tied off his rubber apron. 'Why didn't you tell me about Zach getting kicked out?'

'Because he wasn't kicked out.'

'You sure about that?'

'More than you know.'

'Then why hasn't he been at school all week?'

'He's just hanging at home until I get it sorted.'

'Really?'

'He didn't do anything wrong.'

'And you think that matters?' Malong's eyes were dense and clouded. 'Come on Machar, they just got rid of another Sudanese kid. They'll be happy about that.'

'Malong, shut up with that shit.'

'He just another black kid they don't want.'

'I'm dealing with it. Okay?'

'Machar, what's wrong with you? You think they're gonna listen to you?'

'Cool down Malong.'

'I'll go there. Speak to what's his name? Turner?'

'I don't need your help.'

'Really? What you gonna do? What you gonna do for Zach that will make it right? Zach's just like you were. How many times did I have to sort someone out for you?'

'The one time you 'sorted something out' for me, I almost got beaten up.'

Malong ignored him. 'Some kids sized him up. They know he ain't got it in him.'

Hoping he might talk himself into a calmer state, Ottavio didn't interrupt.

'You can't think your way through everything Machar. Sometimes you gotta fight. You don't like it but it's the truth.'

'Who? Who you gonna fight Malong? You gonna go to the school and beat up Zach's classmates. Is that the plan?'

Snorting, Malong shook his head. 'Not talking about that. There are ways. You know what I mean.'

'We spoke to the social worker.'

'The social worker?' Malong spat like he'd tasted something bad. 'You keep thinking this place is special, don't you? Waiting for *kawaujas* to do the right thing, so you can smile and be grateful?'

'And you think it's better at home? Is that it? And Kenya? How about Egypt? Put them on the list of fair and just places?'

Malong didn't reply.

'At least here there's a chance!' Ottavio said, exasperated.

'I don't believe what I'm hearing.'

'Kids can go to school here.'

'You defending them now?'

'Only person I'm defending is Zach.'

'Machar,' Malong said, shaking his head again. 'You never gonna change are you?'

They both pulled on their rubber boots.

'You gotta trust me on this one. I know how to deal with this okay?'

When Malong was frustrated he could change mood in a second. Bouncing on his toes, he took up a boxing stance, fists lightly punching at his friend.

'Rachel asking after you.' He said, taking a step forward, nudging Ottavio's shoulder.

'You know how to deal with her?'

Ottavio smiled at his friend, relieved at the change of subject. 'Rachel's after you Malong, not me.'

'Rachel's perfect for you Machar.'

Ottavio thought of Alice and smiled slyly. He knew what Malong would think.

'She'll be there Saturday night. You got to come, Machar. Now's your chance before someone else snaps her up.'

'Sure you're not that person?'

Malong returned Ottavio's sly grin. 'Machar, she's all yours. You just got to show up.'

Ottavio reached out and slapped Malong's ear. 'I'll show up and you'll have your arm around her.'

'I wouldn't do that to a brother.' Malong punched Ottavio's other shoulder.

'Yeah, you would.' Ottavio said, tapping his chin.

'Not true, Machar. Not true.'

The buzzer sounded and the hydraulics released a row of carcasses. Malong and Ottavio pushed through the swing doors and took their place on the line.

Ottavio was five minutes from home and expecting to pull up outside his house right on time when Rosa called. She had just spoken to Julie Miller.

'She said she had spoken to both parties and their story hadn't changed. Had to speak to their parents now.'

Ottavio pulled the car over. 'Is that all she said?'

'That's all.' Rosa said sadly. 'Ottavio, could you stop at the supermarket and get something sweet for Zach? Chocolate cake, Zach loves chocolate cake.' Ottavio recalled the first time he had it. He ate slowly, taking small mouthfuls, sucking in the mushy sweetness, his eyes dimming with pleasure.

'Sure Rosa, I won't be long.'

Ottavio made up his mind. He could get a cake at the supermarket, but he headed for the bakery at the shopping centre instead.

A bell tinkled as Ottavio opened the door into the smell of flour and sugar and a faded warmth from the ovens. A young woman was at the counter, telling the little boy on her hand to hurry up and make up his mind. In her pram a grizzly baby was squirming. Behind the counter a bored, fat woman in a tight white smock and cap gave the mother a half smile, trying to appear sympathetic. The boy asked for the jam donut. His mother tugged his arm, exasperated. 'A custard square or a lamington Tommy, they don't have any donuts.' Tommy pouted and dropped his head, stubbing his sneaker against the counter. The fat woman glanced at Ottavio as though he was a species she didn't recognise. Without blinking, she turned towards the kitchen and bellowed, 'Kel!'

Red hair pulled back into a long ponytail, Kelly appeared at the counter. With widened eyes and pink blooming across her throat, she stared at Ottavio as the baby began to scream. The fat woman impatiently bagged a lamington and snatched two bags of sliced white from the rack.

Ottavio watched Kelly's attempts to disguise her alarm. Pretending she had not recognised him, she asked in a nervous voice, 'What would you like?'

Ottavio ran his finger across the cool glass on his watch. Here she was, right in front of him, big greenish eyes, a pretty freckled face and that red hair.

'Chocolate cake.'

'Sorry, none left.'

The baby's scream changed to a higher pitch as its mother

pushed the pram out the door, the boy running ahead with the paper bag held tightly in his fist. Kelly pulled her ponytail over her shoulder and flicked the end of it around the tip of her finger as Ottavio studied the glass display case. The fat woman leaned on the counter for a few seconds, sizing up him up. He avoided her challenging eyes and after a moment, she heaved herself up from the counter and waddled back into the kitchen.

Ottavio considered the sponges, dried-out scones, custard squares and bright-yellow rock cakes. When he moved back to where Kelly was standing, she flicked her eyes away from his. 'I'm getting something for Zach,' he said carefully. Her throat flushed pink again. Ottavio stared at her hard, anger pricking his throat. She flinched but managed to speak. 'Oh?'

'He misses school,' Ottavio replied.

Kelly sucked in her bottom lip.

'I know you didn't see him take it.'

Tears threatened to spill from her eyes, but she blinked them back.

The fat woman stuck her head around the kitchen door and yelled, 'You right, Kel?'

Not giving her a chance to respond, Ottavio picked a cellophane bag of chocolate chip cookies and passed Kelly the money. Quickly she got his change, placed it on the counter and went back to the kitchen. Ottavio left the shop with the bleary eyes of the fat woman boring into his back.

Ottavio knew what he had to do.

28. Alaya

When the chief was old and he knew he was going to die, he asked for his grave to be dug and he lay down in it. For three days people came to him to say goodbye. The last person he spoke to was his eldest son. I wonder what he told him? I am sure he did not say war and suffering would come to everyone in the land. Maybe he told him that the nhalic angic nhialic, the spirit known only to God, was coming?

29. Alice

A tingle of fearful excitement spread through her as she paired a long, floaty orange top and black leggings with a pair of low-heeled orange shoes. She had decided not to cancel her date with Ottavio after all, but she did wish she'd bought the blue silk slip she'd tried on in the lingerie shop the day before. How could she pretend it wasn't a date when she really wanted it to be? She took in some deep breaths and started applying mascara. Out loud, she said, 'Fuck it. I'm going to do this.'

Stefan was still on the couch like it was some kind of life-raft. She had not been able to tempt him into walking to the park or seeing a movie in the city. He'd just smoked and drunk coffee and watched the TV, until this morning when she'd persuaded him to play chess. A game he had taught her. Alice felt his mood shift as he concentrated on the board, warning her of potential wrong moves just like he used to. Alice had felt encouraged. Maybe he was recalibrating.

Alice added lipstick and grabbed her bag, 'I won't be late, Stefie.'

'You look good. Someone special in that class?'

Alice wanted to tell him, to blurt it all out. After all he'd been advisor on all her teenage crushes. But she held back.

'Nothing like that, just like to make an effort sometimes,

otherwise I'd leave the house in my track pants all the time. You sure you're good for the evening?'

'Go on. Get out of here.'

Stiff-backed and blank-faced, Mary was sitting at the other end of the table. Melissa had addressed the class the week before, explaining that Achol had been banned. Violence could not be tolerated. Her invitation for anyone to speak was met with an uncomfortable silence. Pages were turned and pencils spun through fingers. Melissa looked about the room, cleared her throat and got on with the lesson.

Alice thought she should go and sit with Mary but stayed with Batool as she carefully pronounced the words on the worksheet. Keeping her eye on the door, hoping Ottavio might be one of the stragglers, Alice tried not to appear distracted.

When Melissa announced it was time for a break, Alice had to concede he was not coming. He'd stood her up. If only she'd followed her instinct and cancelled first.

Melissa approached Alice in the kitchen. 'You look very nice Alice. How's things with you?'

'Thanks. I'm good thanks. Great. And you?'

'I'm really well.'

'Shame Ottavio didn't make it tonight. I hope he's okay.'

'Oh, he rang earlier, said he wouldn't be in. Some family business.'

'Right.'

'He'll be back next week. Very apologetic. He's such a nice guy.'

Suspicion jerked through Alice's brain. Was that an admiring tone in Melissa's voice? Her stomach flipped. Melissa likes Ottavio. Alice stared at Melissa and felt herself tilt again. Ottavio likes Melissa. That's why he's stood me up. Like an out of control train, she picked up speed.

Of course he liked her; pretty and slender, her clothing urbane and perfectly fitted. There was a stud in her nose. Her shiny auburn hair was styled into edgy layers and spiky lengths, with random streaks of fire engine red. A pair of black and red low-cut boots accentuated her long legs.

Alice's heart was pounding, but she could not stop herself. Was Melissa basking in the glow of an attractive man's desire, is that why she was in such a good mood? Ottavio had called her, what else had he said to her?

Alice noticed a large, elaborate ring on her left hand. Filigree silver with a sharply cut yellow stone. Ethnic looking. Not a traditional wedding ring, but it could be. Melissa seemed fairly unconventional but that didn't exclude her from marriage, and being married did not mean she wasn't seeing Ottavio. She might have an open relationship or maybe she kept her affairs from her husband.

'Did he say what the problem was?'

'No. He didn't say there was one. Just that he had family business to attend to.'

A small, quiet part of her brain told her she should stop but she ignored it. 'Do you have family? I mean, I thought, you know, if you had kids, teaching at night must be quite difficult.'

Melissa looked perplexed. 'I don't have kids.'

'Oh. Are you planning to? Does your husband want to?'

Melissa's forehead creased. She looked annoyed. 'I'm not married. But since you're asking, yes, my girlfriend and I would like to have kids.'

'Oh, that's nice,' Alice spluttered, feeling her cheeks flush. Melissa searched her face for an explanation of her crude questions. Alice tried to save herself. 'Sorry Melissa, that just came out wrong. I didn't mean to be so intrusive.' Melissa nodded coolly, gave Alice a tight smile and went back to the classroom.

Filling a glass, Alice gulped the water down, wanting it to rinse away the shame roiling through her; displaying her insecurity like a peacock's tail, humiliating herself for no reason, jeopardising her relationship with Melissa. Why would she even think there was something between her and Ottavio? Alice wanted to cry, hold onto the sink and sob, let her tears splash down the drain. She stayed there as long as she could, then forced herself to go back to the classroom, keeping her head down, and doodling in her notebook, feeling bile in the back of her throat.

Alice left as quickly as she could, holding back tears as she walked to the train station, taking the escalator to the underground platform. A few other passengers were scattered about, white cords attached to their ears, phones in their hands. A derelict man slumped against a wall, eyeballs rolling into the back of his head.

Alice took the bench at the far end and shivered in the cold air blasting out of the tunnel. Staring into the darkness, she wondered if she would ever change. She pulled her collar up. Stefan would be waiting for her. Maybe she should tell him. Let him make light of another romantic disaster; conduct a brutal appraisal, examine all the details then conclude that Ottavio, like all the others, was simply not worth the pain. He was just another miscalculation, not a failed attempt to upgrade her standards. Getting out before she got in deep was something to be proud of.

Or maybe she could just pretend there was nothing wrong. That, after all, was what they were still doing. Her blunt attempt at truth telling had taken some of the tension away but Stefan was still distant. Why had she thought some brutal honesty was going to make anything okay. He wouldn't be up for any light-hearted banter about her terrible love life. And nor was she. Gail would be calling in the morning, demanding details, and it was impossible to pretend with her. She could try ignoring her call, but Gail would be relentless, and Alice would end up telling her all about Stefan, Ottavio standing her up, and probably the exchange with Melissa; just to give her the full picture of her misery.

Tilting her head back, Alice tried to stop more tears spilling. What a joke, Alice thought, demanding Stefan drop the self-pity routine.

There was a distant rumble and the cold air churned, throwing her hair about her face. The train burst out of the tunnel and slid to a squealing halt. Taking a seat near a window, Alice tried to steady herself. She would maintain a brave front with Stefan and not confess all to Gail. How often had Gail felt sorry for her? Every broken romance, that's how often.

Forty minutes later at Central Station, she made her way through the underground tunnel, heels echoing loudly on the tiles. She stopped at her local café for a coffee and a thick slice of sticky date cake. In the absence of strength, sugar would do.

Fortified, she bought Stefan half a dozen raspberry macaroons. She wouldn't let him see how upset she was. The pretence would continue. He had enough to contend with. Stopping at the bottle shop, Alice grabbed a bottle of creamy liquer: she'd make them a coffee, add a nip and together evoke a new era. Everything they had seen in each other when they were kids was still there. His courage. Her curiosity. They just needed to bolster each other, cheer each other on. With rising spirits, she heard Millie meowing as she put her key in the door. But as she stepped inside, she knew, before she could even think it.

Stefan was gone.

30. Ottavio

'**M**r Bol, the girl's father is upset that you took matters into your own hands and frankly I think he has every right to be.'

Lying, Ottavio tried to regain some ground. 'I didn't know she worked there.' He did feel bad about lying, but lying for your family, wasn't an ordinary lie. It wasn't the first time he had done it. On the visa application for Australia, next to 'sibling', he wrote Alpha's name and Malong's.

Julie Miller was firm. 'Be that as it may, speaking to her was inappropriate.'

'She asked how Zach was and I told her.' He sounded weak. Ottavio was losing.

If Miller had been on his side, she wasn't now.

'Mr Bol, I was hoping Mr Johnson would let the matter drop, but I'm not sure now.'

Indignant, Ottavio snapped back. 'And what would he do if he knew his daughter's boyfriend is the problem here? And that she's scared of him?

He heard her take a breath in.

'Mr Bol, please let me handle this situation. I am still trying to speak to Theo's family.'

'If you speak to Kelly again, she might have a different story to tell.'

He hung up. For a few moments cutting her off like that

felt like a victory. But then it felt wrong. Being rude, letting her see his anger, that was a serious mistake. Zach needed allies and he might have just lost him one. Maybe he should call back, make her understand that Zach was different to other kids. His life had only come good these past few years, and he didn't deserve any more wrong. Ottavio told himself to be calm. Maybe Malong was right; he was just wasting his time with this woman. He would be disgusted if he knew Ottavio had thought of pleading with her, looking for her sympathy. Did Theo really frighten Kelly? Or did she tell her father some nonsense to deflect any attention from her? Or was it Theo? Kelly had told him, and he had schooled her with what to say to her father?

Ottavio's mind kept spinning.

He thought of Holden from *Catcher in the Rye*. He didn't care what other people thought, just did whatever he wanted, even if he knew it would get him in trouble. Holden understood how mean people could be, but it did not stop him. A bit like Malong? But if Malong knew he still looked to an imaginary *kawauja* boy, from a childhood book – a book Malong had declined to read – he would shake his head, bewildered. Ottavio had described the story to him but Malong had dismissed Holden; *a white kid in a white world, rich parents and a good school. What exactly was his problem?*

Ottavio sighed. Malong might be more like Holden than he had ever realised; except that Malong hated the ducks. *Who fucking cares what happened to them* he'd said. Little mysteries like that didn't interest Malong. In his mind the world could only ever be black or white. He thought of all the other kids at the school in Nairobi, they were all from rich families. Vaclav's father was a diplomat. Together he and Ottavio used to sneak out of school in the early evening and get drunk under the palm trees in a park a few blocks away. Vaclav told him outlandish stories of the girls he'd had in Russia. Ottavio didn't believe him for a moment but loved all the lewd details. Twice they got caught climbing back over the compound wall, giggling like idiots, falling over each other. The headmaster warned them, but they both knew they would never get kicked out. Vaclav's family had money and Ottavio might have been a refugee with no money at all, but he was one of the best runners the school had.

Ottavio wondered what Vaclav was doing now. Not arguing with women like Julie Miller, he was sure of that. How good would it be to back under those palm trees with him, sipping beer, and imitating Coach Singh's accent.

Coach Singh was the first to offer him a scholarship and he took it without hesitation. He had applied for resettlement, but that took years. There was no other way out of camp. Coach Singh thought he was a good runner, said he could go far. 'You have a gift from God,' he'd told him. 'You are obliged to use it.' Ottavio couldn't tell him he wasn't sure he believed in God.

At first he'd hated the endless training. Up early, stretch, run. The same thing every day. But despite himself, he got used to it. Even looked forward to being on the track and finding the zone. Focusing on the white line, meditating on its narrow width, letting it lead him around the track again and again. In his second year, Ottavio won all his races and found his confidence, like there might be a place in the world for him.

Mr Singh would probably have suggested that Ottavio take a softer approach with the school and Julie Miller. Work around the problem, quietly keep at it until it changed for the better. That was his coaching style. He'd told Ottavio that he could apply this attitude to any situation he came across in his life.

Ottavio felt exhausted. It was still early but he went to bed and fell asleep instantly.

He woke before his alarm and was thinking of Angelina, imagining her lying next to him when there was a loud banging on the front door. Ottavio felt a ripple of fear.

Flicking the curtain open, he saw Malong's car parked out front. Relieved and surprised, he let a few moments pass before opening the door.

'Take your time my man. I'm in no hurry,' Malong said striding past him and down the hall. He banged on the bedroom door and pushed it open. 'Zach get up and get dressed. We're taking you to school.'

Rosa appeared from her room, wrapping her dressing gown tightly around her.

'Morning Rosa. Heard Zach needs a hand getting to school.'

'He doesn't Malong.'

'Rosa, Zach's not a boy anymore. He got problems, he got to face them.'

'We don't want more trouble than we got.'

'Trouble stops today.'

Rosa looked to Ottavio, but he said nothing.

Zach appeared, wide-eyed, Alpha behind him, grinning.

'Don't even bother disagreeing. Go shower.' Malong said. Taking Zach by the shoulders, he spun him around and shoved him in the direction of the bathroom. Zach did what he was told. He could never refuse Malong.

'What are you grinning at?' Malong said to Alpha. 'You coming too.'

'No. Alpha stays here,' Ottavio said firmly. Alpha glanced at him and back at Malong. Malong shrugged his shoulders. 'Whatever.' Alpha nodded and went back to his room.

'Please Malong, don't make this any worse,' Rosa said.

'Things will be better after today Rosa. Zach just got to stop hiding away like he guilty of something. We'll just walk to his classroom with our heads high. Show everyone he's back.'

Rosa tightened the belt of her dressing gown. 'Just drop him at the gate? Ottavio please?'

Ottavio knew Theo wouldn't be happy to see Zach. Fuck him, Ottavio thought, and fuck Julie Miller too. Maybe Malong was right. No more waiting. 'Okay' he said casually and went back to the kitchen to pour tea for all of them.

Rosa set out cereal and milk on the table. Malong yelled at

Alpha to get his lazy arse out here and chatted to Rosa like it was an ordinary day.

Dressed in his white shirt and long grey shorts, Zach walked into the kitchen, backpack hooked over one shoulder. Taking a seat, he leant his chin against the palm of his hand, eyes big with worry. Said he didn't want any breakfast, but Rosa insisted. Ottavio grabbed his kit for work and as soon as Zach finished his cereal, they left in Malong's car.

Zach sat in the back saying nothing. Malong drove fast and braked hard and spoke non-stop. 'Nothing to be concerned about, leopard. Whoever been giving you a hard time gonna stop now. You act proud. Don't you ever let them see you scared. You hear me?' Malong stared at Zach in the rear-view mirror.

Ottavio let Malong do his thing. Let him lay it down thick. He wanted Zach to hear it. Ottavio regretted letting it go this far. It didn't matter to the school. The social worker didn't care either. Made no difference to her. He could see that now.

At school, kids were pouring out of buses. Others scrambled from their parents' cars in the one-minute drop-off zone. Malong parked across the zone, blocking anyone from pulling in. They all got out as other drivers glared and sounded their horns in protest.

With Zach between them, Malong and Ottavio strolled up to the gates, taking their time. Kids streamed past them when they stopped at the entrance. Taller than every other person, they were impossible not to notice. Malong looked about casually, checking if anyone wanted to catch his eye. Ottavio did the same. There was no one he recognised.

Slapping Zach on the shoulder, Malong spoke quietly, 'Like a leopard. Don't forget.' Zach smiled a little and quickly walked off.

He didn't look back.

※

Ottavio and Malong drove to work in silence. As they pulled into the car park Ottavio turned the music down. 'You were right. Thanks.'

Malong looked at him hard but spoke in a soft voice. 'Brother, if you were truly a Dinka man you would not thank me. You wanna thank me, you show your appreciation. Do it. Don't speak it.' Before Ottavio could answer, someone banged on the roof. Malong was out of the car in a second, Ottavio followed, moving around the car to stand next to his friend. The *kawauja* was beer bellied, hands on his hips, shoulders hunched. 'Which one of you fellas been talking to my daughter?' The man glared at Ottavio and then Malong. Greying curls of chest hair sprouted above his dark blue singlet, climbing toward his throat. His shorts and work boots were stained with paint and grease. Ottavio smelt his sweat and saw the tension in his shoulders. His eyes were yellowish bright.

Beside him Malong flexed his hands.

'You Kelly's father?' Ottavio held his voice steady.

'You don't speak to her. You speak to me.'

'Happy to sort it out.'

'Sort what out? Your kid had my kid's phone in his bag.'

'Zach didn't take the phone. Theo put it in Zach's bag. Everyone knows that, but nobody's saying. Why would that be?' Ottavio tried to control the fear rushing his brain.

'How would I bloody know?' the man snarled.

Ottavio knew he was in dangerous territory, but Malong was beside him.

'Because they're all scared of him.' Ottavio paused. Then he pushed his luck. 'And Kelly is too.'

'I fucking told you to leave Kelly out of this,' the man said, but Ottavio saw a flicker in his resolve and pushed again. 'This is Theo's fault.'

'Whadda ya mean by that?'

'Theo's the problem here.'

'Is that right?' he said, shifting his stance.

For a panicked second, Ottavio thought he'd gone too far. The man leaned toward Ottavio. 'Since when do you know so much about my daughter?' Malong stepped up to the man, but he stabbed his finger at Malong's chest. 'You stay out of it.' Malong stared back, eyes hooded, chin raised. But in the man's bravado, Ottavio caught a glimpse of concern and he gave one last push.

'If you ain't worried about Theo you should be.'

'I don't know what all this is about, but I'm telling ya, talk to Kelly again and you'll regret it.' Then he looked at Malong. 'Both of ya will.'

He turned to go, but Ottavio wanted the last word. 'Leave Zach out of it.'

He hesitated, as if he might turn back, then got into his battered ute, revved the engine hard and drove off.

Malong slapped Ottavio's shoulder and gave him an approving smirk.

31. Alaya

Little brother and I walked to the church at Mayen Aben with our mother and baby brother. He was nearly three, but we called him baby brother because he was so skinny. His father was our uncle. A few months after our father died, mother married his brother. We were part of his family and he would look after us, but there was no food left. People were dying. Others left, saying they would follow the trail to the east, to another country. The horses still came, but now planes did as well. Bombs fell. The earth exploded and so did people; into pieces across the ground.

Mother did not know what to do. Nobody could tell us, not the spear master or the chief. Not our uncles. So, Mother decided we should go to the big church and pray. It was dangerous. As we walked, we saw no other people. Either they were hiding in the bush or they had run away.

We reached Mayen Aben in the afternoon. Our mother led us to the church. It was the biggest building we had ever seen. The pointed roof touched the sky. Mother said the colours in the walls were made from glass. Surely God would hear if we prayed in this building?

But the door to the church was shut, so we sat on the step to rest. There was no sound, not even birds singing. Then little brother pointed to the wall. Bullet holes. We walked around the building and the glass with the pretty colours was broken. The walls of two small buildings nearby were smashed and blackened by fire. There was a terrible smell. Mother told us to wait and walked behind the broken buildings. Then she reappeared, running; her eyes blank with fear. We followed her into the bush, away from the church. It was not in the direction of home.

In the silence we all heard it. The kuei telling us to go and don't stop.

32. Alice

Stefan had taken the ashtray from the balcony and washed it, leaving it to dry in the dish rack. The cushions on the sofa had been fluffed and the furniture straightened. There was no sign he had been there. Sitting down, Alice shivered, as though the cold wind from the train tunnel had followed her through the door. She fumbled about in her handbag for her phone and with shaking hands she called him. His phone was off. Fear dropped through her. She leaned back and tried to slow her heart. Then her phone rang. It was Gail. Alice didn't hesitate to answer.

'Technically that's not a good sign,' Gail said.

'What?'

'You, answering the phone. I was kind of hoping you were busy doing something else. Although these days, answering your phone when you're with someone—'

'Gail, please—'

'—would be no surprise. So, are you with someone? Naked I mean. Please tell me you've got a big black man on top of you and your hand is over his mouth so I can't hear him panting.'

'He stood me up.'

'He didn't? Oh God. Men are such pricks. So, what happened?'

'Nothing happened, he just didn't come.'

'Clearly not. So, no call?'

'He doesn't have my number. But he rang Melissa, the teacher, and said he had some family business.'

'No message for you?'

'No.'

'Oh, that's such a shame. You going to give it another crack?'

'I don't think I want another crack.' Alice burst into tears.

'Doll, don't, he's not worth it. No man is.'

'It's not that. Stefan's gone.'

'Your cousin Stefan?'

'Yeah.'

'I thought he got locked up?'

'He did, but he got out early. A few weeks ago. He's been staying with me.'

'Oh.'

'He tried to kill himself and now he's gone.'

'What?'

'He took an overdose Gail.' Alice wiped tears away with the back of her hand.

'Oh, doll.'

'I told his mum and dad I'd look after him. I wasn't even going to go to class, but he said I should. We played chess and I thought he was better. There's no note and his phone's off.'

Sobbing, Alice doubled over.

'Jesus.' Gail whispered. 'Catch a taxi over here. I'd come over but Tony is out, and I can't leave the kids.'

'What if he comes back? He doesn't have a key. I have to call his mum. She might know something.'

'Are his things gone?'

'He didn't have anything. He just came in what he was wearing. I have to go Gail. I'll call you back later.'

'You promise. You will call, won't you?'

'Soon as I can.'

'I'll be ringing if you don't get back to me.'

'I promise.'

Alice called Bronwyn, heard the phone ring a few times and then hung up. What would she say to her? Maybe she should wait. Stefan might be coming back. He could have just gone out for a walk. His phone had been off all week. Not having it on now didn't mean anything.

She needed to calm down.

❖

Showered and changed, Alice sat on the balcony with a glass of wine. Feeling a little more composed she told herself Stefan was fine; probably just getting some fresh air. If he wasn't back in an hour, she'd call Bronwyn and leave a message. Or maybe she'd wait until morning. Alice took a long drink and almost laughed at herself. Less than half an hour ago she was convinced she and Stefan were going to turn a page. No more dwelling on their mistakes. No more pity. They could have gone overseas together. Somewhere completely out of their comfort zone. Forget about their lives and try out something new. She'd thought about Vietnam. She loved Vietnamese food. And there was Thailand and Cambodia.

But where was he?

As she lay on the couch, Alice patted Millie and considered stacking her new bookshelf. Alphabetical order would keep her occupied. In fact, she could re-do all the shelves. Dust the books. Check for any folded corners or silverfish. Millie purred loudly and Alice refilled her glass. When Gail called, Alice felt quite drunk. She didn't answer. Sliding the phone under a cushion to muffle the ringtone, she waited. But true to her word, Gail kept ringing. Alice gave in.

'Is he back?'

'No.' Alice tried not to slur.

'Oh Alice, why didn't you tell me?'

'I don't know. I thought he'd want some privacy.'

'But you could have told *me*.'

'Well you know now.'

'Was it an accident? Or…you know. Did he mean to?'

'I'm sure he did.'

Gail fell silent and Alice gulped more wine.

'What did his mother say?' Gail asked tentatively.

'I didn't tell her. Decided to wait until morning, hopefully he'll be back by then.'

'Yeah. That's a good idea. I'm sure he will.'

'It's my fault,' Alice blurted out.

'How could it be your fault?'

'I told him he was selfish.'

'Oh, come on Alice. You told him he was selfish, and he tried to kill himself?'

'No! This morning. I said things to him. I shouldn't have said it.' Alice could not hide the slurring.

'You're not making much sense. Whatever you think you did, this is not your fault love. You need to get a good sleep. It will look different in the morning. I promise.'

Alice could not hold back her tears.

'Call me as soon as he gets back? If I don't hear from you tonight, I'll call in the morning. Okay?'

'Okay.' Alice managed to hold back her sobs until Gail had hung up.

33. Ottavio

Malong sounded his horn in a loud farewell, yelling he'd be back later. Ottavio let himself into the house. Tired, he sat in the kitchen and listened to silence until his phone interrupted it. Julie Miller was calling. Ottavio made her wait a little, just to remind her she wasn't entirely in control of the 'situation'.

'Hi Ottavio.'

Ottavio noted her overly friendly tone.

'I was surprised to see Zach is back at school today?'

'He wanted to go.'

'Well, that's good.' She hesitated. Ottavio smiled, enjoying her uncertainty.

'We waited long enough.'

'Well yes. I've not long spoken to Theo's family. His mother doesn't speak English very well, so I spoke to his older brother.'

Ottavio wondered if he was the driver of the black car. How many brothers did Theo have?

'He said Theo knew nothing about the phone.'

'Of course, he did.'

'We can't accuse Theo of anything.'

'Why are kids scared of him?'

'I can't answer that Ottavio. Unless anyone reports an incident with this boy, there is nothing to look into. But I can say that he is known to the school.'

'Meaning?'

'I can't say more.'

'So that's it. You leave it at that?'

'Kelly's father has contacted me. He said he didn't want any further action taken, so Mr Turner has decided Zach will not be on probation.'

Ottavio felt a small sense of victory. In the absence of an apology, it would do.

'Well, Zach's back at school where he should be. That's what we wanted.' Ottavio couldn't bring himself to thank her. There was a brief silence and Miller said goodbye.

Ottavio looked at his watch. School was out soon. He would have to be fast.

Zach was out front with all the kids waiting for their buses. His face lit up when he saw Ottavio's car. Running across the street, narrow shoulders loose, long arms swinging, he got in and slammed the door.

They drove without speaking, Zach fiddling the radio dial looking for a station with the kind of music he liked; girls chirping cheesy love songs over a fast, tinny bass. The lesson in the greats of American hip-hop could wait for another day.

'How was it?'

'Okay.'

'No problems then?'

'Nup.'

'You see Theo?'

Zach looked at him wearily.

'He say anything to you today?'

Zach shook his head.

'That kid even looks at you the wrong way, you're gonna tell me. Malong's right. Okay? Don't let anyone push you around.'

Ottavio let that sink in.

'Did you see Kelly?'

Zach nodded. 'I didn't speak to her.'

'You change your mind about her?'

Zach shrugged.

'You be careful around her. Okay?'

This wasn't over. He just knew it. Should he warn Theo off? Ottavio let the thought race round in his head. Malong would, no doubt.

They pulled into the carport and Zach undid his seatbelt. 'His name isn't Theo, he's called T.'

'T? Like black tea?'

'No, like the letter T,' Zach said.

'You sure about that? I'd say he likes his tea with sugar and milk.'

Zach sniggered at Ottavio's little joke.

Ottavio opened the front door just as Malong pulled up, music booming. He jumped out and ran over, playfully pushing them both into the house.

'Need some help with your homework?' he said.

Zach and Ottavio both laughed out loud. Malong doing homework was ridiculous.

'What? What's so funny?' Malong said pretending he didn't understand.

Shaking his head, Zach went to his room. Ottavio put the kettle on and Malong pulled up a chair. He would have nothing more to say about Zach and the school. To him there was no longer an issue. When he spoke, Ottavio recognised the tone. The one that meant that Ottavio shouldn't even think about arguing.

'Saturday night's sorted. Rachel's gonna be there. I told her you were asking after her.'

'Man, I don't believe you. Why get her hopes up?'

'She got all excited and grateful. Said she'd bring her cousin for me.'

'Which cousin?'

'You'll see and you won't believe it.'

'So that's the deal? The two of us and the two of them?'

'And what a sweet deal. You can let me know later how you're gonna show your appreciation.' Malong beamed.

'Is that right?' Ottavio laughed.

'It couldn't be more right.' Malong jumped up, stretched out his arms in front and lewdly swayed his hips. Ottavio thought of Rachel and Alice. There was a rhythm to their names that he liked. Why not have them both?

34. Alaya

Mother took us into the swamp. We waded through the water and the reeds. Little brother climbed a tree and searched for others. We kept walking. Hours later we saw people on an island. They pointed to where the water was not deep. I carried little brother on my back, mother carried baby brother the same way. There were many people. Some were from Mayen Aben, others from Wunroc. There was no food except the water lilies. The women pulled them from the soggy ground and pounded the bulbs. It tasted like nothing.

When night came, the adults talked of the missing and the dead. A woman cried for her husband; the Arabs had pushed him into their burning tukul and jammed shut the door. She could only hear his screaming. Another cried for her little girls, taken by men on horses. An old man said the war had come back. He knew. He had fought the first time when the British had left. The past had come back. In the east, government soldiers had rebelled. They had guns. He would find them and carry a gun too.

A woman spoke, she wanted to stay in hiding until the Arabs went away. An old man laughed bitterly; the Arabs would not stop. They wanted land. They wanted us to kneel down and pray. They had taken all of his cattle, nearly one hundred. He had nothing left.

Another man spoke of people walking. He had climbed a tree and seen them. A long single line of people, more people than he had ever seen. Some carried small bundles. Others had cooking pots. Many of the children were without clothes. They made no noise as they walked away from their homeland.

Little brother and baby brother were asleep next to me. We lay on a pile of reeds. They were hard and scratchy. Mosquitos buzzed all around us. The stars were looking down on us and so was the nhalic angic nhiali. *I was sure of it.*

35. Alice

The sound of traffic was building to a distant roar. Alice had slept badly all week and lay in the darkness, exhausted, listening to the city waking up. Hydraulic brakes hissing on Cleveland street, the grind of a rubbish truck emptying bins. Bronwyn did not hide her anguish when Alice told her he was gone. Today, Bronwyn and Jack would be going to the police to list him as a missing person.

She called Stefan's phone again, was shocked to hear it ring and click onto message bank. Alice listened carefully to his voice: it sounded mellow. The message clicked off and she called to listen again. Alice felt sure it was meant for her. He said he would return calls ...eventually. Alice called again, wanting to leave her own message, but when then the phone beeped, she didn't know what to say. She held the phone against her chest and relief swept through her. For the first time in days, she wanted to get out of bed. In the shower, she twisted her head in a figure of eight, hot water pounding the back of her neck. She felt like screaming with relief. She let the water gurgle into her mouth and spat it out.

On her way to work she called Bronwyn and told her about Stefan's phone message. Bronwyn was still crying when Alice said she had to go. Then she rang Gail.

'See, I told you not to worry. He just needs time away from you all. Families can drive you mad.'

'I don't think this is about his family.'

'Oh, come on Alice, family is always involved.'

'He can't blame family all the time.'

'Well, it must have been a hell of a shock getting out of prison.'

'I was so relieved to hear his voice.'

'You going to class today?'

'I guess.'

'Just go straight up to him and say hello like nothing had happened. Never let a man see you upset.'

'Easier said than done.'

'You can do it, I know you can.'

Alice put on her a dark blue chiffon shirt and a long skirt that hugged her hips. Then she washed and blow-dried her hair telling herself she was not dressing for Ottavio. She just wanted to feel a bit better after a terrible week.

When Ottavio arrived at class, she ignored him. He took the last seat at the far end of the table. At the break, Alice's stomach fluttered nervously. As the students filed into the kitchen she went straight to the bathroom and lingered at the mirror. Drying her hands slowly, she heard Gail telling her not to let him upset her.

Ottavio approached her as she walked into the kitchen, 'Hi Alice, sorry to have missed you a few weeks back.'

'Miss me?'

'For dinner.'

'Oh, I'd forgotten all about that.'

'If you're not busy maybe we could have a coffee after class?'

'Sorry, but I have to get home, I've got things to do.'

'Another time then.'

'Sure, another time. Excuse me but I just have to have a word with Batool.' Alice walked off with her chin high, wounded pride hidden away. At the end of the class she said goodbye to a few of the students, but not to him.

Half a block from the centre, she was about to cross the street when Ottavio pulled up in his car. 'Want a lift?'

'No, I'm fine. Not far to go.'

Ottavio smiled and opened the door. 'Jump in.'

Alice hesitated. Ottavio looked relaxed behind the wheel, hip-hop playing. She got in.

'Been reading that book you lent me,' he said as he waited for a gap in the traffic.

'What do you think?'

'It's okay. Obsession and tropical diseases are an understandable combination,' Ottavio said dryly.

'I think he means that love is like disease generally, not that it feels like cholera.'

'I get that,' he said with playful eyes. 'But he was obsessed.'

'Maybe love and obsession are the same thing?' Ottavio

said as he changed up a gear, going straight past the train station.

'Uh, that's the station just there. I'll get out.'

'I'll drop you at home.'

'No, don't do that, it's too far.'

'I have to go that way.'

Alice's heartbeat quickened. He did like her.

Turning the music up, Ottavio asked, 'You like hip-hop?'

'Don't listen to it much.'

'You're missing out.'

His cockiness made her stomach flutter again and she stumbled for something to cover her nerves. 'Melissa said you were having some family problems?'

'Did she?'

She knew it was the wrong thing to say but hadn't been able to stop herself. 'I was having a few of my own,' she said hastily. 'Families can be a pain can't they?'

Ottavio looked at her curiously and Alice stumbled on. 'Somehow I've become the responsible one. Like I'm supposed to sort out all the problems. I don't know how it got to be like that. I'm not very good at it.'

'We all have responsibilities.' Ottavio said as he changed lanes.

'Oh sure. Of course, I'm just saying it's a struggle sometimes.'

'Meaning?'

'It's just hard I guess.'

'Being responsible is hard?'

'Yeah, what if you do the wrong thing?' Alice felt heat in her cheeks as Ottavio searched her face.

'Depends if you meant to or not.'

'No, I umm, I guess I mean… I don't know what I mean.'

'You think you're doing the right thing but it doesn't turn out right?'

'That's exactly what I mean.' Alice glanced at Ottavio and caught his eye.

'Happens all the time.' He said quietly.

'Do you think?'

'I know.'

'I wanted to help my cousin, but I don't think I did.' Alice said.

'I could be saying the exact same words.'

'Really?'

'Thought I was doing the right thing.' Ottavio gave Alice a wry smile. 'But someone else sorted it out in the end. I wasn't going about it the right way. Just couldn't see it.'

Alice saw the exit sign coming up. 'Don't think I was going about it the right way either. He just got up and left.'

'Your cousin?'

'Yeah. My only cousin.'

'You only have one cousin?'

'Small family. What about you?'

Ottavio laughed, 'No one has just one cousin. Some have more than they can count.' Perplexed, Alice asked, 'How does that happen exactly?'

'Exactly?' Ottavio said with a cheeky smile.

'You know what I mean,' Alice said shyly.

'Polygamy. Multiple wives. Lots of children. Lots of cousins.'

'Your father was a polygamist?'

'He would have been if he'd had the chance. He was killed in the war.'

'I'm sorry to hear that, Ottavio.'

'It's okay. I don't really remember him. But after he died, my mother married his brother. My younger brother Alphonso, is really my half- brother, as you say in this country.'

'His father is your uncle?'

'That's right. Wife inheritance. If a man dies, his wife marries one of his brothers and any new children carry the dead man's name. That way his children get looked after and his name is not forgotten.'

'Alphonso has your father's name?'

'Not just his name. Alphonso is considered to be my father's son.'

Alice watched him change gears smoothly. 'It sounds complicated.'

'It's not really. It's just a different way of doing things. There's no government help. Family is all you've got.'

They sped along the M4 and Alice relaxed back in her seat. Her dress slipped down off her knees. She didn't try to pull it back up, instead she crossed her legs and revealed some more of her thighs. Ottavio turned the music up and nudged the speedo just over the limit until they reached the end of the freeway.

Nearing Central, Alice gave him directions to her flat and when they pulled up outside, she asked him in for coffee.

'I don't drink coffee,' he said. Alice's heart sank. But then in a teasing voice Ottavio asked, 'Anything else on offer?'

36. Ottavio

The sun was only just up and the traffic flowed. He moved easily along Parramatta Road. Without much delay he was back on the M4. Checking his watch, he gave himself forty minutes to get home.

Ottavio could smell the sweetish odour of her skin. She had been warm and smooth and had drunkenly stripped for him, slowly dropping each piece of clothing to the floor. Lying across the bed, he let her undress him. Her lips slid down his neck, lingering at his chest, biting his nipples softly. He let his hands glide over her thick, soft body, following the curves: shoulders, hips and thighs; the cleft of her arse. Clutching his hips, with closed eyes, Alice pulled him in, panting in his ear. She'd been in a hurry and he was fast and hard, wanting to end quickly. A deep groan pressed against his throat, but he held it in, his heart pounding in his chest. Thrashing under him, her breath came in tiny gasps.

Dropping into sleep, he'd woken to find her watching him. Ottavio didn't like being watched. He rolled out of bed and noticed the rows of books on tall shelves. In the kitchen as he poured a glass of water a fluffy black and white cat curled about his leg. He drank a glass at the sink, and then another, hoping to drive the throb of a minor hangover away. He filled another glass for her.

Alice snuggled up to him and rested her face on his chest. She'd wanted to be held. Cradling her, he listened to her breathing until she seemed to fall asleep. Ottavio felt his own eyelids drooping, but he batted them open and gathered himself. It was time to leave. Alice seemed to sense he was about to move and opened her eyes, sliding her hand down the length of his body, lingering close to his groin, teasing him. He got hard again instantly and pulled her on top. His urgency had gone, and he wanted her to set the pace, but felt himself building quickly. He did not try to hold back. The explosion at the base of his skull jolted through his body. Intense and blinding, sound escaping in a deep long grunt. God, he had missed this. Shame it only lasted a few seconds.

Ottavio didn't look at her as she climbed off. He'd been selfish but he didn't care. He told her he had to go soon, ignoring the part of him that wanted to feel more of her warm skin. Taking his hand, she thanked him and asked for his number. Hurriedly he wrote it down and let himself out.

In the car he turned on his phone; two calls from Rachel and one from Rosa.

Ottavio took the freeway exit. He hoped Alice would be cool when he next saw her. He didn't want her ringing him all the time like Rachel was. It was a good night and he might just want to repeat it. Turning into his street, he saw a police car parked outside his house. He pulled up, his heart racing. Alpha. Fucking Alpha: the cops had finally got their chance. Panicked, he got to the front door and fumbled his keys. Snatching them up, he let himself in.

Two policemen stood in the kitchen, looking uncomfortable. Rosa was sitting at the table, weeping and looking at him with bewildered eyes. She spoke and Ottavio did not believe what she was saying. One of the policemen stepped toward him. Ottavio yelled at them to get out of the house. Leave them alone. Get away. *Lor*!

Rosa started screaming his name, her voice furious with pain. 'Zach! Zach!'

She pleaded, sobbing. 'Where is he! Zachariah!'

Stumbling against the wall, Ottavio slid down, clutching his head.

Inside him something was breaking.

37. Alaya

We waited until the day was passing. Then, with three other women and their children, we waded back through the water. We would find the others walking and follow them to a place where there was no more dying.

38. Ottavio

Word had spread quickly, and the house was full of people to cope with. Stony-faced, Paulino sat amongst the men, quiet with shock. Rosa had not spoken since the uniformed police had left an hour or so ago. When the old women arrived they had taken her to her room and stayed with her. Other women were in the kitchen cooking and making tea for the mourners. Cigarette smoke wafted out from under Alpha's door. His friends had arrived with bottles of beer, discreet in brown paper bags, and went straight to his room. Ottavio's phone was ringing non-stop but he was not answering. He did not want to speak to anyone. He waited in the back yard for Malong. Where was he? His head was fuzzy, like his brain wasn't working properly. He could not understand what was happening. It couldn't be true. It just couldn't.

Ottavio kept seeing Zach lope through the front door and toss his backpack onto the couch. He heard Paulino's voice at a distance, asking him to come outside. Someone wanted to see him. Ottavio got up slowly.

Waiting on the verandah was a *kawauja*, stocky, grey-haired, in a grey suit and pale blue tie.

'Detective Inspector Dennis Peters,' he said, his handshake firm and damp. He offered his condolences and asked if his men could look in Zach's room. Ottavio felt himself nodding in agreement. He had lost contact with his body, could not feel his feet on the ground. He felt like he was looking down from above. Everyone's voices were faint and hollow.

Standing in the doorway with Peters, Ottavio watched as two plain-clothed officers searched the room, looking under the bed, in his schoolbooks, patting down his clothes. Peters asked if they could take some of it away and Ottavio nodded.

'It would also very helpful if you and Rosa could come to the station. We need to ask some questions and it is better done there.' Ottavio wanted Rosa to stay and Paulino did too, but when Ottavio went to her door to say he was going with the detectives, she insisted. The women around her protested quietly, clasping her arm, patting her hair, but Rosa was determined.

At the station Peters offered them tea or coffee but they both declined. Clearing his throat he began asking questions about Zach, who his friends were, how were things at school. The questions were carefully formed, and he was polite but business like, jotting down their answers on a yellow lined pad. Rosa wiped tears away as she described Zach coming home from school the night before and telling her he was going to play soccer with some boys from school. He got changed into his Bulls shirt and track pants and ran out the door with his boots. He was excited. She was pleased he was making friends. He never really had any in the time he'd been in high school.

'He had trouble making friends? Why was that?'

'He is shy.' Rosa answered.

'Did he say where he was going to play?'

'No, I didn't ask. I had to go to work. I told him to call Ottavio if he needed a lift home.' Rosa doubled over, weeping into her hands. Ottavio blocked Rosa's words from his mind. He could only think of Theo.

Peters passed Rosa a box of tissues and poured her a glass of water. Turning to a fresh page in his notepad, he turned to Ottavio.

'Mr Bol, did you see Zach that night?'

'The school can tell you where to find him.' Ottavio replied flatly.

Peters looked at him carefully. 'Find who, Mr Bol?'

Ottavio hesitated, if he said his name aloud, then this nightmare would be real.

'Please, ahhh…Ottavio.' Peters carefully sounded out his name. 'Who are you referring to?'

Rosa was staring at her cousin. 'What are you saying Ottavio?' Rosa's voice was wavering. 'What do you mean?'

Ottavio couldn't look at her. His guilt had filled the room. Dried his mouth. He sipped some water. He wanted to trust the cop. If he told him, it would become his burden. 'Zach had trouble with a kid at school called Theo.'

He told Peters everything; Kelly, the phone, the social worker, the black car and the two guys. The one with the tattoos was Theo's brother. Kelly and her father. How he and Malong took Zach back to school only a week ago. Peters wrote it all down. He read back through his notes and asked Ottavio for more details. Days, times, the make of the car.

By the time they had finished, Ottavio's head was throbbing. Tears were dripping from Rosa's chin. She was shaking her head in disbelief. He had kept so much from her.

'Thank-you both. I appreciate your time and I know this is very difficult. There was just one more question Ottavio. Can I ask you again, where were you last night?'

Ottavio didn't hesitate, 'With Malong Chol.'

Peters gave them both his card and told them to call any time they needed to. He would be in touch.

It was close to midday when they got back to the house. Blurry with exhaustion, Ottavio worked his way through the crowded room, shaking hands and being hugged. Malong was in the back yard with some of their friends, sagging against his chair, arms folded limply across his chest. He stood up as Ottavio approached him, a look on his face that Ottavio had never seen before. His handshake felt weak and heavy.

Speaking quietly, Ottavio told him he had to get out of there. Malong said they could go to his place. There would be no one there. Malong left and after a few minutes Ottavio went down the side of the house, through the carport. Hoping no one had seen him. He ran down to the corner where Malong was waiting in his car, engine running.

❖

They passed the cognac back and forth until it was all gone. Malong lurched off towards the kitchen, returning with two cold beers, he handed one to Ottavio. Grunting, he waved it away, but Malong didn't move until Ottavio took the beer. In unison they gulped them down, Malong draining his first. Exhaling loudly, he dropped the bottle on the carpet. Ottavio did the same, his head lolling back, eyeballs liquid hot, head like concrete.

'Shouldn't have told them about Theo.' Malong slurred.

Ottavio concentrated on the red light of his eyeballs.

'Those dumb fucks just gonna get in the way.' Malong sniggered, 'I'm gonna find that kid and play some soccer with his head.'

'Me first.'

Malong leaned over his friend and nudged him. 'Machar you don't have it in you.'

Ottavio got up slowly. Malong did the same, accepting the challenge. Ottavio punched as hard as he could. Grunting, Malong doubled over and Ottavio hit him again, making him stagger backward. Malong found his balance and shaped up to Ottavio, slapping him across the face, shouting, '*arrouc, arrouc*'. Ottavio stumbled. Even drunk he couldn't believe his closest friend would call him a coward. Rage surged through Ottavio, the alcohol turning his vision into pinholes. He yelled at Malong. 'You fucking *jong*.' Malong pulled him into a headlock and they crashed against the couch, rolling to the ground. Ottavio tried to get up but Malong was on top of him. Gasping for air, his throat felt ragged, heart slamming against his chest. How could it be still beating?

'Cool it Machar. Be cool,' Malong slurred.

Ottavio strained against him but Malong held him down.

'Motherfucker. Let me up.'

'Rachel's been calling.'

'Fuck her.'

'Did you?'

'Fuck you.'

'Who you with last night?' Malong growled. 'It wasn't her.'

'I was with you. I told them I was with you.' Ottavio struggled weakly. Malong pressed down on him again and Ottavio gave in. He didn't have the strength. It had left him that morning when he slid down the wall, Rosa screaming at him.

Malong fell off, lying down next to him. Ottavio heard his voice close to his ear. 'It's not your fault Machar. This is on me.'

Ottavio woke up on the couch. His head pounding, mouth tasting of vomit. Malong was on the ground, spread-eagled on his back, snoring loudly. Carefully, Ottavio stood up and stumbled along the corridor to the bathroom. At the toilet, trying to steady himself against the wall, the stench of piss made him heave.

In the fridge he found a jug of water. Spilling at the sides, he poured the water in his mouth. On the table was a bag of sliced white bread and a jar of peanut butter. He pulled out a chair and sat down carefully, and slowly made a sandwich. Taking a bite, he gagged when he tried to swallow. His vision was blurry, and he tried focusing on the window. Then he heard a faint noise and looked up. Zach was in front of him with that sad, lopsided grin, his skinny arms buried in the pockets of his long, grey school shorts. Lurching back, Ottavio tipped out of the chair. Gasping, he lay face down on the floor. He wanted to crawl away and hide somewhere in the bush. Drag himself into the river and let the crocodiles eat him. That's what he deserved.

39. Alaya

We couldn't find the walking people and we had nothing to eat. When the evening came, we stopped under a tree and rested. Baby brother started to cry, so little brother and I went to look for food. Maybe some mangoes were near. Mother told us to not go far.

I grabbed little brother's hand when I heard the horses and I ran as fast as I could pulling him with me. Then he fell. I could not leave him. I could not run anymore. I dropped to the ground next to him and held him to me. His heart beating hard.

They tied our hands and put us across the horses like sacks of dura and took us away.

40. Alice

At work Alice kept catching herself staring into the distance, wishing she was still in bed with him. She was hungover but didn't mind. There was none of the usual misery. She felt light-headed, almost giddy, and had done nothing all morning but rewind the night in all its blurry detail. The gleam of his skin, the narrow width of his shoulders, the slight curve of his lower back.

She was doodling on a note pad when Gail appeared, knocking on her desk like it was a door. 'Hello? Why aren't you answering your phone? What's wrong?'

'Nothing,' Alice said lightly, knowing what was coming next.

'You sure?'

Alice nodded enthusiastically.

'Well? Are we walking today?'

'Yes, of course,' Alice said, realising she'd forgotten her runners. 'Actually, maybe we could go to lunch instead. My shout?'

'What? Why?'

'Oh, no reason, I just didn't bring my shoes. We haven't had lunch for ages.'

'Something's up and you're gonna make me wait until lunch? It had better be good,' Gail said. 'Meet you at that place on the corner at one.' She stalked off.

Alice sat back in her chair and sighed. Two more hours and her little secret would be no more. Gail would demand all the details and she would oblige. Alice swung her chair around to face the wall and she closed her eyes for a final, private replay.

Gasping, her hand over her mouth, Gail's eyes bulged with delight. 'You didn't? Oh my god you did. You really did!'

Alice smiled, enjoying Gail's surprise. She teased her with just a few of the details, taking her time, ordering a salad and a fresh carrot and ginger juice.

'So?'

'So, what?'

'Oh come on. You have to tell me the rest. What happened when you got home?'

'You know what happened.'

'Alice, I'm your oldest friend. We have shared everything, you can't hold back now.'

'Yes, I can.'

'No,' Gail said crisply. 'Girlfriends are supposed to tell each other everything. Everything.'

There's that word again Alice thought. Stefan came to mind, but she flicked him out of her head.

She dodged Gail's most intimate questions but shared with her what she could recall of her fumbling striptease, blushing as she did. Gail was delighted and insisted Alice tell her again how he had managed to get her from the classroom to her bedroom. She was enthralled by his cheekiness. They giggled so much, they lost track of time and were late back to work.

Moments after Alice got back to her desk, Gail emailed her with the subject heading; 'Best root ever, including the barrister...?' In the body, in capital letters, she had written just two words, CALL HIM. Alice had considered it. Truth was she was hoping to hear from him. She wanted to call but told herself to wait until she saw him at the centre early next week.

But later at home, after dinner, she worked up the courage and rang. No answer. She told herself men didn't like pushy women.

In bed she smelt him on the sheets and fell asleep feeling his hands underneath her hips.

The week dragged by and Alice had managed to not call him again. She couldn't wait to get to class and catch his eye.

Melissa started the class with an announcement. 'I have some very sad news. Ottavio has had a death in his immediate family. Some of you may have seen a story on the TV news. It's been in the newspapers. It was a violent death and the police are investigating the cause.'

The class was silent. The news pounded through Alice. She'd heard on the radio a young African man had been found dead in the western suburbs.

'I have a sympathy card here, if you would all like to sign it. I will send it to Ottavio and his family. The funeral is in a few days and I will be going if any of you would like to come with me.'

When the card reached Alice, she picked up her pen with shaking fingers. She could not think to write anything more personal than, 'sorry for your loss.' Alice helped Batool to write a few words and they passed it on.

At the break Alice approached Melissa before she went into the kitchen. 'That's terrible news Melissa.'

'Isn't it awful. Poor Ottavio.'

'When did it happen?'

'This time last week.'

Alice blinked, taking in what she'd said.

'Are you all right Alice? You've gone pale.'

Alice put her hand to her forehead and felt herself sway. Melissa grabbed her arm and led her to a chair, telling her to put her head between her knees. Alice took a few deep breaths and sat up. 'I'm sorry it's just such a shock.'

Melissa knelt next to her, searching her face.

'How is Ottavio?' Alice asked.

'I don't know. A friend of his rang and told me. I tried Ottavio's phone yesterday, but there was no answer.'

'He must feel terrible.'

'I'm sure. Some are calling it a hate crime.'

'A hate crime?'

'He may have been attacked because he was Sudanese.'

'Why do they say that?'

'Media's been stirring up bad feeling for years, saying Africans aren't settling. Gangs, crime. That sort of rubbish.'

'What's his death got to do with that?'

'Nothing, but they want to make it his fault. Blame the victim. It's an old tactic. Ignore the real story and pretend this is evidence of something else. All kinds of crazy things are being said. Some are saying he was in a gang himself.'

'In in a gang?'

'They've got their own agendas, I guess. It makes me sick. A fourteen-year-old kid's been murdered. If he was white there would be marching in the street.'

'What have the police said?'

'They haven't. Except that they're looking into it.'

A tear slipped onto Alice's chin. Melissa patted her shoulder. 'Would you like to come with me to the funeral?'

'Do you think that would be okay?'

'I'm sure it will. It would be good for the family to see they have support.'

Alice blew her nose and Melissa offered her some water.

'I'd better get the class back in. I'll call you tomorrow.'

The church was cavernous and cold with bluestone walls and stained-glass windows soaring to the ceiling. The sun glowed through the blues and reds and yellows. Melissa and

Mohammed signed the attendance book ahead of Alice. On the table was a large framed photograph of a young man. Dressed in a white shirt and long grey shorts, he had a fine and delicate face and a lopsided grin.

They squeezed onto the end row. People were lining the walls and spilling out into the grounds. A group of women, their heads wrapped in white cloth, sang in Dinka – one voice a single note higher than the others. Alice strained to see Ottavio, but the front row was beyond her line of vision.

Speaking in Dinka then English, the priest asked everyone to stand and the service began. Sniffles echoed about the church and the priest introduced a grey-haired man called Paulino. He spoke slowly. 'Our community's heart is broken. After so much suffering we came to this place for a better life and now we lose one of our sons here.' Pausing, Paulino looked out across the church, then cleared his throat. 'We pray for Rosa who was his sister and mother. For Alphonso. Ottavio and Malong. God bless them all.'

The congregation knelt for prayers. The priest then asked for Malong Chol to come to the microphone. He towered over the lectern in a suit jacket and open necked shirt. When he spoke, the microphone barely caught his words. 'Zach was my little brother. He was clever. Had a quick mind. Everyone knew he'd become a doctor, but he could have been a pro soccer player too.' Pausing, Malong swallowed hard. 'Zach got here three years ago. If anyone was going to make it, he was. Nothing's fair in this world.' Malong's voice broke with anger and grief and all restraint crumpled, the priest placed his hand on his shoulder. The church echoed with wails and sobbing. The priest asked all to stand for a hymn. Wiping away tears, Alice got up and squeezed past the others, saying sorry. She would wait outside.

Outside in the bright sunshine, Alice saw a group of school children dressed in uniforms of white and grey. Two of the girls clutched each other wiping away tears with the palm of their hands. The sun glowed on the red hair of one of them. Other students stared morosely at the ground, chins dropping to their chests.

She listened to the singing and the prayers echoing from the church. Nodded to others who were also waiting. She looked at the sky and wondered how anyone could bear the pain of losing someone so young. And in that way. How could this have happened?

Malong and Ottavio appeared at the entrance, at the front, either side of the coffin. Two younger men were in the middle and two older at the end. A young woman, clutching the framed photo of Zach across her chest, wiping at her tears with a soggy, balled-up tissue, followed them out of the church. The congregation flowed out slowly behind them. Alice watched Ottavio load the coffin into the hearse, his face blank, eyes dull. It pulled away, and the young woman cried out, dropping the photo, she collapsed against the women who were gathered around her.

Melissa drove, talking with Mohammed about the differences between Muslim and Christian funerals. In the backseat Alice decided to take the rest of the day off. The sadness in the church had settled in. It was the first time she'd been to a young person's funeral. Her thoughts drifted back to the crumpled, distraught faces of the school children outside the church.

Melissa dropped her off near Central and Alice waved goodbye as she manoeuvered her car back into the heavy traffic.

Alice made her way to her local café. Flicking through the newspaper, she searched for anything about the boy. There was nothing. She would try online when she got home. Alice felt heavy with sadness. It had wiped away the loveliness of her night with Ottavio. The world felt unjust. How could something like this happen to his family? As she was finishing her coffee, her phone rang. It was Stefan.

Alice took a deep breath and answered. 'Stefan.'

'Cous.'

'Are you okay?'

'Yeah, I'm good.'

Nothing stirred in Alice. The stress of his disappearance, the panic she had felt was very distant from where she was now.

'I'm relieved to hear it.'

'How's things?'

'Fine Stefan. Things are fine.'

'Sorry, about…you know.'

'No. I don't know.'

'I just had to be on my own.'

'You could be on your own and still tell me you were okay.'

'There was stuff I had to do.'

A small spike of suspicion jabbed at Alice.

'Like what?'

'Like getting my life back in order.' Stefan sounded annoyed and defensive.

'I still don't understand why you couldn't let us know.'

Stefan did not reply, and Alice waited, hearing him take a drag on a cigarette.

'Who's the black guy?'

'What?'

'The guy I saw you with.'

Alice felt queasy. 'You saw us where?'

'Outside your place the other night. I was coming to see you but you looked busy.'

Not knowing what to say, Alice stayed quiet. Acid from her stomach hit the back of her throat.

'He one of your refugee mates?'

'You came by?'

'Didn't think I should interrupt.' Stefan said lightly.

Alice could not make sense of what he was saying.

'How's the olds?' Stefan asked.

Irritated, she snapped back, 'Well what do you think? How many messages did your mum leave on your phone? There must have been dozens.'

'Yeah, there were a few,' Stefan said with a little snort of laughter.

Feeling anger prickle across her throat Alice tried not to raise her voice, 'Funny is it Stefan?'

'What?'

'Your mum being worried about you?'

'No. I didn't mean that.'

'Well, what did you mean?'

'There were a lot of messages,' Stefan mumbled. Alice's suspicion returned.

'Are you stoned?'

Stefan did not reply.

'Listen you selfish prick, you leave us all wondering if you're still alive, then call out of the blue, like there's no problem. You must be stoned.'

'Look I'm sorry, okay?'

'Not sorry enough.'

Alice hung up.

41. Ottavio

It was late and Ottavio was driving for the sake of it, just to get out of the house, to get some time to himself that didn't involve drinking with Malong. Every evening at one of their houses, they drank until they passed out. In the mornings they alternated as driver and nursed each other through work, the intense cognac hangovers keeping them both numb. Uncle Paulino had dropped by last night, found him and Malong drinking beer in the back yard. Told them sternly, to leave the alcohol alone and come back to church. Malong had laughed and Uncle had left, furious at the insult. But Ottavio knew the old man was right, at least about the drinking.

Nearly three weeks had blurred passed. The shit that had been in the news had died down. But everyone was still talking about it. Politicians, newspapers; nothing could be done about them. They'd say anything they wanted and get away with it. Ottavio refused to discuss it with anyone, the racism, the hatred. It burned him how they talked about the Sudanese, but he could not deal with that as well.

Rachel had given up calling. Angelina hadn't, but he did not pick up. At the funeral she had hugged him, and he had not wanted her to let go. Rosa and Alpha had barely been home. Rosa was staying with Paulino's family. He missed her. She called in the evenings and he would answer if he hadn't drunk too much. He could barely stand to hear her voice, how it creaked with sadness. She wished Samuel was here. They talked every night now. It would be time for the prayers again soon and they would come together again.

Detective Peters took his calls whenever he rang him. Polite and firm, he could not confirm who the suspects were. Ottavio had stopped relaying this to Malong, who drunkenly threatened every night to go and 'deal with it.' Ottavio did not know how to make Malong believe he was not responsible. He could not tell him about Alice.

Alice. He'd not returned any of her calls either, but had thought of her soft warmth. She knew what had happened on that night. The sympathy card from the class was on the coffee table at home. Ottavio pulled over, listening to the throb of the engine, trying to clear his mind, let it be blank. He didn't know if it was a good idea or not, but he turned the car around and headed for the M4. He let the windows down, feeling the warm air, heavy with car fumes, on his face. The sky blazed a metallic orange on the horizon as the sun disappeared. He'd just call by and see how she was doing. It was the Sudanese way after all.

Alice stood on the doorstep, surprised, a bit awkward.

'Hey Alice.' Ottavio said carefully, trying to gauge how welcome he was.

'Ottavio.'

'You busy?'

'No. Sorry, please come in.'

The cat meowed at him as he followed her into the lounge. There was a glass of wine on the coffee table and a take-away pizza box.

'I'm interrupting your dinner.'

'No, not at all. Would you like some wine?'

'Sure, okay.'

'Please sit down.' She went into the kitchen and Ottavio sunk into the couch noticing an open suitcase by the bedroom door. Returning with a glass, Alice poured the wine then sat in the armchair opposite. Both took a sip.

'Some pizza?'

'Sure there's enough for two?'

Opening the box, Alice broke the pizza apart and passed him a piece on a paper towel.

Ottavio folded it over and took a bite. Alice drank some more wine. 'I'm so sorry about your little cousin.'

Avoiding her eyes, he nodded. He didn't want to speak to her about it.

'I came to the funeral.'

Ottavio looked at her, quizzical and surprised.

'I went with Melissa and Mohammed from class.'

'Okay.'

She looked uncomfortable. Ottavio knew he should say something. 'I didn't know you were there. Thanks for coming.'

'It was very sad.' Alice said quietly.

Ottavio's mood dropped, he almost got up to leave. He hadn't come for sympathy. That was all he ever got these days, no matter where he went. Sometime in the blurry weeks, at work, the *kawauja* Brian had approached him at the end of the shift. Said he was sorry for his loss and offered him his hand. Ottavio reluctantly took it. Somehow, the kindness of strangers made his guilt far worse. But Alice wasn't a stranger. Not anymore. Ottavio cleared his throat. 'It still doesn't feel real. I don't want it to be real.' He dipped his head. A man did not show such strong emotion in front of a woman. Alice hesitated, then went and sat next to him, close enough for their bodies to touch. The warmth of her thigh seeped into Ottavio and he felt like a blanket had been pulled around him. Relieved to be out of her gaze, he relaxed a little and moved his arm so it was touching hers.

'I've never lost anyone close to me.' Alice said.

'That makes you lucky.'

Ottavio rested his head against the couch, not wanting to talk about death. Alice must have sensed it because she changed the subject. 'I guess you haven't read that book?'

'Sorry?'

'The book. *Love in the time of Cholera.*'

'No, I only read a bit.'

'That's okay. Guess you had other things on your mind.

'What happens in the end?'

'They live happily ever after.'

'Really?' Ottavio thought she was joking.

'They finally get together when they're both old and grey and spend what's left of their lives together.'

'Very romantic.'

'You don't like romance?'

Ottavio shrugged. 'Nothing romantic about obsession.'

'You don't think it's possible to love someone for a lifetime – someone you hardly know?' Alice asked. Ottavio shrugged again. He didn't want to be drawn on the subject, did not want to talk about love.

'Well, a good writer can convince you of anything and he convinced me.'

Ottavio found himself softening. 'So, you could fall in love with someone you see on the street?'

'Yes.'

'Women are crazy for this stuff.'

'The author is a man,' Alice said, 'and so what if women are crazy about love? What's more important than love?'

Ottavio saw a flash in her eyes. She hadn't struck him as defiant. He drank some more and looked closer at her over the top of the wine glass. She was thinner, her hair was shorter, shinier. She returned his gaze. Ottavio changed the subject. Nodding at the suitcase, he asked. 'Going somewhere?'

'Thinking about it.'

'Where?'

'Asia.'

'What's there?'

'Don't know, that's why I'm going.'

There it was again, Ottavio thought. Defiance. 'By yourself?'

'Looks like it. Original plan included my cousin.'

'Your only cousin?'

'Yes.'

'Thought he'd disappeared.'

'He's back.'

'That's good news then.'

'I was relieved to hear from him.'

'Where'd he go?'

'Didn't say. Just called one day. Out of the blue.'

'Out of the blue?'

'Out of the blue. It's a saying; an idiom.'

'What does it mean?'

'Something that happens without warning. A surprise.'

'What's blue got to do with it?'

'Don't know,' Alice shrugged. 'Maybe it's referring to the sky.'

Ottavio swallowed the wine, imagining the sky in Sudan. More white than blue.

'Your culture must have sayings like that. Expressions. A group of words that have a special meaning?'

'Yeah, sure we do.'

'Tell me one.'

Leaning back Ottavio scanned his memory, 'Ok, how about; a lion is still a lion even when it is dead.'

'And that means?'

'Dead or alive, people are the same.'

'Okay,' Alice sounded uncertain.

'The spirit doesn't change,' Ottavio offered.

'Spirits?'

'Every living thing has a spirit. A person might die but they remain the same person they were when they were alive. Good or bad.' Ottavio stopped. He didn't like the territory he was in. He didn't even know how much of it he believed. Alice was waiting for him to continue. Ottavio put the glass down. 'Okay if I use the bathroom?'

'Sure. You know where it is.'

Ottavio looked at himself in the mirror. His jaw was rough with stubble and his eyes were dull and glazed. What was he doing here talking about spirits? He should be at home booking a ticket. It was time to go, to get the hell out of here.

Sighing, he washed his hands and patted cold water on his face. Go home, he thought. Just tell her thanks for the wine and leave.

But Ottavio felt hollow and tired. His body was aching. He had come to spend the night and didn't think Alice would say no.

42. Alice

Alice gave him gentle instructions and he did not resist. He gave in easily, doing what he was told. Stripping, he dropped his clothes into a pile on the floor and lay face down on her bed. Alice dropped a fine red scarf over the bedside lamp and filled her palms with oil. Rubbing her hands together to release the rose scent, she spread it across his shoulders with slow strokes, working it down his torso. Ottavio groaned as she plied his taut, corded muscles, persuading them to release. Pressing her palms across his butt, she fanned out to his hips, rolled down along his thighs and back again, repeating the move half a dozen times until she felt him soften a little more into the bed. Moving on, she pressed her thumbs into his calves, making him wince. She moved down to the soles of his feet and he giggled in a sleepy protest. By the time she had finished his arms and slid her finger through each of his, he was snoring softly. Pulling the sheet over his shoulders, she examined his fine cheekbones and wide lips. She carefully kissed his forehead.

Alice went to the kitchen and made a cup of green tea, sipped it as she rested on the arm of the couch. Since the funeral she'd felt distracted, and sad, for Ottavio and for herself, but she hadn't thought she would ever see him again. She had been thinking about travel again, maybe she could give it another go. Sitting in the darkness, the blended odour of the oil and his skin on her hands, she knew escaping from what scared her would be as easy as she let it be.

Lifting the sheet, she slipped in next to him. His chest rose and fell in a shallow, rapid beat. She touched his shoulder. He was hot. As his breath quickened into gasps, Alice put her palm to his forehead. Ottavio jerked awake, his chest heaving in panic. Snatching away her hand, he sat up, eyes flicking about the room, Ottavio looked at her then slumped back onto the pillow.

'Are you okay?' Alice wanted to touch him again.

'Yeah,' Ottavio whispered and turned away from her. 'Just a dream.'

'What was it?'

'Nothing.'

He rolled onto his side, placing his thumb and finger on his eyelids. His chest had returned to an even rise. Sweat gleamed on his forehead.

'Horses.'

'Horses?'

'I dream of horses.'

Alice waited for him to say more. He turned to face her. 'What do you dream of?'

'Don't really remember my dreams.'

'That's odd.' Ottavio said, pressing his hand against her breast, rolling her nipple between his fingers. Her eyelids drooped, breath catching in her throat. Ottavio put his hand on the back of her neck and pulled her mouth to his.

They lay side by side, the sheet discarded. Ottavio was describing Malong. 'You would have seen him speak at the funeral.'

'He found that hard, didn't he?'

'I think he was still drunk.'

Alice smirked. 'So, he's your brother?'

'Might as well be. Immigration records say he is. We were neighbours in the village. We were both lost in the war. His family was all gone. When we got to the camp, we said we were brothers and were put in the same hut. We shared everything; the sleeping mat, the cooking pot. We had the same thoughts. Same dreams. No one knows me like he does.'

'What about the rest of your family?'

'Dead and disappeared.'

'So how did Alpha get there. To the camp?'

'A woman carried him. She found him by himself, alone in the bush. We arrived at the camp at different times. One day I saw him walk past me. I found him just like that. Alpha was with our mother when we got separated. He couldn't say what happened to her.'

Alice felt the flatness of Ottavio's grief, of not knowing. Those two things combined like an endless desert.

'So, Zach was your cousin?'

'Is my cousin.'

'Sorry.'

'He and his sister Rosa moved in with me when they arrived in Australia.'

'I'm really sorry about what happened to him.'

'You said that already.'

'I can say it more than once.'

Ottavio gave her a brief smile.

'Do the police have any idea who did it?'

Ottavio shook his head, looking at her with hard eyes. 'You don't know anything do you?'

Alice swallowed. His tone hurt.

Neither spoke. Alice heard a bird outside. Dawn was near. He would leave soon.

Rolling onto his side, Ottavio lay his head on his hands. He'd been unkind to her.

'There's a kid at Zach's school. I told the cops about him. He didn't like Zach.'

'You think he's involved? A boy at his school?'

'Yeah, I do. But I doubt the cops will do anything about him.'

'This stuff can take a long time.'

Ottavio snorted. 'It's been almost a month. The cops don't care.'

'They don't care if a kid gets killed?'

'They don't care if an African kid gets killed.'

'I don't believe you.'

Ottavio rolled back to face her and spoke gently. 'For you everything works just fine. It's not hard to get what you need. Your life is comfortable. Right?'

Alice didn't reply.

'It's not like that for us.'

'But you're still new in the country. The culture shock must be huge. Surely that's why it's so hard?'

'That's one of the reasons it's hard. The other one is that we are not wanted here.'

'That's not true.'

'Maybe not in your middle-class mind.'

Again, Alice felt stung. Her reply sounded defensive. 'But it's got to be better than war?'

'Anything's better than war.'

'Australia can't be that bad?'

It was Ottavio turn not to reply. In the silence, Alice heard more birds.

'That's why you're here isn't it? Because it's safe?'

'Africa's a big place. Not all of it's in chaos.'

'You know what I mean.'

'Yeah, Australia's a highly developed country, a shining example of a western democracy. But democracy only works for some people some of the time.'

'But nobody dies of starvation.'

'But people do die.' Ottavio said without irony.

'That could happen anywhere.'

Ottavio shook his head wearily and Alice regretted what she said. 'I'm sorry Ottavio.'

'Stop saying you're sorry. *Kawauja's* use that word all the time.'

Alice cringed. The half-light was seeping into the room, 'What do you mean?'

'In the past, there was never a Dinka word for sorry.'

'What did they say instead?'

'You didn't. Your actions made up for what you'd done wrong.'

Alice took a few breaths in. 'Well, I'm still sorry about your cousin. I might be middle-class but that doesn't mean I can't see injustice.'

'Injustice?'

'Some people suffer so much more than others.'

'The paradox is, if you suffer too much, the *kawauja* turns away. You don't know how to handle too much pain. To you it is unimaginable.'

'It? What do you mean it?'

'Two wars, famine, genocide, slavery.'

'Slavery?' Alice stared at him. 'Slavery? This century?'

'Find that hard to believe?'

'Of course, I do. It's …it's unimaginable.'

Ottavio stopped himself laughing at her innocence and pulled her to him, kissing the top of her head. Alice pressed herself against his warmth, thinking they should be the other way around; she should be comforting him.

'Why doesn't someone do something about it?'

Ottavio snorted. 'There you go again.'

Alice felt a flicker of annoyance. 'Yeah, I know, I'm middle-class, but it's still a reasonable question.'

'Okay. It's reasonable but what makes you think someone will 'do something' about it? People would have to care first.'

'You mean white people?'

Ottavio didn't reply.

'Tell me. I want to know.' Alice said quietly.

'The militias took whoever they wanted. Mostly young women and children. They shot the men.'

'Where did they take them to?'

'The North, as farm labour, or to Khartoum or neighbouring countries, sold as servants. They are given Arab names. Made to convert to Islam. Women have to have sex with their owners. Their children are born into slavery.'

'How many?'

'Thousands. Maybe hundreds of thousands. No one really knows.'

Alice swallowed and hurried to her next question. 'Were they ever freed?'

'Some. Maybe. Some escaped.'

'Is there a word for slavery?' Alice asked.

'*Alouny*. The Dinka word is *alouny*.'

'Do you know anyone who was taken?'

Ottavio said nothing. It was so long before he spoke, Alice thought he might have fallen asleep.

'Everyone knows someone,' he said quietly.

43. Alaya

The children were so frightened, none spoke. They were dusty and skinny and looked at me with wide, blank eyes. I was the oldest.

They put us all together under the tree, next to the horses, and gave us water. The other men sat around a fire cooking meat. The smell of it churned my stomach. I tried to think of Mother and baby brother, with the other people, walking away.

A man gave us a bowl of dura and the children pushed handfuls into their mouths, swallowing it down as fast as they could. A little girl vomited then grabbed some more. I waited for all the children to have some and ate what was left. Night came and the children fell asleep in the dust, pressed against each other.

The man came back and took me over to the fire. One after the other they got on top of me. I closed my eyes. I did not let myself make a sound.

44. Ottavio

Ottavio kept in the right lane on the M4. Tailgating, flashing his lights, forcing slower cars to move to the left. He drove fast, not checking the mirrors for cops. Traffic out of the city was far lighter than what was coming in, but it didn't really matter what time of the day it was, this city's roads were always thick with traffic.

Pulling into the car park, Ottavio checked his watch. He was late.

Malong was already dressed and on the line, face loaded with disapproval at the sight of him. The first carcass glided toward them.

'Where you been Machar?'

'Nowhere special.'

'If nowhere ain't special, why you going there?'

Ottavio ignored him. He'd thought of telling him about Alice, but he was so raw, he couldn't guess how he would take it.

They worked without speaking until the five-minute break.

'What is it you got to hide from me?' Malong demanded.

'You got plenty others you can drink with,' Ottavio deflected. Hurting Malong was usually the only way to get him off track, but Malong persisted.

'Who is she and why are you hiding her?'

'I'm hiding nothing.'

'Something about her you don't want me to know?'

'You're wrong Malong.'

'What's wrong is you lying to me.'

'It's nothing.'

'More you say it isn't, the more I know it is.'

The buzzer sounded and the line began moving again.

At the end of the shift they changed in silence. Malong walked off. Ottavio made his way to his car and saw Malong roar out of the gates, spinning gravel, exhaust louder than it should be. He still hadn't fixed the hole in his muffler.

Turning on the engine, Ottavio thought of driving back to the city. He checked his watch. It would take him at least an hour to get to her place. He didn't want to go home. People were still dropping by, sitting in the lounge talking about Zach. His phone rang. It was Rosa.

'Rosa what's up?'

'I'll be home tonight. We can all sit down together?'

Ottavio heard more than the usual pain in her voice.

'On my way.'

Rosa was in the kitchen. Ottavio could tell she'd been crying,

'How's things?'

Rosa shrugged. 'You?'

'Fine.'

'Uncle Paulino called me.'

'I'm sorry Rosa. Malong was an idiot.'

'Said you were both drunk.'

'Well that ain't true.'

'Prayers are this weekend. You know that?'

'Rosa how could I forget?'

Rosa stared at him. 'Detective Peters called me.'

Ottavio's stomach flipped.

Rosa looked like she was going to cry again. 'He's bringing us something. A report that says how he died.'

Ottavio's voice was rising. 'Did he say why he hadn't arrested the guys who did it?'

Rosa began to weep and Ottavio instantly regretted speaking to her like that.

'Please Rosa.'

He waited until she wiped her eyes and blew her nose.

'Lots of people are angry Ottavio. Boys who want revenge. You got to calm down. Be calm in front of the community, they're looking at you. We can't do more bad things. We have to turn the other cheek and pray they find who did it.' Rosa's voice broke. 'All we can do is pray.'

Exhaling through his nose, Ottavio told Rosa he was sorry. 'You right, I know you are, you know why people are angry.'

'No one has any more right than I do. All those years we struggled and he dies here?' Rosa's tears dripped off her chin.

Ottavio put his hand on her arm.

'We all failed, Rosa. We all feel the same. Malong, Alpha, you, me. Why him and not any one of us?

'I'm giving up my studies. Going back to Kenya. Samuel and I will get married.'

Ottavio took it in, wondering if they would lose the chance for him to come to Australia with her, if she had been resident long enough to apply for a spouse visa. But it made sense. Going home made perfect sense.

'I want to make a home for our children. I don't need a diploma for that.'

Ottavio searched Rosa's face. He could not guess if she was punishing herself or trying to move forward.

'When will you go?'

'After prayers. As soon as I can.'

He thought of telling Rosa about Sudan. He didn't feel so bad now. They wouldn't be so far apart after all. He was pleased for that, but it was still not the right time.

'Have you seen Alpha? I've been calling him, but he won't answer. I want him to come home and have dinner with us.'

'I'll send him a message.'

Rosa turned back to the stove and Ottavio thumbed a message into his phone telling Alpha to be home tonight or he would come looking for him. Then he erased it and sent another saying they needed to support Rosa through the prayers on Saturday and he'd appreciate him being home tonight.

In his room he lay down on his bed, he fell asleep for a short while and woke up tired and anxious. He set up his laptop and began searching for flights. There was a knock on the front door. Checking through the curtain, he saw Alpha and carefully opened the door so Rosa couldn't hear. Alpha looked exhausted.

'Why you knocking?'

'Lost my keys.'

'Where you been? You look like you been sleeping on the street.'

Pushing past Ottavio, Alpha went straight to the bathroom. Ottavio heard the shower. Alpha stayed in there a long time.

Back in his room, Ottavio's phone rang. It was Alice. He let it ring, then sent her a text saying he would call her later, and joined Rosa in the kitchen. Alpha came in and took a seat without speaking. Rosa asked Alpha to say a prayer and he mumbled under his breath, his head bent over the table. Rosa waited until they finished before telling Alpha. He took it well; giving her a smile. Rosa reached out and clasped his hand for a few seconds and gave him a sad smile in return. They were just finishing up as Uncle Paulino, his wife and their three oldest sons arrived. Paulino shook Ottavio's hand and told him more elders were on their way.

It was near to midnight when they all left. Paulino asked him to walk with him to his car. Ottavio listened to the old man telling him again that it was time to get married. He could not let the tragedy hold him back, if anything it should spur him on. It would help with the grief, and the community would have two weddings to look forward to.

Ottavio let him say his piece and ended the conversation politely, thanking his Uncle for the good advice. Back inside,

Alpha was in his own bed. His room was quiet. Ottavio decided it was better he left the conversation he wanted to have with Alpha until the morning.

Returning to his room he called Alice. It was late but he wanted to talk to her, to be soothed by her voice. He rang her number. She answered straight away.

45. Alice

During her lunch break, Bronwyn called. Alice was reluctant to take it, but felt sorry for her. Stefan had been calling her, asking her to lend him money to start his own business. Bronwyn thought it was a good idea. Jack didn't and Bronwyn was furious with him. Jack had asked Elspeth to speak with her sister and when she had tried, Bronwyn told her to keep her nose out of it. Now Elspeth wasn't talking to her. Bronwyn wasn't giving up though, Stefan had really got to her.

'Stefan's very upset with you too. Why won't you speak to him?'

Alice didn't answer her question. 'Bronwyn, I think he needs professional help. A lot has happened. You don't just bounce back after trying to kill yourself. I think you should ask him to go to counselling'

'I did,' Bronwyn said, sounding slightly indignant. 'I offered to pay for it, but he said to give him the money and he'd pay. I want to help him, but I can't tell Jack.

'You want to help him start a business?'

'Really Alice, I don't know what to do. Jack says he's probably using drugs. Do you think he is?'

'Yes I do.'

Bronwyn continued as if she hadn't heard her.

'He's trying to find Carmel.'

'Oh God, why would he do that?' Carmel's father had threatened him at the courthouse. Alice had no doubt he would kill Stefan if he ever saw him again.

'He wants her to forgive him.'

'Is that what he told you?'

'Well, not in those exact words.'

Alice didn't know what was worse, Bronwyn's determination to believe Stefan, or Stefan pretending that what he'd done wasn't so bad after all. An odd mixture of naïveté and narcissism? Maybe they were family traits.

'Bronwyn, I think you should let Stefan work this stuff out himself. Try not to help him too much, if you know what I mean.'

'I can't abandon him.' Her tone made Alice wince. She sounded like she trying to make up for already having done that.

'I wasn't suggesting you do. It's just that I think Stefan has some growing up to do and he has to do it by himself.'

'I don't know what you mean, Alice. Stefan's just had a lot of bad luck.'

Alice rolled her eyes. 'I'm sorry Bronwyn, but I do have to go now. Got to get back to work.'

Gail appeared, carrying a bag of chocolate-covered peanuts. Leaning against the edge of Alice's desk, Gail offered her the bag.

'You're feeling depressed?' Alice asked.

'Is it that obvious?'

'Yep.'

'What's up?'

'I think Tony's having an affair.'

'Oh God, not this again.'

'How can you say that?'

'Gail, about twice a year you decide that your devoted husband is off shagging someone else, rather than you acknowledging that you are just bored or about to have a mid-life crisis. Or both.'

'Well, excuse me, that doesn't mean he isn't shagging someone else.'

'If you really thought that, you wouldn't be bingeing on chocolate peanuts. You'd be stalking him, eyeballing the culprit and planning to do her harm.'

'Yeah, alright, maybe I am bored.'

'Maybe?'

'How's the family drama?'

'Ticking along nicely thanks. No one's speaking to anyone else and everyone is refusing to admit that Stefan's probably using. I'm trying my hardest to stay out of it.'

'Good on you. Sounds hideous.'

Gail scooped up some more nuts. 'You're looking very… very…perky.'

'Perky?'

'Yes, like a girl who is … Have you seen that guy again? You have haven't you?'

'Well, actually…'

'Oh, I see. So, great sex and everything is right with the world. Is that it?'

'Yes, more or less.'

'More or less? You are having great sex?'

'Yep,' Alice tried not to look too pleased.

'There's something else isn't there?' Gail stepped back, appraising her friend. Tossing another peanut in her mouth and sucking on it.

'You're in love with him aren't you?'

'God! What? No!'

'You are. I can tell. It's written all over you.'

'Gail you're being ridiculous.'

'And you're being coy.'

'Take your peanuts and go back to your own territory thanks.'

'This conversation isn't finished.'

'Funny, I have the same feeling.'

Gail walked away then doubled back and told her sternly 'Be careful. Okay?'

'Gail. Go. Away.'

Unnerved, Alice settled back into her chair. She wasn't in love with him. Definitely wasn't in love with him. Yes, she liked him. She was attracted to him. He'd had a life so completely different from hers, how could she not be interested? She had started to admire him; he had lived through all that and was still a decent person. But admiration was not love was it?

Alice heard an email arrive and glanced at her screen. The

heading said, *In Love But You Don't Know It?* Below there was a link to a women's magazine. Alice wrote in a reply; *Bugger Off* and pushed the send button.

Picking up a client folder she leafed through the forms, telling herself she should action it: get it done by the end of the week or they'd be ringing her. Contacting the other assessor would be a good start. They'd take at least a day to get back to her, which would buy her some more time to think about Ottavio.

In the staff kitchenette, Alice made tea and passed over the packet of biscuits on the table. She should be going to class but had decided not to. She made her way back to her desk. Alice did not want to admit that she wasn't going because Ottavio had stopped going; he'd said he wanted to give it a break. She wanted to spend time with him, to be naked next to him, listening to his stories. There were so many questions she had, but so many reasons not to ask.

Alice went to the search engine and typed in Slavery in Sudan.

46. Alaya

It was just before dawn when I got up and went back to the children. It was hard to stand, and I was bleeding, but I made myself walk. The children were still sleeping. I put my hand over little brother's mouth so he would not make a sound and shook him until he woke up. He was very sleepy. I untied his hands and squeezed him. Told him he must go and not get caught. Find mother and the walking people. Little brother did not want to go, he held onto my arm, but I pinched him and told him he must. He said he would find me and together we would go back to Mayen Aben. The men were waking. I could hear them, coughing and farting.

I pushed little brother away and whispered to him. Thueny.

He said I must go with him. I told him they would chase after both of us, but they would not care about one stupid little boy. Pushing him, I told him again. Thueny.

Little brother's dusty skin slipped from my hands. The horses stayed calm as he pressed himself between them. Then he was gone.

47. Ottavio

Ottavio got home from work and went straight to the fridge. He opened a beer, wandered into the back yard. The humidity was high, and he could feel sweat rising. The rustling clicks of cicadas filled the air as he tried to stop thoughts of Alice swirling through his mind. It had been good talking to her, when he lay next to her he'd felt …soothed. The hollowness was just a tiny bit smaller.

He thought of how he would tell Alpha that he was leaving. He would be the first and he had to promise that he wouldn't tell anyone else. Ottavio couldn't stand the thought of all the questions. It was Alpha's turn to be strong. He would have to stop smoking weed and do something. Do a course. Anything that would give him a purpose. Ottavio had no doubt Alpha could make something of himself, but Ottavio had barely seen him since the funeral and couldn't guess if telling him the truth would bring him back from the edge or tip him over it. Ottavio swigged his beer and decided to speak to him after prayers. One more day wouldn't make a difference.

Ottavio's thoughts veered back to Alice and her pale blue eyes and sliding his fingers through her fine, pale hair. His groin twitched. Hearing his phone ringing inside, Ottavio ran for it, thinking it might be her. It was Malong. Ottavio hesitated; he'd be drunk for sure. They'd worked side by side, but had barely spoken, since Ottavio had stopped their nightly drinking session. Malong would peel off his work gear, at the end of the shift, and leave without saying a word. Ottavio felt bad, but wanted some space. Malong's grief was suffocating.

Against his better judgment he took his call.

'Machar where the fuck are ya?' Malong slurred.

'In bed.'

'Who with?'

'All alone Malong. Want to come join me?'

'Fuck you Machar.'

'You talking to me now?'

'Ain't not. Just got nothing to say.'

'Whatever man. Where are you?'

'Home.'

'Okay. See you at prayers.'

'Machar.'

'Yeah?'

'Who is she?'

'Go to bed Malong.'

Ottavio hoped Malong was too drunk to remember being hung up on.

His phone beeped. The message was from Alice. She was still awake if he wanted to call. He rang her straight away.

❈

In the morning Ottavio woke to an echo of Alice's voice. Then Zach reclaimed his rightful place and the dull ache appeared exactly as it had for the last forty days. He was tempted to start the day with a beer. It was the only thing that quelled that ache.

Ottavio heard a tap on his door, Alpha edged it open, peering at him, hollow-eyed and hesitant. Ottavio nodded for him to come in. He closed the door carefully and sat down on the end of his bed, shoulders hunched, chest sunken.

'You sleep?'

Sniffing, Alpha shook his head no.

'Weed keeping you awake.'

'Weed make you sleep,' Alpha mumbled, adding, 'But I don't have any.' Then he paused and Ottavio waited patiently, giving him time.

'I keep seeing Zach.'

Alpha's words trickled down Ottavio's spine like cold water.

'Can't stay in that room no more.' Alpha squeezed his bottom lip between his thumb and finger. 'Can I have this room? You sleep in there?'

Guilt rolled through Ottavio. Cavernous guilt. I didn't help Zach when he needed me. Now its Alpha he needs to be around. Ottavio shrugged. 'You can move but he might come with you.'

'Maybe he's waiting.'

'Waiting for what?'

'Someone has to pay.'

'That's what you want? Revenge? That sounds like Malong talking.'

'You telling me you don't?'

'Yeah, I do but Zach wouldn't want that. He wouldn't do that if it were one of us. Not Zach.'

'Then why he still around?'

'Maybe he just likes your company.'

Alpha snorted and shook his head.

'Maybe he wants you to get sorted out. Go back to school.'

'You think?'

'Stop wasting your time. He'd want that.'

'That's what you want.'

'True. But he would too.'

For a while, neither spoke.

Ottavio's thoughts gathered and he knew for sure he had made the right decision. Without thinking more, he told Alpha. 'I'm going back.'

'Back?'

'Home.'

'Home?'

'Sudan.'

Alpha raised his head. 'What the hell? You leaving too? When?'

'Sunday.'

'Two days?'

Alpha leaned back against the wall.

Ottavio spoke quietly. 'There's something else you have to know. Only other person in the world knows is Malong.'

Closing his eyes, Alpha hunched a little.

'She didn't die. Our sister didn't die.'

'Whadda ya' talking about?'

'I was there.'

'You were where?'

'The Murhaleen took us both, but I got away.'

Alpha's face broke with disbelief. He shook his head. 'Man you are unbelievable.' He got up to leave.

Ottavio grabbed his arm. 'Alpha!'

'Leave me alone.' Alpha said, shrugging him off, leaving the room, slamming the door behind him. Ottavio wandered into the kitchen. The silence was worse than it had ever been. He drank some water to stop his stomach quavering; his skin felt alive with the memory of dust and fear. Sitting at the table, he regretted what he had just done. Alpha didn't have to know that part of the story. Not now. Why rain more anguish down on him? He'd fucked up, he told himself. Again. He just kept getting it wrong. He called Alpha and, of course, he didn't answer. He thought of sending him a text. What could he say that would make this better? He didn't know. Instead he wrote, 'Don't worry about this. I'm going to make it right. That's why I'm going to Sudan. Please don't tell Malong about that. I'll tell him after prayers. Okay?' Then he thumbed Malong a message, asking him to find Alpha, and to make sure they were both at the grave.

Exhausted, Ottavio fell asleep on the lounge.

■

In the morning when Uncle Paulino arrived, Ottavio was not ready. He was on the lounge, his phone resting in limp hands.

'What is it son?'

The old man eased himself down into the armchair. 'What has happened?'

'Peters. The detective. He called just now. They have arrested two men.' Ottavio let the news settle between them. The old man nodded, taking a pressed handkerchief from his pocket, he unfolded it and dabbed his forehead.

'Now is not the time to say this son. It is better if we wait. Tell people after. It is better that way.' Ottavio felt relief that Paulino was there. The old man had more strength than he did; he needed to lean on it.

'Now it is time to get ready.' Paulino gently urged him on. While Ottavio was in the shower, Paulino chose a shirt and tie for him, brushed down his suit jacket and trousers, and left them on his bed. Ottavio dressed slowly, thinking of the black car. Knowing he had been right wasn't any kind of salve. Paulino was waiting patiently in the lounge. He held him at arm's length, appraising his appearance.

'Be strong son. You must be strong. For everyone.'

Before the call from Peters, Ottavio had decided to tell Uncle about Sudan, but now it was far from his mind.

When they pulled into the cemetery car park, Ottavio saw Malong and Alpha standing side by side. Shaking hands, slapping shoulders, Ottavio made his way through the crowd to join them, by the grave. They stood together. Ottavio was relieved to be beside them. Rosa approached, her hair wrapped in a white cloth. She looked at them approvingly. Ottavio was sorry that he had kept so much from her. He had given her so much to forgive. The headstone was uncovered and blessed with prayers. Ottavio could not look at it. He could not stand to see Zach's name carved into the grey stone. It took the last of his strength to hold himself in check, to not let any tears fall.

The crowd moved from the cemetery to the house, overflowing into the backyard. There were stories and songs and tears. Alpha and Malong sat together talking quietly.

Uncle Paulino came and guided him outside, a comforting hand on his shoulder. Ottavio had been touched by his kindness. He knew he should tell him. 'Uncle. I am sorry to not have spoken, but in a few days, I will go back to Sudan.'

Paulino took in the news, calmly nodding his head, hand still on his shoulder.

'This is good news son. Good. Your family there will be happy to see you.' Paulino gazed at Ottavio. 'These have been hard times. Both you and Rosa to go home. It is the right thing to do. Don't worry about Australia. We will help Rosa with her arrangements. I will see to it. She will be fine. And this other business, it is over now. It is a good time to go.'

'Thank-you Uncle. People will be upset when they hear.'

'Son leave it with me. I will speak to them when you have gone.'

The old man would visit people, shake their hands, quietly answer their questions, explain. Ottavio knew that much about him. He also knew enough of him to not be surprised by his next question.

'Perhaps you will get married there?' Paulino asked lightly, smiling. Ottavio smiled as well, as he shook hands with him, knowing his joking was entirely serious.

People had begun to leave and Paulino shook hands in farewell, saw the last people out, then left himself.

Ottavio went to find Alpha. He was lying on his bed, but he seemed to be asleep, so he let him be.

It was late. Ottavio joined Malong in the back yard. Odd distant sounds reached them; a burst of shouting, squealing wheels, cats spitting and growling. Ottavio didn't have to wait for Malong to speak.

'You thought telling him now was the right time?'

Ottavio let him say it. But he would be feeling bad too. He was the only other person who knew. But they were not the only ones. Nobody talked about those who were taken to the end of the earth. But Malong was right. Now was not the right time.

Ottavio felt emptied. His secrets, his silence, they weren't strengths. They were failings.

Malong lit a cigarette, blowing the smoke high into the air. Ottavio buried his hands, deep into his pockets. 'The detective called. Peters.'

Malong smirked, leaning back against his chair.

'Those two guys in the black car. At Zach's game. It was them. None of the kids at school knew about it. Theo, Kelly; they didn't know. Those guys saw Zach on his way to the game that night. Told the cops they just wanted to give him a hiding. Didn't mean to kill him.' Ottavio didn't know what else to say. They'd both thought life in Australia would be paradise, but the violence, the loss; it had all come around again.

Stubbing out his cigarette, Malong made fists of his hands and cracked his knuckles. 'You believe that?'

'I don't know.' Ottavio's voice was barely above a whisper. 'But if I had been at home that night, this wouldn't have happened.'

'Where were you?'

'I told the cop I was at your house, because I didn't want Rosa to know I was with a girl. A *kawauja*.'

Malong nodded like he had known all along.

48. Alice

She'd avoided her mother's calls throughout the week. Then the text arrived. 'The usual meeting place, 'Be on time!' Alice had caved in, but she was deliberately late.

Elspeth didn't comment but barely gave her time to order before launching into a diatribe about Stefan, Bronwyn giving him money—quite large amounts. Jack had seen the bank account, demanded to know what was going on and Bronwyn had told him to mind his own business.

'Elspeth, I think you should just stay out of it.'

'How can I stay out of it? Bronwyn is my sister and Jack asked me to speak to her.'

'How could you help the situation?'

'I told her she was being irrational.'

'Oh God Elspeth.'

Elspeth looked at her sharply, but Alice took a deep breath and continued. 'She is not the problem here. Stefan is.'

'I don't know what you mean,' Elspeth said, brushing imaginary crumbs from her lap.

'I mean he's very good at getting people to feel sorry for him. He's manipulating her. He's done it to all of us at some time.'

Her mother did not like it, but Alice was not going to stop. 'Yes, I know in our family we don't speak the truth, but the truth is Stefan's got Bronwyn wrapped around his little finger. He's using her.'

'Bronwyn wants to give him the money.'

'Yes, but that's not really the problem is it?'

'What do you mean?'

'Elspeth, do you really think Setefan is starting a business? He's probably spending it on drugs. Hasn't that occurred to you?'

'Yes, it has, which is all the more reason to talk to Bronwyn.'

'Do you really think that will stop Stefan?'

'Alice, what has gotten into you? Are you working too much? You seem very…cantankerous.'

'Look, I care about Stefan too, but he's got you all running round in circles.'

'Well, why don't you talk to him?'

'I have and I told him he was a selfish prick.'

'Alice!'

'There was a whole lot more I should have said, but I hung up on him.'

'Really Alice, this is not like you at all.'

'Actually, it is like me. The new me, no more keeping quiet in case I might offend someone.'

'I don't know what you're talking about.' Elspeth said, taking a gulp of water.

Alice felt a twinge of sadness for her mother, but she pressed on. 'There's something I want you to know.' Blank-faced, lips pursed, Elspeth readied herself.

'I'm seeing someone.'

Elspeth's face softened and she pushed herself back against the chair. Her demeanour completely changed. 'Well,

I'm delighted to hear it. Really Alice, it has been such a long time.'

Alice knew she was on thin ice. The announcement was premature. A few nights with Ottavio didn't mean it was official. She wanted to keep seeing him but had no idea what he wanted.

Elspeth leaned forward, eyes bright with interest. 'Tell me about him. What does he do? When are we going to meet him?'

Weighing up her options, Alice glanced at her mother. She hadn't expected her to be so pleased. She couldn't retract now, but couldn't she hold off on the details? Elspeth clearly loved the idea of a man in her life, but that would change when she knew who he was. Her approval would be withdrawn. And that's what she hated about her mother. Her power to disapprove. Alice wanted to hurt her in return. Show that her approval no longer mattered to her.

'He works at a meat factory.'

'A meat factory? What does he do there?'

'Cuts up carcasses.'

Elspeth looked so uncomfortable, Alice almost laughed. A waiter approached and asked if they would like to order anything more. Alice shook her head as Elspeth inspected her nail polish.

'How did you meet him?

'He volunteers at the community centre. In the English class.'

'I see.'

Alice sat back in her chair and held in a sigh. Fuck it, Alice thought. 'His name's Ottavio in case you're interested. And he's African. From Sudan.'

Elspeth carefully folded her napkin into a neat, tight square. Alice's conscience stabbed at her. She shouldn't have said anything. Ottavio liked her, she could see that, but she had no idea about any future with him. She'd gone too far.

'I'm sorry Mum,' Alice said, her belligerence gone. Elspeth sipped more water as Alice gathered her things and left.

In her car Alice started to cry, unsure who she was more ashamed of, her mother or herself.

Millie ran to her as she came through the door, meowing for food. Alice scooped her up and petted her soft fur. Alice fed her and ran a bath. As she shaved her legs and armpits, Millie sat on the edge swiping at the foamy bubbles. Rubbing rose-scented cream all over her body, she put on her brand new red and purple silk underwear. Sipping her wine, she put on one of Ottavio's CDs, laid open her suitcase on the bed and started to go through her wardrobe piece by piece. If it didn't fit, hadn't been worn in the last year, or was just plain ugly, she threw it in the corner. If it made her feel good and was lightweight, it went into the suitcase. Half an hour later there was more in the corner than in the wardrobe and the suitcase was half full. Alice repeated the process with her underwear, socks, pantyhose, shoes, belts, bags and hats. Some of them she'd had since high school. She retrieved two large garbage bags from the kitchen she filled them with all the discarded goods. Lying back on her bed, feeling tipsy and a whole lot lighter, she wondered if Ottavio would like to come to Vietnam. She was interrupted by the buzzing of her phone. It was Gail. She didn't answer. Ottavio would be here soon.

Three hours later Alice was drunk and stumbling about her kitchen making cheese on toast. He had not called or replied to her text. Alice had replaced her silky underwear with a pair of sweat pants and an old white t-shirt from the garbage bag.

She popped the cork from another bottle of wine, just as the smoke alarm started screaming. Alice spun around to see smoke pouring out from under the grill. The bottle slipped from her grasp as she ran to the stove, grabbing at the blackened toast. Burning the tips of her fingers, she dropped them on the floor and then saw the spilt wine pooling across the floor. Taking a single wide step to clear the puddle, lost her balance and slipped over, landing hard on her back. Dazed, she lay there, blinking back tears and realised someone was knocking on the door.

'It's okay,' she yelled. A neighbour must have heard the alarm. 'There's no fire.'

There was silence, then another knock. Hair in disarray, tears and snot on her face, her t-shirt stained pink with wine, Alice got up slowly and made her way to the door.

Ottavio took in the sight of her and laughed out loud.

Throwing the burnt toast in the bin, he mopped up the wine with a tea towel and told her to get in the shower. Under the steaming water, Alice felt dizzy and stupidly happy. She squeezed a dollop of shampoo onto her palm and transferred it to her hair. Naked, Ottavio stepped into the cubicle. 'I'll do that,' he said, massaging her hair into a lather. Alice leaned against his chest, his long fingers pressing firmly into her skull. She wrapped her arms around his waist and held him.

They lay on the bed in the dark. Alice still felt drunk, but she was calm, happy to have Ottavio's head resting on her groin. Rolling over, he pressed his lips against the soft rolls of her stomach. Alice squirmed and twisted underneath him, as he shifted on top of her. Holding her head between his hands, he kissed her roughly and she wrapped her legs around his waist. It was like the first time, he was hard and fast and did not wait for her. When he came, he cried out like he was in pain.

49. Ottavio

The day was humid, and clouds were gathering in the sky. Ottavio wanted it to rain as he was leaving. To be rained on was to be blessed. After tossing his passport, wallet, anti-malaria tablets, phone and copy of *A Catcher in the Rye* in his shoulder bag, he packed a small case; clothes, toiletries, sandals. He removed his watch and left it on his bedside table. Snatching his keys up he pulled the front door shut, put his bags in the boot and saluted the giant gum farewell as he drove out of his street. It was early afternoon and the suburb was still. When he'd first arrived, he used to think, where are all the people? There was nobody on the street just hanging out. Neighbours barely said hello. It was one of the things he'd never gotten used to.

Malong's street was packed with cars. Ottavio recognized most of them. Music was thumping and laughter was coming from the back of the house. Double-parking, Ottavio called Malong and told him to come out front. Barefoot, he appeared on the doorstep. Ottavio pushed open the passenger door and Malong strolled over.

'So, where is she?'

Ottavio didn't take the bait. 'Shut up and get in.'

To Ottavio's surprise he did.

'Where we going?'

'You'll see.'

Nudging the speed limit, Ottavio raced through the streets to the freeway entry. Malong glanced at him, questioning as Ottavio pressed hard on the accelerator, merging into the traffic. Ottavio ignored him.

'Whatever.' Malong said, sitting back, squaring his shoulder against the seat and fell asleep.

In the silence Ottavio could hear his breathing, shallow and steady and he remembered when they had slept on the same mat, when they first got to the camp. The nearer they got to the airport, the harder it was for Ottavio to swallow. Excitement and anxiety. Finally, he was doing what he said he would.

He reached for the smooth glass of his watch, then remembered where he had left it. Searching the radio channels, for something Malong would like, he found a shouting and angry song, and turned it up. Startled, Malong opened his eyes.

'You stay cool okay? Paulino going to talk to people.'

Malong turned the music down. 'That's why we're going for a ride, so you could tell me that?'

Ottavio glanced at him, teasing. 'Nope.'

Ottavio maintained his speed, until he reached the turn off for the international airport. Malong, seeing their destination, sunk low in his sear. Manoeuvering into a departure lane, Ottavio slowed, waiting for a gap, ignoring a blast of car horns wanting him to keep moving. A car pulled out right in front of him and he smoothly moved into the space and stopped the car. Jumping out, he got his bags from the boot. Malong was waiting on the curb.

'Here,' Ottavio said, offering him the car keys. 'It's yours.'

Malong shook his head, refusing.

'It's not a thank-you.' Ottavio smiled weakly. 'Take it. How else you gonna get home?'

Ottavio feigned a punch, but Malong didn't react. He stared at Ottavio and when he spoke his voice broke. 'I shouldn't have made him go back to school.'

Ottavio shook his head. 'We all feel responsible, but it ain't anyone's fault. It's just the way the world is.'

Malong would not look at him.

'Prove them wrong. Okay?'

'Who's them?

'Everyone.'

Malong folded his arms loosely across his chest.

'Are you coming back?'

'Soon as I find you a wife.'

Malong smirked.

'Nice village girl; obedient, sweet, never argues. Gets down on her knees when she brings you your food.'

'Get out of here.'

Ottavio lobbed the keys into the air. Malong snatched them and they bumped fists. Malong got back in the car, sounding the horn hard and long as he drove away.

Ottavio turned and walked through the sliding doors into the crowd of departing people.

There was barely a queue for his flight. He was early and flights to East Africa left late at night. The smiling attendant checked his ticket and passport, weighed his carry-on luggage, then waved him through. Ottavio cleared customs, then immigration, and looked for a quiet corner in the departure lounge. He bought himself a coffee and sat down to send Alice a text. First, he wrote he was leaving, and he didn't know when he would be back. Then, taking a deep breath, he tapped in that he thought about her a lot. Deleting that, he tried again, this time saying he wanted her to be more … more what? he thought. Delete. Finally, he wrote, *I'm off overseas. See you round some time.* He pressed send. Turning the phone off he zipped it into the inside pocket of his bag.

Doha airport, three a.m., Ottavio stepped down from the plane into the hot desert air. Crossing the tarmac, he guessed it was at least thirty-five degrees. Inside the huge air-conditioned terminal, he wandered, walking out the stiffness, waiting for his flight to Khartoum. People of all cultures milled about. Women in black burkas, their curious eyes watching those less pious. Chinese businessmen, Pakistani workers. Everyone was waiting.

Leaning against a wall, Ottavio closed his eyes against the fluorescent glare. The agony of the last six weeks made him feel like lead. Flipping open his wallet, he found the photo of Zach he'd put there that morning and grief heaved inside him.

Khartoum appeared on the dust-shrouded horizon. Ottavio peered out the window, fear and anticipation churning through him. The city had been so far away for so long and now, within minutes, he would be overhead quicker than he was ready for.

Touching down, Ottavio tried to breathe calmly. He didn't rush to leave the plane, staying in his seat until the aisle had cleared. There were no questions in immigration, just a cursory glance at his Australian passport, then a smudged stamp.

Ottavio caught a bus to Omdurman, quickly bought a long loose *jellabiya* when he got off at the station, and asked for the nearest guesthouse.

The man who opened the door eyed him carefully, taking in his western clothes; a southerner but foreigner as well. He showed Ottavio the musty room and murmured the price. Ottavio handed it to him in Sudanese pounds, took the key and closed the door on the man's lingering gaze. There was a shower recess without a curtain and cracked tiles surrounding the uncovered drain. The sink had a rusty stain from the dripping tap. A plastic table in the corner held a small television and a remote control. A tiny lizard clung motionless on the ceiling. Ottavio hung the cream-coloured *jellabiya* on the coat hanger on the back of the door and took a cold shower.

It was nearing evening and he was hungry. Not wanting to draw any more attention to himself, he put on the *jellabiya*. The soft, thin cotton reached his ankle, as it should. Ottavio sat on the bed for a few minutes, absorbing the quiet of the room and the muffled sounds of the street outside. Tempted to lie back and sleep, Ottavio forced himself to get up. Sweat was already breaking under his arms and across his forehead. Outside, the air was warmer, and the lane bustled with people. Women balanced their purchases on their covered heads and children scuttled about, traders in tiny shop fronts, selling foodstuffs and fabrics, DVDs and batteries. Craftsmen displayed their silver and copperware, fine filigree jewellery, gleaming ebony carvings, low round stools woven from brightly coloured plastic cord. Produce stalls overflowed with vegetables: fat red tomatoes and the varied greens of okra and beans. There were lentils and spices of every colour. Nobody took any notice of him and he began to relax.

The humid air thickened with charcoal smoke. Ottavio followed his nose to a stall under a torn and faded canopy. A young boy was turning skewers of beef and onion above glowing coals. Ottavio held up two fingers and nodded at the row of brightly coloured drinks on the shelf behind the boy. He did not want to speak and let the boy hear his accent. The boy ran his finger along the top of the drinks until his customer indicated the drink he wanted. Handing the boy a grimy note, Ottavio sat on a plastic stool with his back to the stall, avoiding any chance of conversation. Gobbling the kebabs, the taste lingering on his tongue, Ottavio drank the warm lemonade, searching the face of each African woman he saw, looking for the v-shaped lines on the forehead. How much would she have changed? How many children did she have? She had seemed so tall to him. Maybe he was taller now. Would she recognise him? Would that be possible? Had she spent years searching for his face?

Ottavio went back to his room. In the corridor the man who had received him nodded with stony-faced approval at his *jellabiya*. Ottavio saw no other guests and wondered if he was the only one. Lying on the bed, Ottavio instantly fell into a deep, black sleep and woke mid-morning with no idea where he was. The narrow bed screeched as he got up. Scuffing his sandals across the dusty floor, he rinsed his face at the basin, dressed in the *jellabiya* again and went back to the market.

As he wandered the rubbish-strewn lanes, Ottavio tried to look as though he had a purpose. If any of the faces he looked into returned his gaze, he dropped his eyes and hurried on. The lane led into a narrow street in a run-down residential area. Women swept dust from their doorways. Chickens pecked at the earth amid playing children. He followed the street until it became wider. Occasional cars rolled by. He could see rooftops behind high compound walls. These were the kind of houses that would have a woman like her. The owners were well-off, they could afford a slave to wash their clothes and cook the family meals.

Stopping under the shade of a palm tree, he pressed his back against sharp ridges of the trunk, smelling the fine dust in the burning air. He told himself a family could have been kind to her. It was possible. Not all slave owners were monsters. The practice used to be common. A tradition. The tension and the heat had started to make his head throb.

A young girl, perhaps fifteen, came towards him. She was tall and thin, and her head was covered but the darkness of her skin declared her a southerner.

They were the only people in the street and her eyes flickered towards him. As she passed, he fell into step with her. 'What is your name?' he said, trying to appear relaxed, so she could see he meant no harm. But it didn't work, he felt the girl tense, her step quickening. Not only was he speaking English, there was also a strange flat sound to it. Veering away from him, she increased her pace, glancing back to see if he was following her. Ottavio changed direction too, hoping nobody had seen his stupid mistake. What was he going to say to her? Are you a slave? Do you know any others?

Finding his way back to the market he bought bottled water, went back to the hotel, stripped off the *jellabiya* and rinsed the sweat off his face. Ottavio fell into another deep sleep, waking to the call to prayer rippling across the city, the room airless and hot. Gulping down water, Ottavio worked out the time difference. It would be midday in Sydney. He thought of Alpha, he'd do well if he could just concentrate. The thing Malong could never do. He knew Alpha might follow Malong like a puppy. He thought of giving him a call but reminded himself he'd only been gone two days – it felt like weeks.

50. Alice

Elspeth was as close to hysterical as Alice had ever heard. She'd had to ask her to slow down, but Elspeth began crying and her father took the phone from her and told Alice police had issued a warrant for Stefan's arrest for the assault. He'd hit Bronwyn after she'd refused to give him any more money. 'Jack got home and found her on the lounge-room floor with a black eye. He'd been through their bedroom looking for cash. Made a complete mess of it,' Thomas said, his voice hushed with disbelief. Alice felt overwhelmed; the sensation both dark and dizzying. She blinked tears away, not knowing what to say. If she saw Stefan what would she say to him? How could she not slap him? Tell him he was no longer her cousin. He had ceased to exist.

Thomas had given the phone back to her mother. 'Darling won't you come over tonight? Please darling.' Alice was shocked. She had never heard her mother plead or call her darling.

'I'll be there at seven.'

In a voice thick with tears, Elspeth said goodbye.

Alice lay on her unmade bed. The sheets still faintly smelt of Ottavio. She couldn't believe what was happening. First, the message from him the night before. Just like that, he was gone. She read the message again and again, as if she didn't understand what it said. And she didn't. What had just happened? She'd put on one of his CDs and drank steadily until she was drunk enough to let herself cry. 'You wanted something to *go through*', she said out loud. 'Well go through this.'

Waking with a serious hangover that morning, she called in sick to work and spent all day in her pyjamas, wounded and tearful. How could it happen that she finally met someone she liked, someone erotic, unpredictable …and gone?

And now Stefan. Confirming every fear she had about him since he was first arrested. The tiny bit of hope she'd kept stored for him was gone. Alice remembered what he'd said, when she demanded to know why he'd hurt his wife. *Men are animals. Some just know how to control themselves.* Alice forced herself to get up. At least going to her parents gave her something to do. And there was no way Elspeth would ask after Ottavio. She obviously hadn't told Thomas about him. Alice was relieved in a strange way. She wouldn't have to explain that he'd just dumped her by text.

After a shower, with her hair wrapped in a towel, she read Ottavio's message again. Yes, she'd let her guard down and had wanted more, but he obviously didn't. He must have planned to go overseas for a long time. Surely? In anger, she thought, *he'd made a choice and so could she.*

Alice blew her nose and got herself organised. By the time she'd arrived at her parent's place she had made up her mind. She told them she didn't want to hear anything more about Stefan. Yes, what he'd done was horrible and she didn't care if he was back in jail. He was determined to ruin his life, but she, on the other hand, was going to make the best of hers.

And by the way she was off travelling for an unspecified period of time. Elspeth burst into tears and left the room. Thomas poured them both a glass of wine, toasting her with sad eyes, whispering, *could he come too?*

Driving home she felt guilty, but there was another feeling too, like she had somehow just saved herself. At work the next day, she resigned by email, pausing for only the briefest moment, before pushing the send button. Then she went up to Gail's floor and told her what she'd just done.

'You've just what?'

'Resigned. Two weeks notice. Going to pack up the flat, rent it out and go overseas.'

'I don't believe you. One moment you're madly in love, the next you're rushing off overseas.'

'Not madly in love Gail.'

'Are you going with him? Is that it?'

'No.'

'So, he's dumped you?'

Alice tried keeping her bottom lip steady. 'Not exactly.'

Gail sighed. 'I wish you'd told me before you resigned. If we go up to HR now, you could tell them it was a mistake.'

'But it wasn't.' Alice said. 'Can you help me pack my flat up on the weekend?'

'Doll, don't you think you're being a bit rash. You can't up end your life just because some bloke you've known for a few weeks has dumped you.'

'He didn't dump me.'

'So, are you still seeing him?'

'No.'

'I think this requires an emergency intake of booze. Come on, let's go get a drink.'

'I'm serious Gail.'

'That's what I'm afraid of.'

'It's not because of him.'

'Then what is it?'

'Me.'

51. Ottavio

In his room, Ottavio rested on his bed and turned on his phone, checking to see if Alice had replied to his text. Of course, she hadn't. She'd probably deleted him from her phone. He thought of her in her clothes stained with wine, and matted hair; it made him smile. She'd seemed so proper when he first met her, but she'd changed with each encounter.

He thought of calling Rosa but changed his mind and turned the phone off. Familiar voices might make him doubt what he was doing. He hadn't come here to fail.

Sipping water, Ottavio pressed his head against the wall, and let his mind travel back to Mayen Aben.

It was evening and he was being scolded for losing a goat. She rubbed ash on him to keep the mosquitos away. She asked him what kind of man he would be when he grew up. Ottavio spoke as if she was in the room, *he would be a good man, a man who looked after his family.* The words sounded hollow in the smallness of the room. Ottavio waited for a reply, then told himself to stop being foolish. The only way he would find her was to go out looking.

Dressed in the *jellabiya,* he stood in the hotel doorway, letting the smell of the old city engulf him. Exhaust fumes and rotting garbage, dust and cooking oil and spices wafted all around him. He could see the small boy preparing his grill, blowing the coals into a soft glow. Eyeing Ottavio, he took some skewers from a shallow dish, lined them up on the wire and placed a small tin kettle on the coals. He pointed to the stool in front of his stall and Ottavio took it. They both waited for the kettle to boil. As it started to steam the boy took two glasses, spooned a generous amount of sugar into both, then added the tea. Ottavio watched his quick, practiced movements. He would only be about eight or ten but moved like a professional. Ottavio handed him a few extra notes. The kid probably only ate once a day, if he was lucky. That and whatever he could steal from the stall owner. The boy took the money quickly and Ottavio forgot about hiding his accent and thanked him in Arabic. The boy glanced at him curiously. Ottavio instantly lost his nerve. Asking a kid in the market if he knew which houses had slaves, or where in the market they might gather would be another mistake, even if he could say it in Arabic. It was possible the kid could be a government spy. Nobody in this town would ask questions like that. It was a sure way to draw attention to himself and he should avoid that at all costs. If he had any chance of finding her, he needed help. Ottavio decided he should to go back across the river to Khartoum and to El Diem. Urbane and cosmopolitan, the outsiders and the intellectuals lived there, the misfits and artists, dissidents and entertainers. El Diem was famous in the city. Anything you wanted could be bought there. Perhaps there he could ask questions?

From there he could make his way to the shanties where the southerners lived. The thought unnerved him; the relentless poverty and hardship he knew he would find. But was time to make contact with his relatives, he shouldn't leave it any longer. There would be gatherings and he would need gifts. After the greetings and formalities, he'd tell them why he'd come. Maybe someone had seen her, or they knew where she lived. It could be possible, couldn't it?

Ottavio finished his tea, tossed the boy a small coin and went to pack his bag.

The bus from Omdurman had taken nearly an hour. From the bridge he saw the waters of the White and Blue Nile merge around Tuti Island and his mood lifted for the first time since he had arrived.

At the station, he sought shade from the burning sun under a cluster of palm trees. Nearby, a tea seller sat at her small stall, talking loudly in Dinka to a woman next to her selling fresh breads. A skinny toddler lolled across her lap and nearby a mangy dog furiously bit at its haunches trying to dislodge whatever was hurting it.

The tea seller watched him with interest. Stern-faced and tall, she was the older of the two and he could just make out the v-shaped lines on her forehead. Cautiously he approached, '*Cheebuk,* Aunty. *Ekadee?*' The woman nodded, '*Ekadee* son' and motioned for him to come closer. Ottavio offered her his wrist and she touched the back of his with her own, asking him where he was from. He told her in Dinka where he was born and where he lived now, wanting her to understand the strangeness of his accent. The woman nodded sadly, 'I am Akol. My country is Aweil.'

Ottavio was pleased. Aweil neighboured Twic county. The bread seller called out, asking Akol in Dinka who Ottavio was. Akol told her he was a brother from far away.

Ottavio took the plastic chair next to her as she prepared tea. The toddler staggered to him, propping herself on his knee. The dog got up and wandered over but Akol chased him off with a loud hiss. Through the hazy air, Ottavio could see the minarets, scattered amongst the tall buildings at the centre of the city.

Sipping his tea, Ottavio watched other southerners passing by. The war might be over but Khartoum was still a better place to be than the south. At least, here they might find some work. There was more chance of surviving, yet they were second-class citizens in their own country, living amongst their enemy. The irony of it filled Ottavio with despair.

Akol was looking at him, sizing him up no doubt, even in a *jellabiya*. A foreign Dinka would be a rare thing. Wiping the sweat off his forehead, Ottavio put the little girl on his lap and jiggled her up and down until she smiled and reached out for his glass of tea. He moved it beyond her small hand and asked Akol for a bottle of water. Holding the rim to her mouth, he tipped the bottle carefully.

'You have family here?' Akol asked. It sounded more like a statement than a question.

'Cousins.'

'They will be pleased to see you,' Akol said, matter-of-factly.

'I'm not sure where they are.'

Again, Akol appraised him, then with a nod said, 'Come back tomorrow I will know.'

Ottavio listed the people Uncle Paulino had said were in Khartoum, then carefully handed the sleepy toddler back to her mother and paid Akol for the drinks. Ottavio asked her for directions to El Diem and if she knew a place to stay. She looked at him curiously. 'Take a *rishka* to the main street. Look for a big house on the corner, for a blue door. Khalid will give you a room.'

52. Alice

Alice woke, blinking into the darkness, her mind racing. Rolling slowly out of bed she pulled on the hotel bathrobe, stood dazed and unsteady in the dark room. A dull light was glowing through the not-quite closed curtains. She pushed them aside, slid open the glass doors and stepped onto the balcony. Bangkok sprawled out below her, its permanent traffic jam grinding away, clamouring horns dulled a little by the distance. The air was warm and acrid and she was hungry. Alice went back inside and dressed.

It was late but the streets were alive with people. Groups of young men wandered along, jostling each other and laughing, smoking fat cigarettes. A wizen old man was grilling chunks of chicken on long needles of bamboo, the smoke rich with chilli and lemongrass. Jetlag pressed against the backs of her eyes, fuelling the wiry, restless energy that propelled her. She wandered through the night markets, ignoring pleas to buy t-shirts or special-priced sunglasses, turning away from deep fried tarantulas and crickets. Fingering beautiful cloth woven by women in the far-off hills, she thought of Elspeth. She would not appreciate such intricate patterns and bright colours. Alice slid a heavy band of blackened silver onto her wrist, admired it in the dim lighting of the stall and put it back.

Over the road was an open-air tourist bar, a few middle-aged, overweight white men sat at a long high bench sipping plastic cups of cheap beer, watching the bustling street. Sex tourists? Alice found herself thinking, so kept walking until she found another bar, with a few young tourists scattered about. In the garden, fairy lights sprinkled the palms with dots of light. Alice drank her beer quickly, wanting the alcohol to numb her limbs and switch off her brain. Ordering another would be a mistake. She didn't want a hangover *and* jetlag. Then she noticed a young man at another table watching her.

Without thinking she flicked her long hair around her shoulder and smiled at him. Getting up slowly, he came over to her table. Dark hair, average height, a little overweight, about her age: late-twenties. She smiled again and he took the chair opposite her. A waiter immediately appeared. As he was ordering for them both in a heavy Norwegian accent, Alice made a split-second decision about how this would go. After all she was far from home and no longer the person she had been. What did it matter how she behaved? Who cared?

They would have a few more. Drunk, she would ask him to join her for the rest of the night and they would fuck quickly and intensely then talk intimately like strangers do when they've just had sex. Gail would be mighty impressed.

It wasn't exactly as she had imagined. The Norwegian couldn't quite manage an erection and fell asleep while she was trying to help him out. Snoring softly next to her, Alice was annoyed. Sick in the stomach from the beer, she watched the curtains for the first tones of dawn. When the light shifted to a gauzy grey, she woke him. Climbing on top, she worked herself to a climax, rolled off and told him to go.

She woke to bright sunshine edging the curtains. Pulling on a cotton slip in her bare feet, Alice went downstairs to reception and told them she wanted to extend her stay.

53. Ottavio

Khalid was grizzled and milky-eyed and nodded as though he was expecting Ottavio. With a flick of his hand he motioned for Ottavio to follow and led him from the blue door to a shaded alley at the side of the building, only wide enough for one person at a time, the blinding midday sun blocked by the three-storied house next door.

Cautiously following, Ottavio noticed Khalid's limp and a deep slash of scar tissue across the back of his neck.

Stopping at an arched doorway, set deep into the wall, Khalid unlocked it with an ancient iron key and swung the door open. Ottavio quickly inspected the dark room. A narrow bed against the wall, a small table with candles and a box of matches. A plastic stool. There was also a bucket and a worn towel. Khalid pointed to a tap in a recess further down the alley, next to it, a partially open tin door revealed a pit toilet. Ottavio dropped his bags on his bed and held up four fingers for the nights he wanted to stay. Then he counted out pound notes onto Khalid's open palm until he closed his hand over them, indicating it was enough. Handing Ottavio the key, he pulled the door closed behind him.

Ottavio washed his *jellabiya* and hung it to dry on a wire strung across the tiny room and dozed through the worst of the heat, jerking awake with drool running down his chin, lethargic and disorientated. A small window in the thick wall let in some light. It was early evening and the *jellabiya* was dry and hanging stiffly on the wire.

Ottavio retrieved *A Catcher in the Rye* from his bag. Flicking the book open, he sat on the corner of the bed and read the last few pages. Holden had *felt so damn happy* watching his sister go round and round on the carousel. That's what Ottavio wanted, even if it was just for a short time, he wanted to feel like Holden had.

Outside the street was busy. Men sat on low stools in front of teashops, smoking and drinking from short glasses. He passed a group of southerners seated outside a café, smoking and laughing. They looked well dressed and relaxed. Maybe they were students. A few glanced at him curiously but he kept going. Not greeting them was impolite, but even a wave felt risky. They could be government agents. For all he knew, Akol could be as well. Khartoum was full of the regime's spies. Ottavio told himself to stop, be calm. El Diem was the safest place to be in this city.

Midday he was back at the station. Akol was exactly where she had been the day before. A young man with yellowed eyes sat next to her, but as Ottavio approached he jumped up and hurried over to him, offering Ottavio his hand, shaking it vigorously.

'Welcome, brother, welcome. I am Victor, Mador Alor's

third son. You are my cousin. Welcome, welcome.' Victor beamed and slapped Ottavio on the shoulder. 'Come, come with me. I will take you.' With that he walked off. Ottavio waved to Akol. Smiling, she raised her hand in farewell as he rushed to keep up with Victor. Skipping ahead, he turned to ask excited questions. 'How is Australia? You have been there a long time? What is it like there? I have heard it is a good place.'

Ottavio smiled and nodded. 'Yeah, it's good. It's okay. It's been a long time now.'

Ottavio followed Victor along the street crowded with other southerners. Skinny, dressed in worn-out clothes, Ottavio felt their eyes flick toward him with interest.

Victor waved down a *rishka,* the driver looked them both over with weary eyes. Ottavio flashed him some money and the driver nodded for them to get in and nodded again as Victor yelled out directions in fluent Arabic. The driver skillfully wove through the clogged traffic, dodging minivans, taxis and other *rishka,* working his way across the choking city. Pressed against Victor in the back, Ottavio held his sleeve across his face to block the fumes and the dust, sweat rolled down his temples. They did not try to speak over the noise.

The driver dropped them at the edge of a sprawling shanty. Victor led him deep into its twisting, narrow alleys. Two little boys sensing Victor's excitement trailed behind, trying to pick up the conversation. Victor rounded another corner and stepped up to a hut, flicking the plastic flap open and ushering Ottavio inside.

Ottavio's eyes struggled to adjust to the dim interior. People were seated in plastic chairs. An elderly man stood and reached for Ottavio's hand, gently shaking it. He placed his other hand on Ottavio's shoulder. Close up, Ottavio could see the cloudy film across his eyes. He sat down carefully and Ottavio made his way around the small room, shaking hands with each man. There was one woman who grasped him in a hug and slapped him on the back, telling him she was his father's cousin. Ottavio swallowed at his father's name; the only thing of him he could remember of him. Ottavio would hide that his father was lost in his memory, even as these people would talk of him, to try and bring him back to life.

He took the chair next to blind Uncle. A young girl appeared with a tray of drinks. Narrow tins of coke and fizzy fruit drinks were passed around. Victor sat by the door, vetting others who arrived, telling them who their visitor was and asking them to wait. He looked like he was enjoying himself. Ottavio waited for Uncle Mador to address the room.

'Son, it has made me glad that you have come to us.'

Nodding, Ottavio shifted in his chair. This would take a while.

'Your family here is very poor, we have no cows.'

The men talked about relatives dead and alive, the peace

treaty that was being negotiated. If one day they could return home to the life they had lived before the war had begun. They talked as though this was possible. That the south could become independent, everything would be better, and they would have cows and farms and live peacefully again. Questions were asked about Australia. Aunty wanted to know why he did not have a wife. The men chimed in. There were many potential brides for him to choose from. Perhaps he had come to get married? Ottavio did not reply.

More people came and others went. Word was out that a visitor had arrived. Mador tired after some hours and Aunty suggested Ottavio return the following afternoon. Victor proudly escorted Ottavio out, introducing him to friends squatting outside their shacks as they went. Ottavio's head ached. There were no trees or shade, no water supply. At the road, gusts of wind, gritty with sand buffeted them. Ottavio gave Victor enough money to provide a meal for the family the next day, as they waited for a *rishka* to appear.

It was dark by the time Ottavio got back to his room, he slept fitfully; sweating and turning, the sound of horses galloping. He woke shaky with panic, rinsed his mouth, and spat into the bucket, then drained the bottle in deep swallows. He lay back down and picked up *Catcher in the Rye* and concentrated on the lines on the page, blocking out all other thoughts.

Midday, Victor was waiting at the same place he had left him. Sweat beaded across his forehead, he pumped Ottavio's hand and rushed him through the alleys again to the gathering. There was a festive air inside and it was crowded with guests, children running in and out of the room. Extra chairs were outside in the lane.

There were speeches and laughter. The food was served in small dishes on enormous round trays, elders eating first. Men of Ottavio's age made requests for money, whatever he could spare. He knew what they were thinking. He lived in the West, he must be rich. Ottavio gave a small amount to everyone who asked, until he had no more in his wallet. He was invited to stay, spend the night, but knew this was out of politeness. They had no bed for him and did not want him to sleep on the ground.

Late in the afternoon as Victor walked him back to the road Ottavio decided it was time. 'Victor I need to find someone. Who can I ask?'

'You looking for someone?'

'My sister.'

Victor stopped. 'Your sister? She died in the war.'

'She was taken.'

'You're sure. You saw this.'

'I was there.'

'Cousin, it was so long ago. If she was here how could anyone know? We do not see the *alouny* on the street.'

'Maybe she's in one of the big houses. They would have given her another name.'

'You cannot know she is alive Cousin.' Victor spoke with kindness.

Ottavio felt the truth of his words push hard against him. He knew how true that could be but he always refused that thought. Denied it entry into his world. But could not think that for a moment. He would not.

Victor was watching him closely. When he spoke it was in a whisper. 'The only way is to find an Arab who will look for her. You must have a lot of money. Even if you could find someone to trust, maybe they never find her and all your money will be gone.'

'I have to try.'

'Cousin, it has been how long?'

'Twenty-three years.'

With distant eyes, Victor shook his head. 'Tomorrow you must speak with Aunty Ajak.'

54. Alice

Lying next to the rooftop swimming pool, Alice watched the sun sink into the hazy band of pollution that was the horizon. She still felt disorientated, but she didn't mind. The risk she'd taken seemed to be working. After ten days in the seething grime of the city her list of nots was growing. Not tending to her broken heart with wine and tears. Not maintaining her usual intake of refined sugar and homogenised fat. Not feeling guilty about abandoning the family drama. That morning an email from her mother said that Stefan had not been bailed. Without thinking, Alice had pushed the delete button. That's how easy change was, she had told herself. All this time and she had never realized, how simple it could be. She was changing shape in other ways too. The clothes she had packed in Sydney no longer fitted her as tightly. She used the looseness to her advantage. Since the Norwegian backpacker there had been other nationalities. She thought of them as experiments in sex. The possibilities seemed unlimited, but she didn't want to rush. Didn't want to lose the memory of Ottavio on her skin.

Alice dropped into the pool sinking low, pushing herself along the bottom, holding her breath for as long as she could. Through a stream of bubbles, she burst through the surface gasping the torpid air and was surprised at how close she was to the other end.

55. Ottavio

Ottavio carried his gifts of tea and sugar in thin plastic bags that flapped in the hot wind. Victor was carrying more bags. Cigarettes and oil. Sweets for the kids. Weaving around the tents and shanties that all looked the same in their patchwork of plastic and cloth and pieces of tin. Dogs yapped as they passed and they veered around women lighting charcoal, fanning it into glowing lights with plastic plates.

Victor led him to a doorway covered in yellow cloth. Calling out, asking for permission to enter, he gestured for Ottavio to step inside.

Aunty Ajak was seated in a plastic chair in the middle of the room. One of her eyes drooped, almost closed. With a wave of her head, Ottavio stepped further into the room, offering her the bags. She nodded for him to put them on the rickety bed. Underneath there were a few cardboard boxes with some clothes and cooking utensils. They seemed to be her only possessions. Aunty pointed to the other chair and Ottavio sat, placing a bottle of water in front of her.

Gazing steadily at him with her one eye, Ajak nodded again, then sat back in her chair, head bowed praying, her hands clasped on her lap. Ottavio watched her closely, knowing why Victor had brought him to her. She knew the spirits. Her chin rose up and tilted toward the ceiling, and she swayed a little, then moved as though she was listening carefully. Nearby a baby screamed, but she was not disturbed.

Ottavio waited, lulled by the stifling air. Ajak opened her eyes and raised herself up slowly. Limping over to Ottavio, she took his hands. Turning out his palms, she spat on them as a blessing. Reaching for the water, she tipped a little into her hand. In another blessing, she sprinkled it over his head. 'She is lost.'

'Dead?'

'You cannot find her.'

'Is she dead?' Ottavio insisted.

The old woman ignored his question. 'Go home,' she said kindly. 'It's time for you to go home.'

He knew she did not mean Australia. There was desperation in his voice. 'Please. I have to know.'

Sternly she replied, 'The *nhalic angic nhialic* only knows this.'

Ottavio staggered out of the tent, careening blindly past the shanties, Victor scrambling after him calling. 'Cousin! Cousin! Wait.'

When he found Akol she was her packing away her meager things. The sun was dropping in the milky sky.

'Machar. Are you well?'

Emboldened by despair, Ottavio spoke frankly. 'Aunty,

please. I need you to help me. I will pay you. I want to find a woman.'

Akol kept stacking her cups, as though she had not noticed the desperation in his voice, as though his request was of no surprise.

'A woman?'

'*Aluony.*'

Discreetly glancing about to see who was nearby, in a quieter voice she asked,

'Who is this?'

'My sister.'

Nodding, Akol took a grimy cloth and wiped down the plastic tablecloth. 'It is dangerous.'

Ottavio did not reply. They both knew she was stating the obvious.

'Many bad things happen in this place. Foreigners are not protected.'

'Will you help me?

'The missionaries will help you.'

'I don't want them involved.'

'Then you will need a lot of money.'

Ottavio nodded.

'You are in El Diem. The person you need is also there. He will come after dark.'

Before Ottavio could say anything more Akol told him to go.

Anxiously, Ottavio waited in his room that evening. He checked his phone for messages, wanting to see something from Alice, even some abuse would be okay, but there was nothing. He listened to music on his phone until the battery line shrank to empty.

The next morning, weary and frustrated, he went to the market and drank thick, sweet coffee then bought a dish of *foul* with a dollop of sour cheese and a small round of spongy bread. As he ate, he caught glimpses of the small television in the next stall. Unable to keep up with the speed with which they were talking, he barely understood what was being said. As he wandered through the market, he passed a group of men in a café reciting poetry. He was certain he'd heard *hurriya*, the Arabic word for freedom.

The streets were crowded with Africans and Arabs and those with the skin of both. The atmosphere was lighter here, yet Ottavio still felt wary. He walked past an open café and saw a man well-dressed man in Western clothes, reading a newspaper through dark glasses and sipping a coffee. Ottavio told himself to be calm. Not everyone was a potential enemy.

It was past midnight and Ottavio was nearly asleep when he heard a tap on the door. Scrambling off the bed, he swung the door open and the man stepped backwards into the darkness. He could barely see his features under the white *ima* wrapped around his head, but Ottavio guessed he was not much older than he was. When he spoke, his English was halting and Ottavio could hear an accent but could not guess its origin.

'One thousand US,' he said.

Blinking into the darkness, Ottavio knew he should not hesitate and snatched a fold of one hundred-dollar notes from his pocket, and showed it to the man but did not hand it over. 'Older than me, tall, she is marked here.' With the tip of his finger, he drew v-shaped lines on his forehead. 'Born in Mayen Aben. Her name is Alaya.'

Nodding, the man took the money. 'Two days.' He said and stepped back into the darkness. Ottavio heard his sandals crunching on the fine sand as he made his way down the alley.

Feeling a mixture of elation and fear, Ottavio stepped out into the darkness and leaned up against the wall, it's heat seeping into his body. The smell of the toilet drifted on the fetid air. Was he a total idiot? Was that the stupidest thing he had ever done? What if that man did not return? Handing cash to a total stranger. Was he with his friends now, planning to return and take whatever else he had? Had he told an agent about the foreigner? What was the chance this man could find her?

Ottavio went to the tap and filled the bucket. Using the toilet door as a screen, he soaped himself and sloshed the warm water over his body. In two days would he know? Could that be possible? All night he lay sleepless in his uncomfortable bed with Aunty Ajak's words ricocheting through him.

The following night Ottavio walked to the top of the alley, thinking of the man. Maybe he had simply stolen his money, Ottavio looked for him on the still busy street. The car that pulled up in front of him was old and battered: no different to dozens he had seen pass by. Two men got out and approached either side of Ottavio. 'Looking for someone?' The man was stocky and his face grizzled. There was no mistaking the menace in his question.

Ottavio's instinct was to run, but they read his panic and gripped an arm each. Ottavio jerked away from them, but they held on. Ottavio felt the air suck out of him, when a fist slammed into his gut. He buckled and they dragged him to the car, slammed his head against the roof and forced him into the back seat. Winded, bleeding, close to vomiting from the blinding pain of his broken nose, Ottavio tried to find his breath. The man next to him forced his head down between his knees and yanked his arms behind him at a rigid, painful angle. Ottavio tried to struggle, but the hard edge of a gun pressed at the base of his skull stopped him. The car was silent except for his own gasping breath and the roaring engine. Lurching through the traffic, the driver swerved left and right, accelerating hard, braking suddenly, then speeding up again.

Blood ran from Ottavio's mouth and dripped from his chin. His nose was swelling He took small gasps of air through his mouth. His arms were aching, and he tried to shift his head off the front seat, enough to relieve the thumping pressure. But the gun pressed harder into his skin and he stopped moving. The car filled with cigarette smoke and he heard a window being wound down and smelt the stench of the lead fuelled air. Traffic sounds were loud; horns sounding and truck engines grinding slowly through low gears.

Suddenly the car swung left and Ottavio heard the whine of gates swinging open. The car moved forward slowly, then dipped and Ottavio knew they were going down into an underground car park. A cloth bag was pulled over his head. He grunted with pain as they yanked him from the back seat. Tripping, they shouted at him to get to his feet, but he did not move quick enough, so they dragged him. His feet scrapped on the concrete floor, his sandals left where he had been standing. A door opened and he was shoved into a room, bare except for two chairs and painfully bright fluorescent lights.

One of the men pushed him onto the chair and the other backhanded Ottavio, from one side to another, until he went limp. Eyes swelling, blood and mucus dripping, he choked and spat on the floor. The man hit him again and Ottavio's head tipped back. He could see only slits of bright light. His breath came in jerks and he thought now he would die here in this room.

The man lit a cigarette and Ottavio heard him exhaling loudly. The door opened and Ottavio could not see the man clearly, but he knew he had not been in the car. His presence in the room held more menace than the other two men together.

'Mr Bol. It is good to meet you. To put a face to the name.' There was a long pause and the man came closer. 'Mr Bol, you are a foreign national in this country behaving in a manner that suggests you are engaging in or are planning to engage in illegal activity.'

The speakers' voice had a lyrical quality to it. His English was perfectly correct and evenly measured. This man was in no hurry.

'Well? What do you have to say for yourself?'

Ottavio's mouth gaped, but he could not form any words.

Again, he was back-handed and he thudded to the floor, kicked in the stomach, twice, three times. Then a pause and the foot thudded into him again.

'Surely you know, in this country, there is no such thing as prostitution or slavery. They are illegal. Do you not understand that? Perhaps you have been away too long.'

Ottavio was hauled back up onto the chair, his arms jerked behind him and his wrists handcuffed.

'Yet you would have the audacity to attempt to procure, one or both? This is correct, is it not? You were planning on both?'

All Ottavio could feel was pain. His face felt massive and he was swallowing his own blood. His thoughts a blurred panic. Did the man in the *ima*, have it all planned? Or was he given no choice but to betray Ottavio? Was he in the same building, bloody and begging for his life? Or beating someone like him?

Ottavio tried to slow his thoughts. In the panic and pain, even if he was going to die soon, Ottavio would not beg. It was the one thing he would never do. Not with these men.

The man's voice had become distant, and he heard another sound. Was it in the room, or outside? Was it in his head? The distant screeching cry of a *kuei*.

'Now would not be the time for you to remain silent, Mr Bol. Now is the time for you to explain yourself.'

But Ottavio didn't even try to speak. Inert, he waited. A fist thudded against the side of his head and he crashed to the floor again, the cuffs cutting into his wrists.

Then he heard nothing.

Ottavio woke to the sound of the door slamming. He had no idea how long he'd been unconscious and listened to the movement in the room. Then he felt the cuffs being taken off him. As he was pulled upright, every part of him hurt; his arms sagged, lifeless and heavy. A glass of water was pressed against his lips and he swallowed a little, choking as it trickled down his parched throat. He heard the door bang shut again and he knew he was alone. One of his eyes opened enough to give him a watery view of the room, but he closed it against the painful light. His arms were coming back to life and he tried resting his weight on his left arm, but pain exploded through him and he pitched onto his side again, lying still, trying not to move. His bladder hurt, if someone did not come soon, he would wet himself. Ottavio thought of what could happen next. If they were going to kill him, surely, they would have done it by now? They must have seen his passport; would they really risk killing an Australian citizen? He knew they would not care where his documents said he was from. They would only see his skin.

Hearing a noise outside the door, Ottavio started. The door opened and he was hauled up and dragged, his feet sliding out behind him. Ottavio croaked and gasped in pain as he was swiftly pulled along a dimly lit corridor.

The door at the end of the corridor was yanked open. Bundling Ottavio through it, without hesitating, the men threw him down the concrete stairs.

56. Alice

Lying on the hot sand in her new orange bikini Alice listened to the waves rushing up the beach toward her. The tide was coming in and she had to go back to the hotel and change for dinner with William, a charming older man who she'd guessed was German. He was in the room next to hers and had invited her to a sunset dinner on the hotel balcony. She wanted to take her time getting ready. The dresses she had bought that morning needed trying on and she thought she might have to make a quick visit to the market to buy a pair of sandals to match. Fingering her new, flower-shaped necklace; delicately crafted petals in silver with a jutting stamen, that was hanging from her neck. She thought she'd keep it on, regardless of the outfit, even though the silver stuck to her skin in the heat. Alice thought it would be the one souvenir she'd always keep.

Stuffing her towel, book, sunblock and water bottle into her tote, Alice made her way back up the beach thinking about Melissa's email. Alice had written to her a few days ago, saying she'd really loved the class, apologising for not being in touch until now. She was in Thailand. She'd just had to get away. Melissa's reply was warm, she would make a good ESL teacher, it would be easy to find work in Asia. Alice liked the idea of teaching. Maybe she could even be good at it?

Dinner was just as she imagined. William was well mannered and cultured, pulling out her chair for her and ordering on her behalf. He'd become a widow eighteen months before and his two adult sons had sent him on holiday. Time to get away and revive the heart, he said. Alice laughed and sipped her champagne. She knew exactly what he meant.

The air was warm and the food spicy and fresh. Alice nibbled at her prawns and ate only a little rice. Not that she was dieting, she just didn't have the appetite; she could feel her bones against the wooden chair. When she arrived in Koh Samui, she'd gone shopping at the night markets, as well as the necklace, she had bought clothes, all smaller in size than the ones she had packed.

William was describing his villa, somewhere near the Swiss border, but Alice wasn't really listening, she just smiled and murmured encouragement, letting her mind drift to what she should do next. A plan, unfurling in her like a revolutionary's victory flag. Even though she still thought of Ottavio, if felt like she was in brand new territory.

William took her hand and kissed her fingertips, suggesting they retire to his room for more champagne. Alice graciously declined, deciding a stroll along the dark beach was needed. William protested gently but Alice was not swayed.

As she made her way along the path, under the palms, waves quietly crashing, she let the plan take shape. It was a plan filled with certainty, not doubt. She would have her own family. She would teach her daughter how to avoid the maze of doubt and low self-esteem that she had got lost in. And how to recognise the intricacies of guilt and shame, the way they could work into the most ordinary parts of your daily life. You had to keep them away, be strong enough to let the barrage of it bounce off.

She imagined being a grandmother and showing her grandchildren her flower necklace, telling stories of how she had travelled alone. Of what she had seen and how she had changed. Maybe she would tell them about a man she'd known before she had left Australia. Someone she'd met in her hometown, who had also travelled. A man with a hard-to-believe past, so laden with loss and death that it had not seemed real. And how, in the brief time she had known him, the unimaginable had happened. The place he had taken the last of his family to, a place that was meant to be safe - turned out to be as dangerous as where they had come from. No doubt they would ask how the world could be like that, and she would not be able to explain. But she would tell them that even after all that had happened, he had still been kind, a good person. He wasn't twisted and broken when he could have so easily been.

A wave reached her toes and shocked her out of her reverie. She waded out until she was stood ankle-deep in the foaming water. Yes, she would tell them, but would leave out the way his skin had gleamed in the light of her bedside lamp, of how he had dumped her by text, and that she never heard from him again.

Alice made her way back to her room and reminded herself to buy a postcard before she left in the morning. Alice had been collecting cards; the picturesque, the grotesque and the tacky. In sequence, she wrote a few lines on the back of each one, until the cards told the story of how she had loved someone she barely knew.

57. Ottavio

Ottavio jolted awake as wheels of the small plane banged on the desert airstrip, once, twice, then a third time; the squealing brakes bringing it to a standstill. Engines still humming, it taxied towards a scruffy, single story flat tin-roof terminal.

Outside the heat of the red earth soaked through his sandals. The sun was overhead, and the other passengers passed him, moving quickly toward vehicles waiting nearby. Carefully placing the strap of his bag across his chest and grasping his small case, Ottavio walked slowly to a straggly tree and leaned against the trunk. Taking deep slow breaths, he tried to smooth out the anxiety that had assembled inside him. He looked about him and tried to take it in. The intense sun, the green of the trees, the fine red dust. The endless, white sky.

He was nearly home.

Had three weeks or four passed since he'd woken in a darkened room with Khalid gently wiping his face? He was lying on a thin mattress on the floor and his body radiated with pain. His arm was bandaged as were both of his hands. He could only lie on his back. Khalid came and went. Ottavio would crack open his swollen eyes and find him peering at him or tipping water into his mouth. Suspended in a bleary nether world, he had felt strangely safe in Khalid's care. He'd stayed on the mattress until he could breathe without hurting. His appetite returned and Khalid spooned *dura* porridge gently past his split lips. They never spoke. Ottavio never saw anyone else but guessed from distant sounds, he was no longer in Khartoum. The noises belonged to a village. Donkeys and chickens. Children. The evenings had been silent and dark.

When the bandages were taken off and he was able to stand by himself, Khalid had brought him a bucket of warm water and he'd slowly washed himself, softening the scabs and fresh scars with a rag and soap, inspecting the last of the bruising. Exhausted, Ottavio limped to the plastic chair outside the room facing the compound's wall, thinking he should go soon. A few more days and he would be stronger.

Khalid brought him tea and sat next to him for a while, saying little. The day was hot and buzzing with flies. His bags had been in a corner of the room all along and he was amazed to find all his belongings. Even the money in the lining of his suitcase was still there. He tried asking Khalid to help him get to Wau, but he seemed unsure of what he was saying. The next day Khalid bought a young woman with him. Ottavio guessed it was his daughter. Her face was covered, and she stood a distance away from him, listening carefully, then speaking quickly with Khalid. He nodded, then began speaking in a lower voice. The woman repeated, telling Ottavio, Khalid had found him on the street where he had been taken. Deliberately left, bleeding and near dead, for all to see. It was Allah's will that he had lived, but he must be very careful now. His cousin would take him back to the city and buy his ticket. But he must make his own way to the airport. Do not stop or speak with anyone. Ottavio went to his bag and offered dollars to Khalid, telling the woman he must thank him this way. Khalid refused.

Breaking hard, throwing up a swirling cloud of dust, Jok stopped in front of him.

'What took you so long?' Ottavio asked, teasing.

'No cousin, the question is what took you so long?'

Jok took in the scars on his cousin's face but asked no questions. He got out of the dust-covered Land Cruiser and took Ottavio's bag from him and helped him into front seat. Ottavio knew he wouldn't ask about what happened in Khartoum. Jok didn't need to know the details. It could happen at any time. Everyone knew that.

'It's good to see you man.' Jok laughed, excited to have his cousin back.

'You too, cous'. You too.' It had been three years since he had left Sydney telling everyone it was time to go back to his people. Now here he was looking exactly the same with his big grin and laughing eyes. The cruiser hurtled along the hard dirt road, dust streaming from behind it. Jok tried to slow before the bumps and Ottavio mostly managed not to wince. They drove on into the coming darkness, Jok telling him stories of his misbehaviour and what he had planned for them.

A flare of excitement burst in Ottavio as they approached the Wunroc bridge, a single lane with no barriers, high above the Lol River—the only way into Twic County.

Jok looked over at him, 'Nothing bad can happen to you now.'

In the headlights they saw a heavy branch across the road. Near a small fire, a boy stood sentry, an AK47 slung around his neck. For the past five years there had been relative peace—but the bridge was under guard again, closed at night and they did not have permission to cross. The sun was down; they were breaking curfew.

Jok turned the engine off. The headlights went out and Ottavio's eyes adjusted to the darkness, focusing on the glow of the fire.

'Don't worry, they'll let us pass.' Jok sounded confident. He asked Ottavio to flick on the internal light. Fumbling to find it, Ottavio saw the boy step back, wary of a vehicle that had not immediately identified itself. Lifting the gun to his waist, he turned it in their direction just as Ottavio found the switch. The boy saw who was inside and relief swept across his face. He called out for them to wait; he had to speak to his superior. Minutes later a man approached, buttoning his shirt. Recognising Jok he offered his hand. The man nodded at Ottavio, noting his battered face. They exchanged greetings then he stepped back and waved them on, the boy dragging the branch out of their way.

Crossing the bridge slowly, at the other end, another young guard pulled his branch aside.

'They know you?' Ottavio asked, surprised at how easily they passed.

'Of course, they do. Not many around here drive. Those who do are known, but that's not why they let us pass. They want us off the road. Don't want anything happening on their watch.' Jok looked at Ottavio, his face serious in the dim light of the dashboard. 'And next time be a bit quicker with the light.'

Ottavio nodded. He hadn't forgotten. War was nervous children with big guns. Peaceful nights ambushed. Fire, bullets and chaos. Even as peace was being negotiated, it could all start again without warning.

As they entered Mayen Aben, Ottavio could only see glimpses of it in the headlights. Jok drove straight to the only accommodation, a high walled lodge with a half dozen rooms. He banged on the gates. In the darkness a voice called out, who was arriving so late? Jok negotiated, the gates opened, he bounced the vehicle over a low barrier into the compound and the gates were shut behind them.

Nothing stopped Ottavio falling asleep; not the sweltering heat or the raucous chorus of countless frogs competing with wheezy donkeys and barking dogs. The dogs won. Across the village they yelped and howled at anything and each other in a rowdy all night loop. The sticks holding aloft the fragile mosquito net collapsed on top of him. Carefully he pulled the net down, not wanting to tear any more holes in it. The night was almost over, when he sensed movement in the room. Something swept past his face, then something else. Alarmed, he ducked under the sheet. Bats, tiny, silent and swift. In the gloom he could just make them out. Detecting his presence, swerving to avoid contact, they were no bigger than the size of his hand. Flitting through the gaps around the window, they circled the room and out again. As the gloom lightened, the air stopped churning. His silent companions were gone.

The village was stirring. Roosters, goats and cows, all added their calls to the morning. He sat on the bed, feeling the layer of fine dust under his feet. The air was soiled with the odour of his sweat. Ottavio dressed slowly then crossed the compound and slipped through the blue metal gates as the suns' rays threw bands of light across the ground. He followed the perimeter of the village along a narrow track that veered south, leading him to the edge of what he had never forgotten.

The land transformed into a vast and beautiful marshland, iridescent green, shoulder-high *kunai* grass growing in knee-deep water. Tree canopies mushroomed above it. Cows waded through, only their horns visible above the reeds. A fisherman in a balaclava and shorts threw his net into a pool then slowly hauled it back in, small fish thrashing and gasping in the air. Birds rose up and disappeared into the blank sky.

With difficulty, Ottavio slowly levered himself up into a tree and looked out, mesmerised by the colours and shapes of the land. A white long-legged bird stalked carefully through the water. Spiky yellow feathers erupted from the top of its head like a tiara. Ottavio watched it step through the reeds, snatching insects off the water. He shifted and the bird spread its wings, lifting up into the sky away from the intruder.

Ottavio saw his seven-year-old self, walking with his sister as she balanced a container of water on her head. Their mother cooking on a fire, smoke curling up into the still air. He'd loved the end of the day, his family completing their chores and rituals before the sun went away.

The sound of his dreams pushed against him. In every bed he had slept in since he had left, the sounds had been the same. On the hard ground under trees, a grass mat in the camp, wire bunks in Kenya. Even on the mattress in Australia that was so soft he thought he might fall through, it was the same. The shouting and running, crying children, horses pounding toward him. Ottavio refused to allow the sounds near, keeping his focus on the swamp, beckoning and unchanged. He watched until the fatigue threatened to unbalance him.

Slowly dropping down from the branch, he landed evenly on both feet, pain jarring through his legs. He limped carefully back to the lodge.

News of Ottavio's return spread swiftly. He spent the morning greeting cousins he couldn't remember. Elders he didn't recognise. Faces drawn with loss and struggle looked at him with hollow eyes. They told him there must be a ceremony to thank the spirits for his survival. Ottavio explained he was there for only a few days, saying he had to return to Australia, trying to sound convincing. This was met with blank faces. His life in a far-off country did not matter to them. Preparations had to be discussed with the most senior man in the clan. He would decide the most auspicious day for the sacrifice to take place. Whatever else Ottavio had to attend to had to wait.

In the late morning before the worst of the heat, he and Jok drove out of Mayen Aben. As they neared the next village, Jok stopped on the side of the red dirt road. They walked through columns of ready-to-harvest sorghum, stepped around drying mud and the last pools of the wet season, following a path to the home of his mother's oldest brother. People rushed to greet them, women singing loudly and joyously: *ayi, yi, yi, yi!*

Uncle Bol was seated outside his hut, waiting. Ottavio offered his hand and the old man took it, steadying himself. To Ottavio, he looked ancient.

'Machar, you have come home. Our son has come back, when others have not returned. We are sorry for your family who are not here. But you are here now.' Uncle Bol told him to stay close. A plastic chair was bought for Ottavio.

Family members milled about, and children ran around, excited to meet a relative from another country. They had heard about men like Ottavio and hoped for sweets or a bottle of fizzy drink. Teenagers admired his T-shirt.

Everyone gathered to hear the negotiation. This was not a private matter. The *agumloung* sat on the other side of Uncle Bol, loudly repeating essential words so everyone could follow the gist of the discussion—which quickly became tense. Ottavio stared at the ground listening intently, dabbing at the sweat on his brow with a handkerchief. The rain clouds that had threatened had been chased away by a blazing sun. Jok sat nearby, listening carefully.

Ottavio asked that the sacrifice be conducted the following day. The reply was emphatic; a ceremony could not be arranged so quickly, it was not appropriate. Ottavio stated he had only a little time. Uncle Bol replied that the spirits would not be happy. Ottavio countered, saying if it rained the road might be cut off, preventing his return to Wau. He could miss the flight, but his protest was half-hearted. The plan to return was feeble. The truth was he had no plan.

The discussion moved from time to resources, and politics erupted. How many bulls will be sacrificed and whose? Whose sorghum would be used to brew the *marissa*? A woman interjected, complaining she had none to spare. She was told to shut up, her opinion did not matter.

An hour passed and Ottavio held his ground, repeating that he would need to leave as he had planned. Reluctantly Uncle Bol agreed. The ceremony would go ahead the next day. They shook hands and Ottavio handed him a bundle of Sudanese pounds.

He and Jok walked back to the vehicle followed by a trail of children and women singing farewell. Just before Mayen Aben, Ottavio asked Jok to pull over and let him out.

Under a burning sun he walked to a clutch of mango trees and rested on a narrow bench made of old branches. The ground was sandy under the thick, green foliage, the air a few degrees cooler. Two boys passed, herding their goats, tapping at their flanks with thin sticks. A young girl with a baby on her hip walked under the canopy, glancing curiously at him.

He couldn't recall what Mayen Aben had looked like when he was young. Now there were a few ramshackle buildings made from bricks and mortar, but mostly it was tents constructed from branches and whatever people could find, plastic sheets or sun-bleached pieces of cloth. First the war destroyed any infrastructure, then prevented anything being rebuilt. No roads were sealed, rubbish was strewn everywhere, there was no sanitation, drainage didn't exist. The area was rife with malaria. He gazed at the shallow pools of green, slimy water, clogged with rubbish and breeding mosquitos. He began thinking like an engineer. How to drain the water away from the tents. To build latrines and pipe water. So much of what was needed could be easily built.

Ottavio lay out on the bench and fell asleep, waking

sometime later. He felt more tired than before he had slept, and his leg was throbbing. Reaching for the cool glass of his watch, he felt only his hot skin, and Alice came to mind. He lay still, remembering when she seemed most sure of herself—when she was talking about books. Groggy, he made his way back to the village, to the bustling market. Arab and other African traders, Ugandan and Kenyan side-by-side, sold small quantities of everything from spices to washing powder, dispensed in cones of newsprint.

A shoeshine boy sat behind a small pyramid of Kiwi shoe polish tins, waiting for those who could afford to wear shoes, to have them cleaned in spite of, and because of, the dust and mud.

He found Maria, the tea seller Jok had told him about. Her tent was the most popular in the market.

Tall and skinny with small, yellowed eyes, Maria told him to sit, dragging a plastic chair across the dirt floor to the spot with the best view. She sat on a low stool next to an old tin sideboard with peeling yellow paint, stacked with cups, a large tin of loose tea and a jar of sugar. At her feet a kettle boiled on a charcoal brazier. Steam whorled from the spout and she held the kettle high, pouring water into the cup through a tiny sieve of tea leaves, dissolving the sugar she had added. Ottavio took the plate of chewy sorghum cakes she offered, his first food for the day. Maria sat with him, asking who his family was and when had he arrived. Ottavio said little in reply; he didn't feel much like talking, so she let him be.

An old man moved slowly past on an old Chinese-made bicycle. Donkeys pulled carts loaded with sacks of grain, splashing through the pools of stagnant water. The occasional vehicle bumped down the road, dust pluming out behind it. Goats and fat-tailed sheep trotted among the flow of people. Passers-by stopped and entered the tent to see who was there. Greeted him, shaking hands, they welcomed him back. An old man asked him what country he had come from. When Ottavio told him Australia, he nodded, uncomprehending and walked on.

Opposite, a boy was cooking chapati on a metal plate resting on top of an old oil drum; a fire burned inside. A young girl, shoeless, in a worn-out dress, sat in the dust watching him, holding her body in an unnatural way. Ottavio wondered if she could walk at all. She raised her fingers to her mouth, '*chum, chum.*' She was hungry. The boy-cook ignored her.

A small herd of goats wandered in, nosing about until the boy chased them out, narrowly avoiding the chapati grill tipping over as they bustled past. The boy snarled at the girl to warn her off as well, but she didn't move. Ottavio went over to the boy, gave him a pound and told him to cook for the girl. He went back to his chair. The boy eyed him cautiously from behind the drum, but did what he asked, handing the hot chapatis to the girl. Shocked, she grabbed them and awkwardly stood up, lurching away, stuffing pieces into her mouth, her clubfoot leaving a wide angled line in the dust.

Restless, Ottavio finished his tea, paid Maria and walked

back to the lodge hoping to find Jok. No one knew where he was. Filling a bucket from the water barrel, he went into the narrow stall that was the washroom, closing the corrugated tin door and rinsed off the morning's sweat and dust. Dressing in clean clothes he thought of returning to his lookout, but instead lay on his bed and slept fitfully until the sun started to sink. Feeling rested, Ottavio wandered across the village and started to relax. They could see he was someone returning from a long time away. He looked like them, but his manner was different. People stepped out of their *tukuls* to greet him, calling out '*Ekadee*'. Children peeked between spindly fences. Girls giggling as they walked past, shying away from his eyes.

Ottavio heard the vehicle get closer and turned just as Jok pulled alongside. Pleased, Ottavio got in beside him. He didn't say where he had been. They spent the evening drinking bottles of Kenyan beer in a tent at the back of the market, joined by other young men keen to hear about life in the West—especially about the girls.

Later they staggered through the village, drunk and lost in the complete darkness. People called from their huts for them to be quiet. 'Go home! Stupid drunks!'

Grabbing Ottavio, slurring, Jok asked, 'What the hell happened to Zach?'

Ottavio stumbled and fell without feeling any pain. Lying on the sandy ground, stars blinking down on him, he mumbled. 'Zach's here, you know? He's here.'

58. Alice

Alice had been excited and nervous, when she'd reached the Mae La camp. But in no way had she been prepared for the sight of it. A mass of people squeezed into a narrow strip of ground between the road and the hills, on the Thai side of the border. Deeply grooved dirt paths had turned to mud in the rain. Bamboo and leaf shacks, pressed against each other, sprawled across the hills. Rows of barbed wire. Alice felt sickened and shaky, but she was determined to not let it show. All the volunteers had been told their presence was tenuous. At any time, Thai officials could decide that foreigners had to leave, because of tensions with the Myanmar military that could change at any time. The foreigners were mostly like her, young, enthusiastic Westerners, wanting to 'give something back'. Alice hated that expression. Hated the unstated truth behind it. They wanted to give something back because so many western cultures had taken something. During orientation, when she was asked why she was there, Alice wanted to say she had learned, only recently, how to go through things, difficult things. And now, on the other side, she liked the person she was. She was stronger, braver. But instead she just shrugged and smiled and let them make up their own minds about her.

In the early morning the hills were shrouded in a smoky mist. The air was fresh and cool, as she washed her breakfast dishes in a basin of water, thinking through her morning lesson. The children were sweet and shy and underfed. Sitting in rows of bench seats, in the rickety bamboo-walled shacks, every morning they chanted in unison, 'Good morning Miss Alice.'

They wanted to know about Australia and on the blackboard, she drew wonky pictures of kangaroos and koalas, making them giggle in delight. It had only been a week, but she loved her job. Teaching made her feel hopeful and inspired. She wanted to hug the children, squeeze them hard.

At the end of each day, one of the children had the task of preparing the classroom for the next day. Tete, a Karen child with fierce bright eyes, stood on a chair and wiped the board clean, then lined up the chalk she'd carefully selected from the box. Tete was tiny for her age and was missing one of her front teeth. Embarrassed by the black gap, she tried to hide, even the hint of a smile, behind her hand.

During orientation they were told to avoid showing favour to any one child, but she adored Tete. She was bossy and loud, organising the other kids, looking out for them as well; even those who were bigger than her. For someone so little, she was tough. Tete had walked with Alice, back to her hut. As Alice answered each of her questions, the next was bolder. 'Would she stay long? Did she have photos of her family? Had she left her husband and children in Australia?' Alice wanted to take her hand as they walked, but resisted, not wanting Tete to form an attachment to her. Alice nearly laughed at the thought. Who was she kidding?

The next day, during lunch break, Alice ate with the children under the glowing green leaves of a banana tree. Plastic cups of water were passed around for them to fill up on, as the portion of rice was small, but none complained. Tete rinsed the plates and cups and stacked them in a box. Alice watched her organise the rest of the class into a game of statues, taught to them by another volunteer. After she was caught out, Tete sat next to Alice and watched the game transform into tag, the children tearing after each other, scattering across the dirt playground.

Alice etched squares into the earth and put a number into each. Tete's face lit up at another new game and the other children began to crowd around. Alice threw the rock across the squares, lifted her sarong and hoped to each number, over the rock, spun around, picked the rock up and came back to the start. All the children clapped and whispered amongst themselves at their teacher's funny game. Alice cut another two sets into the earth, divided the children into three teams to play against each other. Alice pointed to her watch and told them to hurry. The team that finished first won. Without warning heavy rain began to fall, the fat drops dissolving the squares, but they didn't stop the game. Tete hopped over her rock and slipped, landing hard on her backside. Some of the children roared with laughter, but she was helped to her feet. As the rain ran muddy rivulets down her legs, Tete looked shaky, like she might cry. Alice did not resist the urge to give her a quick hug. Her body stayed limp in Alice's grasp and Tete would not look at her. The rain got heavier and started to drop through the classroom roof. Alice told them all to run for home.

59. Ottavio

Ottavio woke to a flint of light. Bats flashed through the room again. Trusting their guidance system, he did not try to hide. Instead he lay still and strained to follow the shadows of their movement through the room until the light drove them away. His head fuzzy from the previous night's beer, Ottavio filled his bucket and went to the stall to wash, taking his time, favouring his sore leg. He went to the compound gate and eased it open. Leaning on the blue metal gates he watched the morning sun glitter through the trees.

Jok roared up to the lodge, braking hard in front of him. 'Machar, you should not have bothered getting dressed. It is not happening today. The ceremony is postponed.'

'What? This is the second time.'

'I don't know.' Jok smiled, as if it was of no surprise. 'We have to go back to Uncle Bol.'

Ottavio shook his head, exasperated.

'You want to go and explain to them that time is not fluid Machar? They don't care about your Western ideas. This is Africa.'

Together they drove back to Uncle Bol's. In the early afternoon, they returned to the market, their spirits low. Ottavio's head pounded. At Maria's, they sat in the back of the tent and asked for syrupy mango juice and the strongest tea.

The elders were insisting that a sudden death in the village was the reason they had delayed the ceremony. Jok thought Uncle was manipulating the situation because he thought his authority had been undermined. He was wanting to make a point. His right to decide had not been respected. Meaning, Ottavio should not have tried to insist on the date. He told them the elders would gather tomorrow and a decision would be made then.

Exhausted, Ottavio left Jok at the market and walked back to the lodge. Outside the gates, he saw two barefoot boys in ragged clothes. Suddenly the taller of the two launched himself at his companion, landing a punch on his mouth, another to the side of his head. His target swung his skinny arms in defence, planting his feet with knees bent, he leant in, trying to connect and hold his ground. The taller boy laughed at him, slapping his ear, then his cheek. A teenage girl ran to them and pulled them apart, yelling, 'Stop it! Stop it! Brothers don't fight!'

Laughing, the taller boy sauntered off. The girl flicked her hand, dismissing him. The younger boy's chest was heaving, fists still raised in front of his face.

Ottavio went over to him and placed his hand on the boy's shoulder. The boy glanced up, surprised. He shifted his shoulder away from the reassurance Ottavio offered. Dropping his fists, he took off in the direction his older brother had taken.

Ottavio returned to his room and waited for sleep and the bats to return. He wondered how long the younger boy would chase after what it was that hurt him.

■

Jok drove deep into the bush. There was no track, he was weaving through the trees and shrubs, finding the smoothest path, knowing exactly where to go.

They parked under a *teet* tree. The branches stretched far beyond the trunk. It must have been hundreds of years old. Tiny purple birds, orange splashed under their wings, flitted about, agitated by the intrusion.

Rain had swelled the river across a wide flood plain. There was no boat or bridge, no other way to reach the place of the ancestors. They had to go through. Hoisting what they needed onto their heads they waded into the warm water. Midway across, Ottavio's chin was wet and water streamed off their clothes when they walked out the other side. Ottavio saw an empty snail shell in the mud that would have fitted in the palm of his hand.

Crossing a scrubby stretch of land, they reached a clearing with two *tukuls* under the shade of another very old tree. Ottavio's great, great grandparents were buried here.

Women greeted them, singing, piercing the air: *ayi, yi, yi, yi, yi!* The elders were arriving, spears in hand. Impossibly tall and seriously thin, the V-shaped lines on their foreheads looked to be sinking back into their skin.

In order of importance they sat in a row of plastic chairs. Some wore the *jellibiya*, others were dressed in suit pants and business shirts. The man in the fake tiger skin cowboy hat was the *bany bith*, master of the sacred spears, responsible for the spiritual life of the village. Ottavio, diverted his eyes.

A plate of meat from the boiled head of a cow was served to the elders. Women strained the *marissa* that had been fermenting overnight. Skinny, rabid, hunting dogs dozed in the shade of the meeting tree. Ottavio was told to take care and not to stand on them. He would regret being bitten.

More people made their way along the path. Two men arrived, each carrying different model machine guns. Ottavio recognised the weapons. The Gem-3 and the AK47s. The Gem-3 was carried with special pride. It had been taken from the enemy.

There were other arrivals. Vultures circled, sensing what was to come. One landed on the pointed tip of *tukuls'* conical roof, and looked down on the ceremony, waiting for its chance.

Ottavio sat in the shade of the tree and listened to the old men discussing the sacrifice. Uncle Bol argued for a bigger animal. The spirits needed a generous offering. Ottavio did not interject and the men did not consult him. He was too young to understand what was required. Only they could make these decisions.

Eventually, they agreed, the sacrifice would be a large white bull.

The sun was directly above them. It had been nearly two hours since the men had gone out to the herd to catch the animal. Children slept under the tree. Ottavio sat next to Jok, listening to the old men trade war stories when a commotion broke out. A very agitated bull with enormous horns was led into the clearing. There were cheers and the sleeping children woke, jumping to their feet.

No time was wasted. The beast was expertly trussed and laid down on its side. The neck twisted to the sky. One of the old men used his spear, carefully slicing across the jugular vein, releasing a fine spray of blood. He handed the spear to another elder and continued the delicate slicing; the wound gaping wider and wider. Blood pooled on the ground. The animal twitched—eyelids fluttering, exposed muscles jerking. It could not struggle, and it made no sound. About fifteen minutes after the cutting began, the animal finally went limp. The jubilant crowd mingled, chanting and singing. While the carcass was being skinned, women danced and sang in small groups. Hands raised in the air, eyes shining: *ayi, yi, yi, yi, yi!*

Ottavio was told to go the man in the cowboy hat for a blessing. Ottavio approached him, hands cupped, to receive the water. 'No man forgets where he belongs,' the man said. Looking Ottavio directly in the eye he thanked God, their ancestors, the elders and those who were with them that they could not see.

The celebration began.

As the afternoon wore on people drank too much and arguments broke out. A young man drunkenly shuffled amongst the dancing women and tried to persuade Ottavio to join him. Ottavio declined, listening instead to the rambling song of the old man sitting nearby. He was singing a song to their enemy. '*The Murhal are near. We hear their guns. They are near. They are near, but we will fight them and win.*'

Ottavio walked off into the bush and found a quiet place under a tree with long fat seedpods hanging from thick vines. He smiled at the memory of playing *yi anyuok* with his age mates. The heavy sausage shaped fruit was swung in a circle above their heads and they threw their pointed sticks at the pods, practicing for manhood and the day they would carry spears.

He thought about the Spear Master's blessing. Longing, remorse, grief, pulsed through him, he closed his eyes against it, trying to keep it at bay. He heard an unfamiliar sound. A distant voice. A young woman telling him to get up. Don't be so lazy. It was time for him to go.

Ottavio opened his eyes and looked about, but he was alone.

Feeling weak, he leant back against the hard bark of the tree. His sweat stained shirt clinging to him. Reaching out, he snapped off a vine, stepped away from the canopy of the tree and swung it above his head.

He was a child; spear in hand, aiming for the long, thick fruit. He threw it and the spear glanced off the edge of his target. He grabbed another and tried again. The spear hit the fruit but bounced off. Young Ottavio breathed in, asking his ancestors to help. He tried again. Keeping his eyes on the fruit as it swung around and around, he stepped forward, with a steady hand, and all the force in his skinny body, he threw his last spear. The fruit split open and dropped to the ground.

Swinging the vine harder, Ottavio let go.

In the distance he heard the celebration. Wiping the traces of the vine off his hands he went back to the party.

Hours later, he and Jok quietly left the party without anyone noticing. They waded back through the flood water which felt hot in the late afternoon sun. They took their time getting back to the village. Jok kept his speed low. As they neared the lodge Ottavio made a decision.

'Can you speak to the Spear Master for me?'

Jok laughed quietly. 'All afternoon you are quiet and then you come out with this.'

'Will you. Ask him if I can meet with him?'

'You can't make an appointment. He isn't a dentist.' Jok joked.

'Tell him it's about family.'

'It's always about family.'

'Will you?'

'Why didn't you speak to him at the ceremony?'

'I don't know.'

Jok snorted in disbelief and waited for Ottavio to explain himself. Ottavio couldn't. Jok looked at him with sympathy. 'Machar, everyone has lost someone.'

'It's not that. I said I would do something …and I couldn't.'

'Who did you say this to?'

'My sister. I should have come home with her. She should be with me.'

Jok looked at him with softer eyes.

In the morning, when Ottavio stumbled out of his room to use the latrine, he found Jok sitting in the chair by his door. The day had hardly begun, and the sky was gathering rain clouds.

'I have a message for you Machar.'

Ottavio waited to hear what the Spear Master had said.

'Malong called last night.'

Ottavio wiped sleep from his eyes.

'He said to tell you Alpha is starting a course soon and next month, Rosa and Samuel will marry in Nairobi. You must be there.'

Ottavio's heart beat a little stronger.

'And if you do not turn your phone on soon, he's going to come here and turn it on for you.'

Pleased, Ottavio made his way to the latrine.

On his way back, he saw that Jok had not moved. Jok gave him a playful smile.

'You didn't let me finish. The Spear Master said go to the Lol river and cleanse yourself. And speak your sister's name.'

334

60. Alice

Alice had finished for the week and was planning to spend the weekend helping Liz, one of the medics, vaccinate newly-arrived children. Alice checked her email on the computer, while Liz gathered her kit. Quickly scanning through the list, ignoring the three from her mother, she opened one from Melissa. They had become firm email friends. It said that she had received a text from Ottavio. He had sent an address in Nairobi, if anyone in class wanted to contact him. Melissa had assumed by 'anyone', he had meant her. Alice read that line again and again, until she understood. With shaking hands Alice wrote down the address.

That evening she found the small pile of postcards, tucked into a pocket of her suitcase. With her heart thumping she removed the rubber band and wrote the address on each one.

61. Ottavio

At the Lol river with the sun dropping low on the horizon, Ottavio stripped off his clothes. Wading in, he cupped the dark, warm water and splashed it over his chest. A fish darted past his leg. He scooped the water over his head. Feeling the sandy bottom beneath his feet, he stepped slowly until the water reached his neck.

Ottavio tried to form the word he had not spoken since he was a boy, but it would not take shape. He tried again, but the croaking sound stranded in his throat and he felt foolish.

'What am I doing here?' he asked the river, its current swirling around him. He ducked his head under the water, and he lost contact with the bottom; the water lifting him away. Ottavio panicked, thrashing at the water with his arms, kicking his legs, he found the bottom again and staggered backward out on to the bank, falling against the scratchy grass.

He lay back and let his breath slow. Feeling the water on his skin drying. The sound was faint, but it rippled across him. He heard it again, louder and closer. Looking up he saw a *kuei*, circling above him, arching across the vast, pale sky.

Ottavio's heart was thumping. He watched the bird wheel through a figure of eight, its eerie cry sharp and clear. Picking up his shirt, he got up, flapped it above him, not to scare it away, but to get its attention, to bring it nearer. The bird kept circling and Ottavio followed its motion until he was dizzy. He stumbled to the ground, something inside him breaking open, and he yelled, 'Alaya!'

The bird dropped lower, its cry ringing across the water. The *kuei* landed on the branch of a tree, twitching its head toward him. Ottavio could see the creamy, feathers of its underbelly. Watching each other, with only the water moving, Ottavio felt his spirit lifting, rising up.

The bird raised its wings, holding them aloft for a few seconds, then it launched itself into the hot air, flying above his head, out across the *toic*.

'Alaya!' Ottavio yelled as the *kuei* sped toward the horizon. 'Alaya!'

Jumping to his feet, his hands reaching out to the sky, Ottavio leapt and danced across the sandy dirt, singing.

'Alaya! Alaya! We're home!'

Dinka

Agumloung	acts as a human microphone at meetings
alouny	slave
arrouc	coward
bany bith	Master of the Sacred Spears
cheebuk	Good afternoon/Welcome
chum	food
kuei	fish eagle
dura	sorghum
ekadee	how are you?
foul	stewed beans
jong	dog
kunai	marsh grass
kawauja	white people
lor	go
marissa	home brewed beer
nhalic angic nhialic	spirit known only to God
teet	mahogany tree
thueny	run
toic	new grassland after the rain
tukul	thatched roof, mud-walled hut
yi anyuok	children's game using the vine of the sausage fruit tree

Arabic

ima	cloth turban
jellabiya	full-length loose robe for men
hurriya	freedom
rishka	three-wheeled covered scooter for hire